Mr. High Maintenance

Mr. High Maintenance

Nishawnda Ellis

www.urbanbooks.net

Urban Books, LLC
78 East Industry Court
Deer Park, NY 11729

ISBN 13: 978-1-60162-366-9
ISBN 10: 1-60162-366-6

First Mass Market Printing October 2012
First Trade Paperback Printing September 2010
Printed in the United States of America

10 9 8 7 6 5 4 3 2 1

Distributed by Kensington Publishing Corp.
Submit Wholesale Orders to:
Kensington Publishing Corp.
C/O Penguin Group (USA) Inc.
Attention: Order Processing
405 Murray Hill Parkway
East Rutherford, NJ 07073-2316
Phone: 1-800-526-0275
Fax: 1-800-227-9604

Mr. High Maintenance

by

Nishawnda Ellis

New Year's Eve, 2007

Marcus dried his wet body off with the towel his wife left for him by their his-and-her sink. The New Year's Eve party they were throwing at their Pasadena, Maryland mansion would start in an hour. He finished applying his Get Fresh products, before brushing his low-cut black hair and putting on his underclothes. He stepped into their master bedroom to look for his clothes. He didn't see them.

He yelled out, "Sheri! Where are my clothes?"

No answer.

"Sheri! Sheri! Do you hear me calling you? Where are my—"

Sheri yelled from the foyer downstairs, "Hanging in the closet!" She needed to get showered and dressed herself, but she still had last-minute party decorations to put out and needed to make the warm buttered rum.

Marcus opened their room-sized closet and saw his black slacks and blue silk shirt hanging in front of the rack. His pants were creased but his shirt screamed, "Iron me!"

He yelled again, "Sheri, what's going on? You didn't iron my shirt. How are you going to iron my pants and not my shirt? You are really trying my patience."

Sheri heard him yelling and almost lost it. She was fed up with her husband's demands and didn't want to live like this anymore. She dropped what she was doing and marched upstairs, where Marcus continued to whine like a child.

"This is ridiculous. One thing. That's all I ask you to do, and you can't even do that. Maybe if you didn't spend so much time back and forth to Boston visiting your family then you wouldn't be slacking on your responsibilities here."

Sheri stormed in. "My responsibilities here? I take care of what I am supposed to take care of, Marcus. You're lucky I even do that."

Marcus looked at her like she'd lost her mind. "Oh, so I'm the lucky one?" He sucked his teeth. "Child, *paleese*."

"You just don't know how good you've got it. How much it takes to meet your demands. How impossible you really are. You just don't even know." Sheri meant every word.

Marcus wasn't buying it. "Just iron my shirt, please . . . if you can handle that." He walked off as if the conversation was over.

Sheri yelled after him! "Fuck you and fuck your shirt!"

"I'm not going there with you tonight, Sheri. I'm not even doing this with you." He kept walking, to get as far away as possible from her.

Sheri taunted him. "And I didn't buy your scotch. We are out. So you'll have to go get some. I'm not doing it." She snatched the steam iron from the bathroom linen closet. Furious at her unappreciative husband, she wanted to ram it down his throat. "You hear me, you-can't-do-shit pain in my ass! I'm not doing it. You're just too damn needy, Marcus!"

Marcus yelled, "Whatever! Just iron my shirt!" He walked into his study wearing his slacks and Hanes white tank top. He'd gotten so used to arguing with Sheri over nothing, it became normal to him.

He picked up the telephone to call his cousin Lamant to stop at the store on his way to the party. Lamant and his girlfriend Melinda lived an hour and half away. He would definitely need his Pinch scotch, if his wife was going to be in a sour mood all night.

Lamant picked up his cell phone on the third ring. "Hey, cuz. We're on our way now. Just leaving the house."

"Cool. You mind picking up some scotch?"

"Pinch?" Lamant knew his cousin well. "One bottle or two?"

"Better make it two. No telling how my New Year will be rung in."

"Damn! You pissed Sheri off already?" Lamant joked. "You sure know your way with the ladies."

"Whatever. Just don't forget."

"I got you. See you soon."

Lamant pulled out of his driveway and reminded his girlfriend to buckle up.

"You are such a rule-abiding citizen, Lamant. Is there any time you just forget about the rules?"

Lamant didn't even think about it. "No."

Melinda smiled. They had been together almost a year, and she knew rules were a part of the package. Feeling full from their late lunch she said, "I think we should have skipped the scampi today, baby. I won't have room for dinner. I don't want Sheri to think I'm being rude."

Lamant smirked. "I don't think she will even notice. Trust me, she's got other things on her mind."

Melinda didn't want to get into Marcus and Sheri's business, so she decided to leave that alone. She checked herself in the mirror and realized she still had things stuck in her teeth. She pulled out her floss from her purse and started to pick her teeth.

Lamant's skin began to crawl. *Here she goes again, after I told her a million times how disgusting that really is.* He could see the tiny food particulars being plucked across the car and he wanted to vomit.

"Melinda, do you have to do that now? It's so gross. I literally feel like I have food and plaque all over me. I might have to go home and change. Why do you do that? It's such a nasty habit."

"I'm sorry, baby. I keep forgetting. It's an awful habit I just can't seem to crack."

"I've noticed." Lamant began to wonder how much longer he would be able to put up with it. She'd been so right in every other department.

Melinda put away her floss and tried to hold off until they reached Marcus's house, or when Lamant gave her two minutes alone. She really couldn't help it.

Lamant's thoughts about Melinda's violation were interrupted by the buzz from his phone. He had an incoming text message. "Baby, can you read that for me?"

As she went to pick up his phone, he said, "Baby, please use the hand sanitizer first."

Melinda rolled her eyes. She loved him, but his obsessive-compulsive behavior got on her nerves quite often. She doused a dot of sanitizer in her hand and rubbed them together. She held them up and said with a smart tone, "There. Are you happy now, Mr. Perfect?"

Lamant nodded. "Very."

Melinda picked up his cell phone and pressed the red button to display the message. "It's from Jerome. It says, 'I can't make it to Marcus's tonight. Something has come up. Please keep your phone on in case I need bail money.' " She shrugged her shoulders. "What's that about?"

Lamant shook his head. "No clue. Dial his number and put it on speaker for me please. I need to know what's up."

Melinda did as she was asked and called Jerome.

His phone rang twice, and he picked up. "Yo, man, can't talk now. I will holla at you."

Lamant barely heard him. "Jerome, what's up? I can't hear you. What's going on?"

Just then the phone call dropped.

Jerome parked his car outside the art gallery, not wanting to believe what he knew to be true. He parked in a no parking zone but didn't care. If he saw her there with another man, he was sure to be going to jail anyway.

He walked up the steps and made his way past security and inside the gallery. He could hear the music coming from a party down the hall. He almost made it to the entranceway when the security guard at the door said, "Excuse me, sir. Do you have an invitation?"

Jerome ignored him. He was too busy trying to spot her from afar. Terri's words were starting to sound like poison. *"Jerome, you wear your heart on your sleeves."* She'd said it like it was a bad thing. *"The way you love is costly."*

"Sir, I am going to have to ask you to leave."

He found her. Rage in his eyes, his heart began to pound as he watched his fiancée-to-be-arm-locked with another man.

Part One

"Mr. Needy"

Chapter 1

Sheri slammed down another heavily packed suitcase on the check-in scale at the Baltimore/Washington International Airport. Either she was moving too fast for the skycap, or he was moving too slow for her. She was so full of rage that cold, wintry Friday night, she could have moved earth with the flick of her fingertips. She "turbo-walked" back to the car and plucked another suitcase out of the trunk of Marcus's SUV, a heavy, overstuffed Spiderman suitcase.

She waited for the skycap to process her two suitcases and Marquise's two suitcases, and give her their gate and seat information in hand. Her freshly done French-manicured fingernails tapped anxiously as she hummed a familiar tune, "I Will Survive" by Gloria Gaynor. She stroked her ten-year-old son's S-Curl Wave fade haircut. He was heavily engrossed in his PSP, watching the movie *Kicking & Screaming*, starring Will Ferrell, to even notice his mother's attitude.

This has been a long time coming, she thought, saddened by what she had to do.

The skycap told her it would be a thirty-dollar charge for each of the two suitcases that were fifty pounds overweight. Sheri whipped out her husband's American Express card without hesitation, and gestured for the skycap to use that.

He frowned after looking at the card. "Sorry, ma'am, but I cannot take this card. I'm going to need one with your name on it."

No time for the bullshit, Sheri barked, "But I'm Mrs. Hill. I use his card all the time. This is ludicrous." She snapped her neck and rolled her eyes.

"Sorry, but I can't accept it, unless the cardholder presents it to me and signs it."

Sheri realized this would only be the beginning of a long road of problems for her. She rolled her eyes for the second time at the rule-abiding skycap, mumbling under her breath, "There goes your tip, asshole." She turned around and signaled for her husband.

Marcus was like a watchdog, looking out for airport security because he was parked illegally. He saw his wife telling him to come over but was reluctant to leave his post. Finally after Sheri gave him the "get-yo'-black-ass-over-here" frown, he decided a one-hundred-and-fifty-dollar fine was less painful than a dose of his wife's Royal Rumble smackdowns.

Marcus's six-foot-three-inch muscular build scurried along the pavement. He knew he was handsome. His dark skin resembled black raspberries, and the texture was as silky as chamomile oil. His Gucci sunglasses hid his dark brown, almond-shaped eyes. He walked over to her and asked, "What's the problem?" as if there should never be one as long as she was with him.

"My bags are overweight. He needs you to sign the charge slip for your card," she said, a few degrees from her boiling point.

"Well, why didn't you pack lighter?" he said, aggravated he could be getting a ticket because of her nonsense. "Can't we put some stuff in one of the lighter bags?"

Temperatures rising. Sheri yelled at him, "Do you want the whole world to see your wife's thongs and bras? Or how about my special toy?"

"You packed that?" He still didn't get it. "Why?"

Sheri didn't respond. She cut her eyes so hard, Marcus didn't know if he would see her iris again. Trying to avoid another lengthy "getting told" session with the wife, he dropped the conversation and said to the skycap, "Charge it. Where do I sign?"

Marcus lifted his wife's stuffed suitcase off the scale. "Damn! You packed like you're never coming back." He wondered why his wife packed so much of her and their son's stuff.

Sheri didn't say anything.

The skycap gave Sheri her boarding pass and Maryland state license back. "Your flight is leaving out of Gate B11." He circled with his pen the number on her ticket receipt. "Make your way through the doors and take a left to go through security check-in."

"Thank you." Sheri ushered Marquise toward the security check-in.

The skycap gave Marcus the okay to tip him now, and Marcus reluctantly gave him two dollars, as if it was breaking the brother.

The skycap took the chump change. *Cheap bastard!*

Marcus gave him the nod then dashed after his wife, who apparently wasn't waiting on him for anything. "Baby, wait up! I can't leave my truck. I'll get a ticket." He chased her to the gate.

The ungrateful skycap threw Sheri's bags on the belt carelessly.

She shot back, "Well, then don't! I've said all I'm going to say to you."

"What's up with that?"

Marcus finally noticed his wife's disposition, something he had missed the entire ride from their five-bedroom mansion in Pasadena, Maryland. For him it seemed like Tuesday, just another day his wife was pissed at him for whatever reason.

Sheri tapped Marquise on his shoulder. He looked up at his mother without hesitation.

"Say good-bye to your father."

He obeyed and gave his father dap.

Marcus hugged him because something in him wanted him to know his love. Marquise went back to watching his movie, plugging his earphones in his ear.

He attempted to give his wife a hug and kiss, but she blocked it with her hand.

"Good-bye, Marcus."

He looked even more confused at his wife's behavior toward him. "What's the matter? I tipped the guy and paid for your heavy bags. What are you so mad about?"

"See, that's the saddest thing. You didn't even notice." Sheri shook her head. "How could you not know?"

"Know what?"

He looked at his truck through the automatic glass sliding doors. He could feel the flashing lights approaching his car. Impatient as usual, he said, "Call me when you get to your Mom's." He snuck a kiss on her forehead and made his way to the truck, to avoid spending more money than necessary.

"Marcus, we're not coming back!" Sheri shouted to him as she and her son made their way through the security check-in.

Marcus spun around, almost knocking over an elderly woman. "What did you say?"

Sheri looked at her husband one last time. "It's over!"

She ushered her son through the metal detectors, then herself and never looked back. Marcus thought her frequent visits to Boston were due to the holiday season that winter. Little did he know, she was enrolling Marquise in a new school and house-hunting with her mother. By the beginning of the new year, her plans to leave him were four suitcases and an expensive lawyer away.

Marcus hurried back, trying to get through security check-in.

"Sir, boarding pass and ID," the female airport attendant said.

He yelled out to his wife, "Sheri! Sheri!"

"Sir, if you're not boarding an aircraft, I'm going to have to ask you to step out of line."

He pushed past her, caring less about airport security.

"Sir."

"Sheri, what are you talking about? Wait!" He shouted.

He got as far as the metal detectors when two airport security guards grabbed him and pushed him back outside the Velcro ropes.

"Identification," the officer commanded. "I need your identification, sir." He and his partner had Marcus pinned up against a wall, face-first, his left arm pressed into his lower back.

More security came rushing over to assist and defuse the situation. Onlookers eyed their every move, wondering if he was a terrorist, or what.

"Wait. You don't understand. My wife . . . she's leaving."

"Last time. Identification, sir."

An onlooker shouted, "Hey, that's Marcus Hill, all-star running back for the Baltimore Ravens."

The security guard who was holding his arm let go. "Sir, I'm going to ask you—"

"My wallet is in my back pocket. I'm Marcus—"

"I know who you are."

The officer took down his Maryland license number and address. Marcus wished he would hurry up. Then he could buy a ticket to Boston and catch Sheri before they boarded.

The officer radioed in to his higher-up and said, "I got the situation under control. There has just been a misunderstanding."

"Can I go now? I need to catch my wife."

"Sorry, Mr. Hill, but I'm going to have to ask you to leave. I could charge you a fine, but instead I'm banning you from this airport for a week. We need to run your info through our system for—"

"For what? You said you know who I am."

"I still have to follow protocol, it's one or the other."

"I have to catch a flight now."

"Not today. Even if you weren't banned, we would take you down to holding, have the Baltimore PD arrest you, and then you would be facing up to a hundred-thousand-dollar fine, or jail time. That may not be any money to you but . . ."

Marcus's frugal fanny heard the one hundred thousand loud and clear. Defeated, he left the airport.

He got a one-hundred-fifty-dollar ticket anyway. Heated, he snatched the white ticket off his windshield and flung it in his back seat. His temporal blood vessel beat through his head as if it were going to pop from his skull. WTF. He'd missed the signs.

Losing his family wasn't an option for him; he needed a wife like he needed air. One couldn't survive without the other.

Chapter 2

Marcus threw another burnt, cooked-too-high piece of fried chicken in the trash, perturbed that ache in his stomach was yet to be handled. *Maybe I should have given her another look.* He thought about his date with Mary the other night, another one of his blind dates he'd thought he was too good to go on, but his mother, Willie Mae, insisted.

That should have been a clue, but no, he went against the grain, and decided to go out with her. Thought, at best, he could coerce this new friend into making him six meals so he could freeze them and be good until Sunday dinner at his mother's house. But just like the one before that, and the one before that, he gave them their walking papers due to their lack of interest in being a cook, housekeeper, and do-as-I-say kind of woman he was looking for.

He turned off the burner and flinched when the churning grease popped him in his cheek then his arm. "Dammit! Fucking shit!" He jumped up and down as if he was hit by gunfire. He quickly ran over to the sink as he held his cheek and turned on the faucet iceberg cold to run over his war wounds from cooking. "This is for the birds," he said, shaking his head. "A man can't even eat. Damn!" He turned off the faucet and marched over to his living room inside his two-bedroom condo located on Florida Avenue in Washington, D.C.

Still holding a piece of wet paper towel to his cheek, he slouched into his black extra-soft fabric sofa and snatched the cordless from its docking station in frustration. He subconsciously pressed memory three, and the usual voice answered, "Good evening. Thank you for calling Red Dragon. How can I help you?"

"Yes, I would like the orange chicken, no broccoli, chicken teriyaki, shrimp lo mein, crab Rangoon, and chicken wings please."

"Phone number please?" the woman asked with an Asian accent

"202-555-91—"

The woman cut him off, finishing the rest of his information, saying, "5681 Florida Avenue, bell four."

"Yeah. How did—"

"Same thing, every Friday night—orange chicken, no broccoli. *Tee-hee.*" She giggled through the phone. "You are our regular customer."

Annoyed that his new single-hood cover was blown, he said, "Yeah, yeah. Just make sure I get a regular discount."

"*Tee-hee. Tee-hee.*" The woman kept laughing. "I will be sure to give you extra sauce, twenty minutes, okay." She hung up without waiting for a response, or asking whether he was paying cash or credit. She already knew it would be cash, like always.

Marcus was feeling like a Magnum without lubricant before. Now he really felt raw, since the Chinese food restaurant lady was *tee-hee*ing him to death.

Ashamed at where he was in life, he fell back into his comfy soft sofa and reminisced about a time when daily home-cooked meals were a given. He missed Sheri and till this day couldn't understand why she left him. He provided, he was faithful, and outgoing, and very tolerant of her family, who turned out to be nothing but a bunch of gold diggers. *Hmm, I wonder if they were the reason why she left and took half of my money with her?*

Marcus's divorce was way more expensive than twelve years of marriage, child-rearing, and half-a-million-dollar wedding combined. Claiming and proving to the divorce judge that Marcus provided this lavish lifestyle for her, and why she should keep it, Sheri walked away with half his money and full custody of his son.

He slumped back and recited out loud, "It was the best of times and the worst of times." *Dickens must have been going through a divorce,* he imagined.

Marcus couldn't fathom how things went from Sheri loving everything about him—down to his sweaty jockstrap—to gutting him and cleaning him out like an endangered white whale. He thought she worshipped what they had. How could she not? "It doesn't get any better than Marcus Hill," she'd told him.

He could recall their courtship like it was yesterday. Thirteen years ago, she was what, planning to go to nursing school and wipe butts for a living? And, by chance, she'd met him, a rookie football player for the New England Patriots, at a bar in Marina Bay, about ten miles south of Boston.

Sheri sang along to Mary J. Blige and Method Man's hit single, "I'll Be There for You/You're All I Need to Get By."

Marcus stared at her from across the room. It was karaoke night, and for all the tipsy, silly-willy "mofos" who took the stage and belted their fifteen minutes into patrons' ears, who would need another round of drinks and earplugs, Sheri could really sing, blowing an impressionable country boy from Harrisville, North Carolina farther and farther away.

He rehearsed as he got closer to her, thinking about a way to get her attention. After all, he was just a rookie, being roped and broken in by some of the finest athletes this side of the northern hemisphere. She, on the other hand, seemed untouchable. Another Yankee girl his mother warned him about from the North.

He got up the nerve and stood in front of the small ten-by-ten stage and stared her down.

She was the least bit uncomfortable. She watched him as he watched her, and it almost seemed as if he was "all she needed to get by."

After she finished her song, Marcus held out his hand to help her off the stage. "Hi. I'm Marcus Hill." He smiled at her, and she smiled at him.

"I'm Sheri."

"Listen, your voice is incredible. I noticed it from the first *hmm*." He innocently tried to hum. "On my way over here, I've thought of a million plays from my playbook to throw at you to get your number."

"Oh, really?" Sheri twisted her lips, prepared to initiate a letdown.

"But you're too good for that bullshit. You're a gem, rare and impossible to find. I am flawed and expendable. Would it be wrong if I just wanted to get a glare of your shine?"

Sheri heard a lot of smooth talkers run the best lines on her, but Marcus was straight-up, no chaser, something she could appreciate. "I see no harm in letting you shine a little."

"Dinner tomorrow?" Marcus eagerly asked.

"How about now?" Sheri was feeling his flow from hello.

"Works for me." Marcus smiled.

"Then let's go," she said with confidence.

That date led to them seeing each other every day for a year until Marcus proposed.

Marcus wasn't kidding either. With her, he did shine. He played his way out of the rookie shadow and into the lucrative contracts and championship rings and endorsements.

Sheri gave up her nursing dreams to be her husband's full-time personal cheerleader, coach, agent, and manager. You name it, she was there for her man. "Ride or die," she used to say to him. Always, played the perfect housewife role, cooking, cleaning, entertaining, and doting on Marcus's every need.

Then Marquise came along, and she had two guys to devote her life to. This went on for years, from the New England Patriots, to the Atlanta Falcons, the Cincinnati Bengals, and finally the Baltimore Ravens.

Marcus didn't notice the more he shined, the less Sheri did or even felt like she did. The years piled on, and she was no longer that gem. He treated her like a dime a dozen. The marriage was always about him, his career, what he needed and what he wanted. Sheri's input didn't matter.

When Marcus finally retired, he thought Sheri would stay the same, catering to his every need, until that one day he thought he was taking her to the airport for a short visit with her family, only to find out she was leaving him and taking their only son with her.

Marcus sipped his Heineken Light and rubbed his head. He still couldn't understand why Sheri up and left, and treated him the way she did during their divorce, like she never loved him. As if he was a stranger.

"What was so hard about being married to Marcus Hill anyway?" he shouted out loud. As a retired forty-something-year-old football player, he found himself back on the market, a place he fantasized about, but never really wanted to travel.

He toasted to himself and said out loud, "Here's to the best of times and the worst of times ahead of me."

Marcus didn't know what to do without a wife, and he damn sure wouldn't be happy until he remarried again. *Back on the market.* He reminded himself, *It doesn't get any better than Marcus Hill.* He was a catch and could hook any fish in the sea. There were plenty of women out there dying to be the next Mrs. Marcus Hill.

Chapter 3

Marcus, as arrogant as he was, assumed he would have no problem meeting someone to take Sheri's place. But after ten months of dating, he couldn't find anyone who fit the description of a good old-fashioned housewife: cook, housekeeper, nanny, penny-saver, and freak.

Meeting women was never a problem for him on or off the football field. In his early days, hot young girls practically begged him to take their virginity. The vibrant young horny boy in him had no problem granting their every wish. The older, more mature man with a kung fu grip on his wallet, however, knew all too well how to spot a ho from a housewife. He never got them confused.

Well, that was until he met Sheri, the holier-than-thou Christian on Sunday, freak in bedroom every Thursday and Saturday he used to call his wife. She proved his gold digger radar skills rusty, taking his son and half of everything he owned, leaving him half-witted and alone at the age of forty. Call him choosy, if you want to. He never planned to make the same mistake twice, or be a chump.

Marcus was sitting at the barstool in a D.C. lounge during the afterwork-networking happy hour. He sipped his scotch on the rocks as he thought of where he was supposed to be as opposed to where he really was. Alone. For the first time in his life, his philandering days had dwindled down as the hot new rookie football players were the new eye candy and he was the retired grandpa that couldn't keep the interest of a young hot thing if he paid them.

Marcus sighed. "That's the problem," he said, reflecting to his longtime friend and bartender George. He took a long sip of his third scotch on the rocks.

"What?" George folded his iron arms across his chest, his bald head reflecting the glare from the wall-mounted LCD fifty-inch flat-screen TV hanging between the two glass mirrors behind the bar.

"These young gals running around screaming how independent they are and sexually free. They trying to turn the tables on us and wear the pants, pay the bills and pimp us. You feel me?"

George nodded.

Marcus laughed. "They can go on with their independent *Sex and the City*-wannabe asses, 'cause the truth is, ain't no man going to marry that. Hell, I ain't."

This was the usual Thursday for George and his friend Marcus. Marcus would bitch and moan about how there are no good women around anymore, and George would listen, agree, pour him another and another, then call a cab to take him home.

George noticed a thirsty patron at the other end of the bar and excused himself from his friend's tirade.

Marcus shook his head. Everything he had ever believed in walked out the door along with his wife and son. He never thought Sheri would be the type to do what she did. And he never imagined being on the opposite end of the dating curb, along with the other undesirables: women over thirty-four. It was baffling to him why he couldn't meet a woman down with his program.

George came back and poured him another.

Marcus put up his hand. "Whoa! Slow down, partner. I haven't finished this one yet."

"It's from the lady at the end of the bar. She told me to tell you that you look like you could use a neat Pinch."

Marcus hadn't heard that phrase from a woman ever. He looked toward the end of the bar and was immediately intrigued. Short haircut, her bang slicked back and upward like a 1980s Sheila E., her eyes resembled an Angelina Jolie, with the lips and skin complexion of Naomi Campbell. Her blouse was slightly unbuttoned in just the right place.

"Tell her I said thank you and that I would love for her to tell me what else she thinks I need." A little fire in Marcus lit up as if he was a fresh twenty-two-year-old NFL rookie. He was feeling his "playa card" slowly becoming reinstated.

George chuckled to see his friend off his pity party. *It was about goddamn time*, he thought and didn't hesitate to relay the message.

Marcus watched from afar her every move as George gave her the message. She grinned a devious smile. To Marcus that meant only one thing. She was digging him. Marcus stuck his chest out just a hair, getting that good old feeling back. The kind of feeling every man needed to make him feel like he was a man. That he was desired, and that for sure, he could still get it.

The woman laid some bills on the bar, her lips mouthing, "Thank you," to George. She slid back from her barstool and flung her oversized designer bag onto her shoulder.

Marcus could hear the click-clack of her heels walking toward him. He made eye contact with her and followed her deep brown eyes without a blink, smiling confidently. Here was this beautiful female creature coming who recognized his needs and was willing to take care of them. He didn't know her from a hole in the wall, but what he did know, he liked.

He didn't take his eyes off hers, as she strutted toward him in a fitted dark grey waistline skirt and white blouse, revealing a plastic surgeon's ideal cleavage.

Marcus watched her plump lips stretch to form a grin. *She can definitely get it.* Her curves were sensational with all the right proportions. The woman got closer and closer, and Marcus's smile got wider and wider. Any bigger and he might as well have been the Joker.

She was close enough now. Marcus got up and pulled out the barstool, like a gentleman. Without a word, the woman smiled with her eyes, and continued to walk past Marcus, the sound of her click-clack heels fading until she was out the door.

Marcus quickly forgot about all the nonsense he was talking just a few minutes ago as he stood there with the barstool still in his hand. Embarrassed and crushed, he slumped back into his barstool, signaled for George to pour him another, and continued his rant about bitch-ass women missing out on a hell of a guy.

George felt bad for his friend and tried his hardest not to laugh. The scene was comical to him, but he tried to be sensitive of his friend's feelings and abandoned the idea of making jokes. He knew all too well how delicate Marcus's feelings were.

"Don't worry about it, man. You are never going to meet the one for you in here anyway. My place screams one-night stand. Why you think I have this happy hour special four times a week?"

Marcus shrugged his shoulders. "I don't know. Why?"

"Because the liquor brings out the freak in everyone, especially the suit-and-tie women."

"I know that. Why you think I am in here? I want a freak, a suit-and-tie hottie," Marcus said, slurring his words.

"No, you don't. You want a wife, and you damn sure ain't going to find her in here. I'm calling you a cab. You've reached your cut-off point, my man." He patted him on his back.

Marcus nodded and sipped down the last of his Pinch scotch. He shook his head again and looked around at all the young fabulous crowd mixing and mingling in booths and at the bar, wondering why he wasn't so popular.

He decided to wait for his cab outside because he couldn't stand feeling sorry for himself any longer. It was sickening.

As soon as he stepped outside it began to rain. He didn't have his umbrella or a jacket to shield him this wet fall night. As he turned toward the bar doorway to run back inside, there she was with an umbrella.

She walked up to him and stretched the umbrella over his head with one arm, and with the other, pulled his face to hers and kissed him. She said, "Soft. I knew they would be soft."

Marcus was so caught off guard. He thought she'd left him high and dry. Now here she was looking out for his needs again. He grabbed her face and returned the favor.

As his cab pulled up, she whispered, "Let's get out of here."

Her forwardness caught him off guard again. *Who is she? And who does she think she is?* Marcus never liked a pushy, bossy woman. They were never his type. He looked into her eyes and without an afterthought said, "Your place or mine?"

She smiled. "Wherever."

Hot damn! His playa card was renewed. Marcus opened the door, popped his collar and got into the cab with a woman he didn't know and nine times out of ten didn't want to know, but tonight he was gonna make her an exception.

Chapter 4

Marcus only fantasized about a woman like this—ready, eager, adventurous, and no holds barred in the bedroom. She'd undressed him with her eyes way before she undressed him physically. He lifted his arms and she pulled off his shirt.

Her hands caressed his back, and she nibbled a bit on his nipples. She tugged at his pelvis as she sat on the edge of his king-sized bed. She unbuttoned and unzipped his pants, not timid about her need to look over the merchandise before trying it out.

His long, thick shaft sprung up to meet her.

She grabbed him gently and stroked him with her hands. She placed her hands on both sides of his waist and moved his pelvis slowly toward her mouth.

Marcus wasn't expecting anything but maybe doggy-style, but this, whoa, what a treat it was. He flung his head back to view his ceiling fan, exhaling with each lip, tongue, and shaft inter-action. He glanced downward, at her undeni-able skills for making a man feel damn good. He grabbed her hair at the roots. He didn't want to cum, he wanted this to last all night.

Before he began to tremble, she pushed him away and proceeded to climb on top of the bed, unzipped her skirt, and pulled it off.

Marcus grabbed her head again and stuck his tongue in her mouth. He reached for her clito-ris and she moved his hand to the right place. He kissed her neck and down to her breasts. He couldn't wait to hold them, touch them, and bite them. And so he did. He put his fingers deeper between her legs. The soft, moist orifice felt like a cherry-baked pie inside. He wondered what it tasted like.

He didn't have to wait longer as she began to mount him like wall climbing, one step at a time. Her legs wrapped around his neck as she braced herself by holding onto the ceiling fan, he pushed his tongue inside her cherry pie and licked and sucked his way to her clitoris, making her giggle with pure glee. Her sweet filling began to drip down his cheek. She giggled louder as her legs shook.

Marcus untangled himself from the grip of her legs and threw her on his bed. She crawled like a tigress trying to get away. He pulled her by the legs to the edge of the bed. She tried to turn around, but he had her right where he wanted her. She stopped him with her hand and held onto his twin sac tightly, and Marcus's face became a little flushed, feeling pleasure and pain at the same time.

He reached for his pants and pulled out a condom from his wallet, but she never let go of his balls. He ripped open the condom, and she began to tug a little gentler. He slipped on the cover and tried to push her hand away from him, but she wouldn't let go, like a dog with a bone. *Fuck it!* He rammed his penis into her cherry.

The feeling of her tugging on his balls as he power-drove into her was exhilarating. Doggystyle was his favorite, but this upgrade had him oohing and coo-cooing like a baby. In no time he collapsed on her back.

She giggled again. "I will give you a ten-minute break," she said with authority. "Then it's my turn to ride you."

Who the hell is she? Marcus kept asking himself. *And where the hell has she been all his life?* The sex was unbelievable. Maybe he could tame her shrewlike, I-don't-need-a-man behavior. Marcus concentrated on how much fun he just had and tried not to think about tomorrow. It was in his nature though. What's a man without a woman to take care of his needs? At this moment, one of his most important needs was met without his usually nightly self-entertainment.

She rolled over and tapped him on his shoulder.

Fuck it! The theme for the night. Whoever she was, he was definitely ready for the next move in her playbook. Maybe he needed to step outside his box.

Chapter 5

Marcus woke up to the sound of a shower running. He rubbed his head and looked at the time. Quickly recalling his actions last night, he hopped up, checked his wallet, and looked for his Tag Huer watch on his wrist. All there. So he hadn't taken home a hooker or thief. Then who the hell was she? *What kind of woman picks up a man, fucks the shit out of him all night, and doesn't rob him? A groupie, maybe?*

He looked for the condoms he'd used last night, trying to match a rubber for each time they did the nasty. If she was a groupie, he didn't have the funds to support another "take-him-to-the-cleaners" kind of girl. All there. He forcefully exhaled.

The shower cut off. He slipped on his briefs and tried to find his silk robe behind the door. Then he saw her purse on the nightstand. He was tempted to take a quick peek, jot down her name and address, just in case.

As he reached for it and began to rumble through her bag, she said, "Can I help you?"

Embarrassed, Marcus laid his cards on the table. He shrugged his shoulders. "Seriously, though, what kind of woman sleeps with a man she doesn't even know?"

"What kind of man sleeps with a woman he barely knows?"

Marcus was caught off guard for the third time by this woman. Feeling defeated, he extended his hand with a smile. "Hello, my name is Marcus Hill."

On the inside, she thought that was cute, but on the outside she didn't melt. "Nice to meet you. I have to go."

Dumbfounded, he asked, "So you're not going to tell me your name?"

As coy as she wanted to be, "Nope." She snatched her purse off the nightstand and proceeded to get dressed.

Marcus scratched his head. She was cold as ice. He didn't know what to say next. "Look, I apologize for going through your purse. I just don't do this kind of thing often."

Still ignoring him, she zipped up her skirt and looked for her shoes.

"Really, I figured you were either a hooker or a groupie or—"

"So wait a minute. A woman can't get her freak on with a complete stranger unless she is some kind of whore?"

Marcus didn't go anywhere near that one. He remained silent with doe eyes.

"So I guess I should be asking you how much then, or if you have a card with a number on it so I can pass you around to my friends, you know, with you being a whore and all." She didn't blink.

Marcus chuckled. "A man whore and a woman whore are on two different playing fields."

"Fuck you!" She stormed off.

Marcus was never in his life attracted to such a firecracker. He couldn't let her go until she told him who she was. He tried his best to behave like a gentleman and pull out his playa card once again.

He was on her heels. "Look, I am sorry again. It seems all I do is offend you." He grabbed her arm. "Let me at least drive you home."

She snatched her arm from his grip. "*Puh-leeze*. My driver is waiting downstairs by now."

"Your driver?" *So she is a call girl.*

She recognized that look. "Marcus, so you are not confused ever again by women . . . I am a businesswoman, a hardworking businesswoman who can afford anything she wants, including someone to pick her up and drop her off whenever, wherever. Maybe it's that fact that makes me feel like I can have anything I want. And last night, what I wanted was you. Plain and simple."

Marcus was again dumbfounded. No woman ever spoke to him like that.

She got closer to him and said, "Haven't you ever seen something you wanted and, without an apology, just taken it?"

Marcus pondered.

Before he could get out an answer, she silenced him with her index finger. "Think about it, Marcus. And when you know the answer, then you may call me." She walked out the door.

Marcus snapped out of her trance. He ran after her outside his front door. "Wait!" he shouted. "I don't know your name."

She looked back at him before her driver closed her door. "Figure it out. If you want it bad enough, you will."

Marcus took a memory snapshot of her license plate and planned to track her down.

Chapter 6

Marcus shifted through the aisles of the Alexandria supermarket, fifteen miles outside D.C. He knew she would be there right around this time. It didn't take long for him to track her down. A quick registration look-up led to a business, that led to a CEO, that led to a name. Kendra Black. He followed her one day from her office and watched her routine from afar. Marcus could have been a private detective in another life if he wanted to. But was it this serious? To him the chase was.

There she was in aisle seven, filling her basket with wheat pasta this and brown rice that. Marcus pulled his cart filled with V8 juices and meats in front of hers. She looked surprised, but her smile quickly turned upside down.

"I'm sorry about that. I was caught off guard by your beauty, and instead of going for the spaghetti noodles, I ran into you. Hi. My name is Marcus. And yours?"

"Kendra. Kendra Black."

It had been two weeks since she saw him last, but she behaved as though it had never been.

"Can I ask you something, Kendra?"

"What?"

"Have you ever seen something you wanted and just taken it?"

"All the time." She grinned.

He smiled back at her. "Then we have something in common."

She rolled her eyes. "Hardly."

He pushed his cart out of his way and grabbed her waist. He pushed his tongue inside her mouth and caressed her back. Then he pulled away. "Hardly." He grinned and squinted his eyes. "Hard, yes, *hardly*, no." He walked away, leaving his cart of groceries.

Kendra smiled with excitement as he left. She didn't care who saw or who made comments. It was about to be World War III with Marcus, no prisoners.

Chapter 7

A month and half later, Marcus still had yet been able to catch up with Kendra. It was always, "I have a previous engagement," or "I have to work," routine excuses that left Marcus wondering if she was even into him. He proceeded with his MO, sending flowers to her job, expensive gifts to her front door, more-naughty-than-nice text messages to her BlackBerry, and explicit photographs to her Gmail account.

He could tell she enjoyed the erotic e-mail forwards he would send, since he always got a smiley face or an LMAO (laughing my ass off) response. He often wondered why she played so hard to get, when he already had gotten it? What was this cat-and-mouse game about?

At his rope's end, he called his younger cousin Lamant to see if he had any idea what women of today get hot enough for. He and Lamant met the following Saturday morning at the golf course on Lowes Island Boulevard, seven miles outside D.C.

Fair-skinned with hazy green eyes, Lamant stood five feet four inches tall. Marcus nicknamed him "the pretty boy of the family" and always mocked him for his height. The Napoleon complex in Lamant made him work out regularly at the gym, seek weekly visits for his manicure and pedicure, and consult with his female fashion experts to tailor his outfits.

Marcus thought of his cousin as somewhat of an expert on women. He never had a problem, meeting, dating and sustaining a relationship with women. It was his picky, rigid dating obsessive compulsive requirements that left him either floating in a sea of different women or sleeping alone some nights.

Marcus teed off first, naturally. After football, golf was the next best thing for competing. He'd invested heavily in two sets of custom-made clubs, with matching leather bags and dozens of gold-encrusted M.H. initials on his golf balls. Thanks to his weekly lessons with a coach, he often won each round.

Lamant played mostly for business. As an investment banker, he never really tried to win, but the competition was always a motivation to play. What male didn't enjoy a little competition, along with a wager, to keep it fresh and interesting?

Pressed for time, they played a nine-hole round and chatted about money, sports, cars, and then women.

Lamant asked, "So what did she say when you gave her the Tiffany bracelet?"

"She called me to thank me, and told me I didn't have to do that." Marcus swung his nine iron, firing his golf ball 150 yards to the green.

Lamant shook his head. "So, didn't you say she is some big executive or something?"

"She owns her own marketing firm."

"Damn! A sista has got to be paid. And you broke her off with a Tiffany bracelet?" He laughed. "Come on, cuz, you have got to come harder than that. She probably has like a hundred of those things." He smirked. Lamant tried to swing his club with enough acceleration to beat his cousin's last shot, but the ball didn't make it anywhere near the hole.

"It cost me over five hundred dollars."

"Still tight with your wallet, I see. That's what cost you your last wife, and it definitely isn't going to get you anywhere with the ladies. Women today have enough juice to upgrade you, so buying them things they can afford times ten means nothing. You have to think outside the box." Lamant drew an imaginary box in the air to emphasize his point. He was able to break it down for him, most of his friends being females from college.

Marcus let his cousin's advice sink in, but he couldn't think beyond the ways he knew how to woo a woman, which had always worked before. *What kind of woman doesn't want flowers, gifts, and for a man to call her all the time? What made Kendra so damn special?*

"Can I ask you something?" Lamant scratched his head in bewilderment. He couldn't grasp why his cousin was going to these lengths when he'd already test-driven the ride.

Marcus shrugged. "What's up?"

"Why are you tripping off this female anyway? Didn't you already hit that?"

"I don't know. There's something about her that makes me just want her. I don't know. It's weird."

Lamant smiled. "Oh, I get it. She made it do what it do." He began to mockingly laugh. "She put it on a brother. Damn!" He put his fist to his lips, grinning, amused at his cousin's predicament.

Marcus waved him off. "Let's go." He didn't want to admit it, but Kendra had his nose more open than the ozone layer.

"Just admit it. She fucked your brains out. Otherwise, there is no way you of all people would be tripping like this." Lamant followed Marcus to the next putt. "Come on, admit it—The nappy got you ready to make her Mrs. Hill."

Marcus ignored his younger cousin's comments. "Not even. I just want to get to know her. No rush to make her the missus. She too damn sassy and independent for me anyway. No way would she want to give it all up to be a real housewife of D.C." He alone laughed at his joke.

"Yeah, right." Not buying his cousin's camouflage, Lamant knew Marcus couldn't stand not having his trophy wife and, even more so, hated being single. "Just admit it, and I will tell you how to get her."

"What did you have in mind?"

After they finished up their nine holes, Lamant filled Marcus in on what he meant by thinking outside the box. He started off by saying, "The question you have to ask yourself is this. What can you give to a woman that she can't already get for herself?"

Chapter 8

Marcus succeeded in getting for Kendra, a woman who had everything, something she couldn't get for herself.

Kendra trembled in her seat of the air carrier. As adventurous as she was, she could never build up enough courage to do it herself. Her knees buckled, and she wanted to escape as the doors to the airplane, 14,000 feet in the air, opened. She shook her head. "I'm not doing it, Marcus, no way. You can forget it!"

Marcus gleamed from ear to ear. Finally he had her right where he wanted her. She needed him. For the first time since he met her, she needed him for something. He finally proved to himself and her that he was surely man enough for her, and he had the balls to show for it. Loving this moment, he commanded her, "Don't be afraid. I got you. I won't let anything happen to you." He smiled and reached for her hand.

She closed her eyes and shook her head. "No, I can't. I can't do it."

"Kendra, look at me. Look at me!" he shouted.

Kendra managed to peek through one eye. She could see the white clouds.

He caught her bare gaze. "When I first met you, I knew you were that superwoman. You're not going to let a little jump defeat you, are you? Are you that superwoman?"

Kendra snapped out of her paralyzing fear. She wanted to kick her own ass for telling Marcus all the things she would love to do before she died. Never in a million years, did she think he was actually listening.

She wasn't afraid of death. Pain, yes, but death, no. Fast cars, action, and excitement were what she craved. She never wanted to be bored. That alone was death. She kept telling herself that as she slowly rose, eyes closed, praying to God to give her the courage.

"Trust me, baby, I got you." Marcus had her right where he wanted her. "I won't let anything happen to you."

She opened her eyes and stared down her fear, 14,000 feet of sky that land never seemed to touch. Trying to shake off her terror, she screamed at Marcus, "If my hair gets messed up, I'm going to kick your ass."

Marcus chuckled at the thought of her five feet three inch frame ripping him a new one. She was cute when she was mad. He liked it.

The tandem skydiver instructors strapped Kendra and Marcus onto their harness. She trembled more but was determined to do it. She wouldn't let fear control her. She put herself in a timeout as she counted and prayed, counted and prayed.

Like a warrior on the battlefield, Marcus chanted, "Let's do this!" He gave Kendra's partner a high five before he and his jumper leaped into the open sky. Kendra watched as Marcus's body quickly became a dot. She closed her eyes. She couldn't back out, and she couldn't let anyone get the better of her.

She nodded her head. "What are you waiting for? Let's go." She said it with more authority than she knew she had.

The instructor didn't count to brace her but just leaped into the humongous blue with the adrenaline of an assassin.

Kendra was as stiff as a board; she wanted to be airlifted back into the plane. Her heart couldn't find its way back inside her chest. She wanted to open her eyes but thought she would lose it and kill them both.

Her instructor yelled at the top of his lungs in excitement, "Whoo-hoo! Cowabunga!"

"Shut up already!" Kendra shouted, her eyes still closed.

"You're missing it. This feels unbelievable. Let go, Kendra. Imagine you're a hawk soaring in the sky, unstoppable, untouchable, looking down, no destination in mind. You're free."

Freedom. Kendra didn't have a lot of that since she'd started her company. Always on the go, always trying to be better at what she did, she was always stressed and never stopped trying to find ways to release it, including sex.

She let the word sink in her head as she opened her eyes, and her body stopped fighting the wind and loosened up. She couldn't believe it. She was literally flying. She shouted, "Oh my God. I am freeeeeee!" She found her moment and started living in it.

The two caught up to Marcus and his partner. Just when Kendra was letting go, her instructor pulled the rip cord to release the parachute.

She jolted to fear again. "What the fuck!"

Marcus laughed hysterically. He loved seeing her not in control. Uncouth. He enjoyed every minute of it. He and his partner parachuted out, and the four of them floated through the air without a care for tomorrow.

Kendra regained her composure. She was in the zone again, feeling untrapped by demands.

Marcus shouted, "Isn't this incredible?"

Kendra nodded. "Yes!"

"Still plan on kicking my ass?"

She nodded. "Oh, hell yes!"

He laughed, knowing he had finally broken her iceberg.

Kendra had her mind on absolutely nothing. It was a rare occasion. She wasn't on her grind, she wasn't engaged in mind games with men, she wasn't trying to control her addiction, she wasn't thinking about tomorrow. More than a release for her, it was a triumphant moment.

They reached the ground and tumbled to regroup and regain their balance. The jumpers released their harness to let Marcus and Kendra go. Kendra unstrapped herself and took off her helmet, which left her hair matted on her forehead.

Marcus took off his gear, apparently not fast enough for Kendra, because she threw her helmet at his head.

He ducked. "You missed me."

Kendra charged at him and began to flail her hands in the air, trying to attack him. "I'm going to kill you. I can't believe you did that to me."

Marcus grabbed her arms, pulled her body into his, and wrapped her arms around him. "You know you loved it!" He stared her down.

She was immobilized. She looked at him, secretly thinking she had the time of her life. No one had ever done anything like that for her that brought her so many emotions all at once, fear, excitement, peace. It was the ultimate high. Marcus had her attention beyond the bedroom. *Could I let him in? Could he be the one to save me from myself?*

Their lips touched gently.

"Are you hungry?"

She nodded her head.

He gave each instructor a high five, with a small tip, and led Kendra to a nearby picnic area where he had set up a table, chairs, and a romantic candlelight dinner at sunset.

Marcus stepped up his game, and Kendra took notice. She felt like she was a mess, sweaty, her makeup was running away, and her hair, Lord, must've looked like a beautician's nightmare.

Marcus pulled out the chair for her and noticed she grabbed the knife to check her reflection. "You look beautiful," he assured her.

She smiled back at him. "Liar."

Out of nowhere, a waiter came with a glass of wine. Kendra did a double take. She couldn't believe how Marcus was shining that evening. She wanted to tell him but couldn't let him throw her off her game. A serious relationship wasn't what she wanted at this time. She enjoyed doing her.

Marcus was in his glory. He thought he had done it, melted his little ice queen in the palm of his hands. With persistence, he knew she could be the woman he needed. He thought, *What woman could say no after this? I can change her.*

Chapter 9

Four months into their relationship, Marcus thought his plans to change Kendra were going well. She'd started leaving personal items at his house, so she could stay over three out of seven nights a week. Those three nights she would cook dinner for him. Spinach lasagna was his favorite. At first, meeting her for lunch was always a no, but now he could catch her at least once a week. She attended charity functions with him, and he introduced her as his lady. Before, she would correct him and say she was his friend, but Marcus got her to see it his way.

Kendra was seeing him at least five times a week, a date here, phone conversation during the night on occasion. He even got her to agree to meet his mother. That was a task, but Marcus was convinced she just might be the one.

Although Kendra fought tooth and nail to keep her independence, Marcus knew he could get her on his program when he proposed. *What woman wouldn't want to marry me? What woman wouldn't want to be taken care of? If all she has to do is manage a household and cater to her man's needs, what else really does she need?*

Marcus was certain that Kendra would want everything he did for them. The next thing was for her to meet his son. If he could get her to be a mother to his child, then it was on. She would be the next Mrs. Hill.

The difference between Sheri and Kendra was that Kendra already had her own money, so he wasn't worried that she would go after his. Together, their empire would be unstoppable. She could easily get someone to run her company for her, and be a mother to his son and their future children. Marcus thoroughly believed all women wanted to be rescued, and all that independent, don't-need-a-man bullshit was just an excuse for those who hadn't met their knight in shining armor yet. And Kendra wasn't any different, no matter how hard she tried to deny it. She needed a man. And Marcus wanted to be him.

Marcus's meeting with his foundation, the Marcus Hill Sports Foundation for Kids, ended early. He and his team were planning to open a recreation center in downtown D.C. for inner-city kids to join, get off the streets, get involved in sports and channel their energy. He loved working with kids, especially young boys, since he didn't see his son as often as he wanted to after the divorce.

"I want to have this center up by the end of the March," Marcus said to his staff at the meeting. On, and now off, the field, Marcus still embodied that team-member spirit and wanted to get everyone on board with his plans.

"We should have it up sooner than that if these next two fundraisers bring in the right amount of capital." Joyce, the wife of a former teammate of Marcus's, assured him. She had worked on all Marcus's projects and helped him start the foundation. She and Sheri used to be very close until the divorce. When Marcus and Sheri split, Joyce felt she knew Marcus longer and decided she would continue to be his friend, especially since he and her husband were still good friends.

"Let's make it happen then. The next meeting is when, Debbie?"

"Two weeks from today. Everyone should have their action items completed by the next meeting." Debra was Marcus's longtime personal assistant.

"Cool. Okay, ladies and gentlemen," Marcus said, referring to his brother Gregory, the only one male on the team of five. "See you then."

Everyone nodded. "Yeah."

Marcus checked his watch. He figured he would surprise Kendra at her job for lunch.

Joyce caught him before he left. "Hey, Marcus. When is Marquise coming for the summer? I want to get him and Jeffrey together." Jeffrey was her son, and he and Marquise were close friends.

"The end of June. He will be here for two months. School for him doesn't start until after Labor Day in Boston. He's been asking about Jeffrey like a mad man. 'Is he going to be home, Daddy? I want to go to the baseball game, Daddy. Can Jeffrey go'?" Marcus mimicked his son. "If he had his way, he would spend the entire summer with Jeffrey and not me. But I will see him in a few weeks for his February break. Maybe they can catch up then."

Joyce laughed. "Those two are as thick as thieves. Jeffrey misses him a lot. He got so excited when I told him he was coming down last summer, but was so disappointed when he didn't make it." She shook her head.

"Yeah, but what are you going to do? That's your girl," he jokingly said referring to Sheri. "Convince her to move back."

"I wish I could. I would have talked her out of the divorce too, but you know how that goes.

I miss her too. Shoot, I miss all the fun we used to have."

"Well, according to her, it wasn't much fun. Anyways, water under the bridge." He shook his head, trying to push out the hurt his ex-wife had caused him. He perked up at his next thought. "Don't worry, I might be coupled up sooner than later."

"You and Sheri are talking reconciliation?"

"Hell, naw!" Marcus couldn't conceive giving her another chance after what she'd done to him. "I'm seeing someone. It could get serious."

"Sure, sure, Marcus. I know what serious means for you."

"What's that supposed to mean?"

"Don't think I don't know all the times you've tried to convince Jeff to go out whore-hunting when he was supposed to be at home with me. I can only imagine what you've found out there. I'll pass on meeting this one."

"For real, this may be serious. Ask Jeff. Kendra is a keeper."

"Yeah, that's what you said about Sheri, and look what happened. You're never going to meet this ideal Martha Stewart, Florence Jefferson woman in the nightclub, Marcus. And not at these groupie-polluted fundraisers either. You don't think these women know who you are and what they want out of you?"

"Kendra's not like that. You'll like her. Watch." Marcus caught himself. "Wait. How did you even know about her?"

Joyce gave him one look. "Come on, you know good and well Jeff can't keep anything to himself. He told me all about her."

"Well, don't believe the shit your husband is shoveling. Kendra isn't like that. You'll see." Marcus made a mental note to get on his buddy about bad-mouthing Kendra to his wife. He couldn't have anyone disrespecting the future Mrs. Hill.

"*We'll see* is right, Marcus. She doesn't even sound like your type, you know, catering to your every need. Sounds like you are catering to hers."

"Whatever." He waved her off. She was like a sister to him. "Just tell your husband to keep his mouth shut about my personal business."

Joyce laughed. "I will try." She had been friends with Marcus since she and Jeff were in college. She loved him like a brother and was very sad when things didn't work out with him and Sheri. She wasn't surprised though. She tried to tell him that his wants were too demanding for any woman to put up with, but he never listened. She figured he would get it right sooner rather than later. For his sake, anyway.

Chapter 10

Marcus drove from Georgetown to downtown D.C. to meet Kendra for lunch. He didn't call her; he wanted it to be a surprise. He parked his car in the garage of her building and took the elevator to the lobby floor. He walked up to the security desk to get a visitor's pass. The security guard recognized him and told him he had to call up to the floor.

Knowing the routine, Marcus told him, "I was trying to surprise my lady for lunch. You've seen me here with her before. Kendra Black. She runs the marketing firm Blackside. I'm Marcus Hill."

"The running back for the Baltimore Ravens?" he said, surprised. "Yeah, I know you. Damn, they could of used you this season. I'm still pissed about them losing the playoffs to those 'bamas,'" he said, referring to the Indianapolis Colts.

Marcus gave him dap. "I agree, man. Thank you. Next year it's going to be an entirely different set, you feel me? No mercy." Marcus figured the security guy must have been from Maryland, rooting for the Ravens instead of the Redskins.

"You can go on up, Mr. Hill."

"Thanks, partner. Let me know when you're trying to go to a game. A ticket is not a problem."

The security guard gave him a head nod.

Marcus made his way up to the twenty-eighth floor, where Kendra's company was located. He was hoping more for an afternoon quickie than a sandwich at the nearby Panera Bread bakery-cafe. He whisked past the front desk clerk and made his way to her office. He could feel Pamela, Kendra's assistant, on his heels.

She stopped him. "Excuse me, Mr. Hill," she said. "She's not in today."

"She's not? That's funny. She didn't tell me that."

"She left early. She wasn't feeling well."

"Oh, really? I'll give her a call on her cell. Thanks. I hope it's not the flu."

Marcus felt bad. He pulled out his phone and called her, but it went straight to voice mail. He left her a message. "Hey, babe. It's me. Hope everything is okay. Call me when you get this."

He made his way back to his car and was going to drive home, but instead he decided to drive out to Alexandria to see if Kendra was home. He stopped and picked up some chicken soup and some Tylenol for cold and flu. He reached her driveway and parked his car behind her brand-new baby blue 2009 Jaguar.

He rang the doorbell, and her housekeeper came to the door. Madie greeted him, "Hello, Mr. Hill. Is Ms. Black expecting you?"

"No. I just left her office after her secretary said she went home sick. How is she?

"She's not here. She left this morning for work."

"Did she call to say she was coming home sick?"

"Not that I know of. I just know she's not here, Mr. Hill. Should I leave her a message?

"No, that's okay, Madie. I'll check in on her later." Marcus gave her the bag of soup and medicine.

"I will tell her you came by, Mr. Hill. She'll be sorry she missed you."

Marcus hopped back in his car. He wasn't born yesterday. *Where the fuck is she really?* He drove home thinking maybe Kendra wasn't who he thought she was anyway. "Hell, look how she met me," he said out loud to himself. He shook his head and began to rethink his plans of introducing Kendra to his son, marriage, and everything else. Maybe things were moving too fast. Maybe Joyce was right. She wasn't his type, and he was kidding himself that he could get her to change.

Ten minutes from his house, Marcus was all set to slow things down with Kendra and start seeing other women. When his phone rang, he wasn't surprised who it was. "Hey. I just left your house. Are you home?"

"I'm on my way. I'm leaving the doctor's office now."

"Is everything all right? Are you okay?"

"Yeah, just feeling under the weather today. Thought it might be the flu or something. The doctor thought I needed a pregnancy test."

Marcus slammed the brakes. The screech of his Escalade's tires could be heard through the phone.

"Marcus, are you there?" she said in a frantic voice. "Are you okay?"

He caught himself. "Yeah, yeah, I am cool. So what did the doctor say?"

She laughed. "Oh, Marcus, don't worry. I'm not pregnant. I take my magic pill every day. Haven't missed one ever." She continued to laugh.

Marcus turned on the air conditioner to his car. He had worked himself into a sweat. He wasn't ready for that, especially if they weren't even married yet. Two baby mamas was straight "project" to him. That just wasn't how he wanted to do things.

"Hello. Are you still there?"

"Yeah, I'm here. I left you some soup and medicine at your house."

"How sweet of you. I might be up to you playing nurse tonight."

"Doctor. I can play doctor." The thought of a male nurse screamed J.L. King and his *On the Down Low* drivel.

"You're so jaded, Marcus." Kendra smirked. "So your place or mine?"

"I can turn around and head back to your house. That's not a problem."

"Okay, maybe in an hour or two. I want to freshen up and get comfortable. Madie probably already has dinner going. See you soon."

Before Marcus could object to waiting that long to arrive, she was gone. He had just left her house thirty minutes ago. Now he had to go home, wait like another hour, then get back on the road to go see her. *Who's wearing the pants in this relationship?* It was starting to feel like he wasn't, and all the things he thought he'd changed in her might have not been his doing at all.

Caught up, Marcus drove home, showered, relaxed and got back on the road an hour later.

He convinced himself that going to see his sick girlfriend was the manly thing to do. What kind of man lets his girlfriend travel so far and so late to see him? Especially if she is sick. He reminded himself the entire drive to her house that he was wearing the pants, that he was in control of their relationship.

Chapter 11

Christmas, seven months ago, was the last time Marcus saw Marquise, who was supposed to spend his February vacation with Marcus, but Sheri took him to Europe instead. Easter came around, and Sheri went back on her word again, and took him to Florida with her family. It was one excuse after the other with her. He talked on the phone to him every day and texted him at night to make sure he had done his homework, brushed his teeth, and said his prayers. Because of his anger toward Sheri, Marcus tried to only have contact with his son, to avoid spilling his venom in front of him. One wrong word or eye-roll from Sheri, and Marcus couldn't keep his composure. He was still devastated by her decision to leave him and break up their happy home, and wasn't over it after all this time. How could he be?

At first he planned to invite Kendra on the drive to Boston to pick up Marquise. He wanted to rub her in Sheri's face, which wasn't a good idea, considering she held all the cards when it came to custody of their son.

Sheri had hired a man-eating, great white shark of a lawyer, and had everyone convinced, including the divorce judge, that all Marcus cared about was football and chasing after women.

Marcus told Kendra he was taking a weekend to pick up his son and explained why he didn't ask her to go.

"I'm looking forward to the summer with my son," he said. "I don't want anything to get in the way of that. And I mean my heartless ex-wife coming up with reasons not to let him stay. I plan to tell her about you soon. Don't worry."

Kendra wasn't worried. She was looking forward to a little time for herself over the weekend. She enjoyed Marcus's company, but she still wasn't ready to make the commitment he wanted. She still wanted to play the field. She couldn't help herself.

"That's okay, baby. It gives me time to catch up on work and other things."

A tad bit curious, Marcus asked, "Other things like what?"

"So jealous, I swear. Marcus, can something possibly not be about you?" His constant wet-blanket routine wore her down. That, and his constant mission to change her made her want to never commit to anything Marcus was planning. He was just too damn demanding, always wanting her around to cook, pick out what he should wear, to attend this event and that event. Kendra felt like she was already his wife and wanted no part in any of that. She remained on his arm though. Torn.

The sex was incredible, and he treated her nice, but she only wished he could loosen up the reins and accept her for her. But how could he, when she hadn't been completely honest with him about her condition?

"I'm just saying, this is like our first weekend apart in ten months. Are you sure you're going to be fine?" Marcus asked, trying to shield his jealousy.

"I'm positive." *Good riddance*, she thought. She finally would have time to see what's new. In other words, see someone new. Monogamy wasn't in her nature. She tried to mask herself and be a better person, like her therapist coached her to be, but her inner desire was her disease. It didn't help much either that her therapist, Dr. Sarkasian, had been missing for months.

"I will be fine. Can't wait to meet Marcelle next week."

"It's *Marquise*, baby," he reminded her for the umpteenth time.

"Sorry. *Marquise*." She knew she messed up again and tried to play it off. "I bet he gets all his looks from his father."

"You're right about that. Maybe Monday or Tuesday night you can fix your special spinach lasagna. We would love that."

There he goes, trying to make me a housewife again. This Samantha Bewitched *shit gets on my nerves.* "Sounds like a plan. Talk to you soon. Have a safe trip."

"I'll call you when I get there, baby. Love you."

"Me too. Call me. *Ciao*." Kendra pressed the end button on her BlackBerry. She typed in a reminder on her calendar so she wouldn't forget: Have Madie make spinach lasagna Tuesday night.

Her deception with Marcus got deeper and deeper by the day. She liked him, and felt a way about him. But was it love? Was this it? Besides, she'd never been the kind of girl to put all her eggs in one basket. She liked to date. She loved to fuck. The adventure of meeting someone new ran her, so she had no intentions of settling down, no matter what Marcus had planned for her. But how long could she keep this up? She was almost caught months ago in her office when

Marcus decided to surprise her for lunch. It was the sheer excitement of not getting caught that thrilled her.

Kendra scurried through her contacts and pressed the call button. The phone rang. "Hey, you."

"Hey, yourself. Haven't heard from you in a while."

"The phone works both ways, you know."

"You know what else works both ways, right?"

Kendra smiled. True, she was looking to get into something new tonight, but sometimes a little something old could be just as sweet. "Ten o'clock tonight, Hilton Plaza. You know the place."

"That I do. Oh, and, Kendra, wear the red one with the straps."

"I've got something even better for you, baby." She pressed end. Finally she was free to do her. She couldn't help herself; sex was her drug, the ultimate high.

Chapter 12

As soon as Marcus walked through the door, Sheri had her anthem playing, "I Will Survive." He knew she did it to annoy him.

"Loud enough for you?" Marcus said to his ex-wife, trying to have as little interaction with her as possible. One wrong word and he and she would start arguing like schoolyard kids, and the next thing you know, Marquise wouldn't be coming with him. He was determined to learn from his mistakes in the past and keep his cool.

"It can never be loud enough for me," she said, parading around in her tight spandex workout pants and tank top. She made sure everything shook where it was supposed to and didn't jiggle where it wasn't. She put down her dumbbells and tried her best not to cuss Marcus out for sneezing wrong. She too was looking forward to the summer off. Time to get back out there and date.

"Where's Marquise?" He looked around their eight-bedroom, four-and-a-half-bath, 8,500 square foot mansion in Lexington. Marble floors, gaudy chandeliers, and museum-sized murals decorated the home. He could hear his echo from down the hallway. He couldn't resist. "Helloooo, is anybody hereee?"

"Don't come out to get me. I'm just a poor humble man looking for a bite to eat," he joked, as if her house reminded him of a haunted mansion. Sheri's taste was similar to Countess Dracula's. The house was dark and empty, with way too much space to fill in.

She shook her head. "I'm trying not to go there with you, but you are trying my patience."

"I apologize. The place is great, fitting of a countess." Marcus worked hard to keep in what he really wanted to say. *Now I know why you needed one hundred fifty million dollars of my money plus alimony. Blood-money-sucking vampire. Lord, let me get in and out of here before I burn down this place with her in it.*

Sheri snapped her fingers to get him out of his trance. "Marcus, did you hear what I said?"

"What?" He shook it off. Leaving his son motherless was an option he'd abandoned a long time ago. "What did you say?"

"I said, wait here. I'll page him on the intercom to tell him you're here."

"Cool." The fewer words exchanged between the two, the better.

Sheri walked off, strutting her tight little bottom in her ex's face. Marcus tried not to take notice but that was the very first thing he noticed about her. That ass. He watched knowing he couldn't stand her any more, but could never get enough of watching her leave.

Sheri knew what she was doing, wearing what she did, the exact same time her ex was to arrive. A little ego boost was necessary, especially since she felt like maybe, just maybe leaving the love of her life and trying to find a new one wasn't the right thing to do. What if she couldn't hook a man at her age? What if she'd made a huge mistake by leaving him? Too many what-ifs kept Sheri working out, eating less, and surfing need-a-man dot-com sites to get her groove back.

Marcus stood in the bodacious foyer staring up at the baby angels' mural painted at the top of the dome-shaped ceiling. It was quite the sight. Perhaps his wife's taste had improved. Or perhaps her ass had him hypnotized again. He heard quickened footsteps from down the hall.

"Daddy!" Marquise yelled.

Marcus opened his arms like he was receiving his son for the first time. Marquise jumped in his arms and he spun him around. They had equally missed each other. Marcus reluctantly put him back down to the ground. Men were supposed to be men. "Look at you, boy. You're about the size of a division one full back," he said, amping up his son at how big and strong he was getting.

Marquise posed like The Incredible Hulk. "You're going down!" He playfully charged for his father, and they pretended like they were on the field playing football.

Sheri looked on at the two. A part of her regretted moving her son miles away from his father, but she felt she had no choice. It was for her own sanity and salvation. Still, the two of them together made her wish they could have found a better way. She knew only a man could raise a man and hoped, whatever her and Marcus went through, he would never turn his back on his son.

Marcus took a break from their horsing around. "You ready, son?"

"Let's roll." Marquise turned to his mother to give her a hug.

She held on tight, teardrops rolling down her cheek. "Have fun, baby. And remember to say your prayers, brush you teeth, and don't let Daddy feed you all that fast food." She hugged him a little longer. "I'll call you every day, baby. I love you."

"I love you too, Mommy."

"Okay, okay, let the boy go. He'll be back." Marcus didn't want his son getting too soft and mushy now.

Sheri wiped her cheek. "You better take good care of my baby, Marcus."

"Not to worry. We're going to have a great time. Right, champ?"

"You know it."

Marcus grabbed his son's bags and almost made it out the door drama-free until Sheri's mother, Lorraine, walked in.

"Nice of you to show up," she snarled.

In short, she and Marcus never got along, mainly because he could smell from a mile away her greed and only hoped it hadn't rubbed off on Sheri. He was wrong.

"And hello to you too, Lorraine. We were just leaving."

"Not without saying good-bye to big mama, you're not." She gave Marquise a big hug and a sloppy kiss on his cheek. Marquise wiped it away; he couldn't stand old nana kisses.

"Make sure your father doesn't have you up late at night and around those sluts he calls his friends. Okay, baby."

Why'd she have to go there? "Watch your mouth around my son, woman."

"Excuse me. Who do you think you're talking to? Don't make me have to call nine-one-one on you. This is Boston, you know. They lock up a black man for trying to get into his own house. Don't get it twisted."

"Here you go, always with the drama. I thought by now you could have bought some class with all my money your daughter stole from me."

"I didn't take anything I didn't deserve," Sheri responded. "Following behind you, tending to your every need, I earned whatever I got."

"Okay, so our marriage was a job to you. You got paid for your services, you got paid for your time. Is that how it went?"

"It might as well been a job. She was always doing for you. It was always about you, you, you."

"Yeah, right. Just like my money was all about you and the rest of your money-grubbing family."

"You leave my family out of this. You don't want to mess with me, sucka. We'll dance." Lorraine gave him the middle finger.

"Tell me this, Sheri. If it was money you were after, why did you stick around as long as you did? You could have left millions of dollars ago without taking the most valuable thing to me."

"Marcus, don't go there with me. I did what I had to do to get past—"

"You did want you wanted to do, to hurt me. You knew taking my son was the deepest cut to me, and you did it anyway. Why? So you could forever be in my pocket with alimony."

"You know that is not true. You didn't even take an interest in either one of us until we were gone."

"Yeah, and you were never around. You're lucky she didn't take the shirt off your back for all you put her through. You're damn lucky."

"Look, old woman, I done told you not to use that language around my son. Wasn't anyone even talking to you. Why don't you just bounce!"

"You can't talk to me that way. Sheri, are you going to let this no-good, sorry excuse for a husband talk to me that way?"

"Marcus, just leave before I change my mind. Just go."

"Come on, Daddy. I want to go with you." Marquise could tell things were about to get overheated as usual between his mother and his father, and he didn't want to jeopardize the time he had long been looking forward to. He tugged on his father's white polo shirt.

Marcus wanted so bad to tell his ex-wife, "Fuck you! Fuck your mother! And fuck your family! None of you is ever going to see Marquise again. I am going to take him far away for good." He put himself in a timeout and said, "We'll call you when we get home." He placed his arm around his son. "Let's go, champ."

Marquise did as he was told and waved goodbye to his mom and troublemaking grandmother. Every kid's dream was for his parents to be together; in his case, he just wanted them as far away from each other as possible.

Chapter 13

Marcus waited a few days before he introduced Marquise to Kendra. He wanted them to spend some "men" time together first. As agreed, Kendra came over that Tuesday night and fixed them up a manly dinner. She thought Marquise was adorable, just like his father. She even thought maybe him being around was a good idea after all, because it kept Marcus busy. And instead of focusing on her, he could focus on his son. She pushed that idea to no limit.

She served the men their lasagna and tossed salad. "So what do you boys have planned this summer? I bet you can't wait to have all kinds of fun with your dad, Marquise." She got it right that time.

Not sure how to read her, Marquise responded with enthusiasm, "Yeah, I want to go to Six Flags, I want to go to Water Rafters, I want to go to the baseball games, I want to go to Kings Dominion, I want to go . . ."

Kendra tuned him out after Water Rafters. She counted the endless nights she would have to herself as Marcus was off busy trying to make up for lost time with his son.

"That sounds great, sweetie." She was dancing inside. Finally she could hang up this Pollyanna routine and be herself. "Your summer sounds full, baby. I don't want to be the third wheel, so don't worry about me. You two should spend as much time together as possible."

Marquise liked her already. He was a little apprehensive at first, thinking his father's girlfriend was going to be like big mama described, slutty and selfish. But Kendra was nicely dressed, she talked real nice, she was real pretty, and most importantly didn't mind him spending all his time with his father. She was sitting pretty from where he was standing.

"Don't worry, baby. There is room for you on some of our excursions. Besides, I want you to get to know each other."

"Why?" Marquise's question was both unfiltered and innocent.

Kendra was on his page. *Why does he want me to get close to his son?*

Marcus wanted to be coy. "Let's just say, I do. That's all."

Kendra began to get nervous. She couldn't believe Marcus would take it there. She started to get nauseous with the "runaway bride flu." She sat down, fixed her plate, and drank three glasses of Pinot Grigio. *What have I gotten myself into? I should have never listened to my fucking therapist. "Start fresh, try building a real relationship based on something other than sex." What a fucking joke!* Kendra's mind began to fizzle with regret.

Later that evening, Marcus tucked Marquise in for the night. He made sure he called his mother to say good night, brushed his teeth, and said his prayers.

Marcus prayed with him in unison, as if they never were apart, "Now I lay me down to sleep, I pray the Lord my soul to keep. May angels watch me through the night and keep me in their blessed sight. Amen."

He kissed him on the forehead and watched him roll over in his football field-crafted bed. He missed tucking him in at night and saying his prayers with him. He may have left everything else up to Sheri to take care of, but brushing his teeth, prayers, and tucking him in was his ritual.

Marcus was hoping he could convince a judge to let him have joint custody with Sheri, especially if he re-married and proved he would be a responsible parent who could provide a stable home.

He shut down the lights and walked out of the room to find Kendra putting on her shoes and getting ready to go. "Hey, you. Stay. He's going off to bed."

"No, it's okay. You two hang out. I have a lot of work to catch up on."

"Hang out? His bedtime is at eight P.M. Ours, well, that's another story." He grabbed her by the waist and pulled her to him.

She wrapped her arms around his neck and gave him a small peck on the lips. "Really, I have to get some work done."

"Is work and no play going to make Kendra a boring girl today?" he teased.

Humph. It's always playtime for Kendra. I don't do boring. She kissed him. "Maybe just a quick run, I have to get home."

"You know you can stay here anytime you want. You can work here."

Kendra started to feel stifled. Relationships weren't her thing, but she was trying. Refusing to go back to rehab, she decided she'd battle her addiction every day.

She kissed him harder this time and undid the buckle to his pants. She placed her tongue inside his mouth, titillating his inner desires. *Why can't I control myself?*

Marcus picked her up and carried her to his bedroom down the hall. He closed the door tightly and began ripping his clothes off and then Kendra's. He tossed her onto the bed, passion flaring in his eyes.

He grabbed her ankle as she tried to move away from him. He pulled her to the end of the bed, and she flushed with exhilaration. She loved to play hard-to-get even in bed, and he loved to play harder.

He grabbed her legs and spread them apart and over his shoulders. He began to kiss her inner thighs deeper and deeper until he reached a sweeter reward. He tugged on her clitoris with both his tongue and bottom lip. As her hips slowly rocked back and forth, he blew the heat from his mouth across her as he sucked, licked, and bit her like a pudding pop.

Kendra reached for his head and pushed him deeper inside her. She loved feeling a man's lips between her thighs, especially a man as skilled as Marcus.

She moaned deeper, her body coming unglued with every wiggle of his tongue, nibble of his teeth, and pursing of his lips. She didn't want him to stop. She grabbed her nipples and pinched them hard.

Kendra giggled with anticipatory glee, embracing the joy coming her way, and Marcus licked every last drop, leaving no crevices untouched.

He pulled her body over onto her stomach and pressed her upper back down to the bed. He grabbed her by the hair and buried her face into his satin sheets. Then he licked his index finger and placed it inside her vagina. He licked three more of his fingers and placed them inside. He licked all five and thrust them inside her, pumping her juices in and out of her.

Kendra reached from behind her and stroked his mister. He was so hard, the head of his dick could have broken a brick. She wanted him inside her. She reached for both sides of his pelvis and guided them into her.

Marcus flung her arms away and grabbed her hair to pull her face toward him. He dug his tongue, dripping wet with her juices, into her mouth, and Kendra licked his mouth.

He whispered, "Tell me how bad you want it."

Kendra groaned with impatience, "Real bad. Super bad."

"Super bad, hey." He grabbed the roots of her hair and pushed her down to the bed again. He slid his mister inside her and savored every moment as he let go of her hair and placed his hands on her hips.

When she flung her arms on his back to grab his muscular behind, he flung her arms right back where they were. He was in charge. Kendra loved it.

With each stroke her body became more glued to the bed. He was so deep, she could feel the mattress springs cling to her body. As he pumped faster, Kendra wanted to pop. When he dug deeper, she wanted to ripple.

She screamed, "Faster! Harder!"

He growled like a werewolf chasing its prey. His fangs were out, his claws were sharp, and his hunger was clear. He piled into her at the speed of a cement drill, roaring and slapping her bootylicious behind.

"Whose pussy is this?"

"Yours daddy, yours. All yours, baby! Whoo!" Kendra knew what she had gotten herself into. She hollered, "Marcus!"

The drill collapsed after shattering the tightly cemented pussy.

In Marcus's mind, there was no question who Kendra belonged to. He gave way to the moment. Caught his breath. And tapped his love on her shoulder.

She really didn't have work to do that night. She just wanted to get a breather from Marcus's demands. Now sex was a different story. Any time he wanted it, he could surely get it.

She rolled him over on his back and began to massage him everywhere. Marcus never had a complaint when it came to the bedroom and Kendra. The two were a match made in heaven. That was one area he never wanted to change. Now if she could fall in line with everything else he had planned, she could definitely get it. In more ways than one.

Chapter 14

"The whole point of us going to the baseball game together, baby, is for us to spend time together and for Marquise to get to know you. It's important to me." Marcus desperately needed to know if she was that one. He had invested all his time, energy, passion and ideas into her being his wife, and mother to Marquise. Deep down, he secretly needed her to convince a judge that he could provide a stable home for his son, but that was a backdrop to his other need. A wife. He couldn't wait to brag to Sheri that he'd really moved on.

Kendra had tried to duck and jive Marcus's "all-of-us" antics as soon as she met his son. She liked the kid, but more than an hour or two was a setup, and she knew it. Giving her all to Marcus at this time in her life wasn't what she wanted. But despite her shady behavior, Marcus wouldn't budge. She found herself trying to figure out, *How do you lose a guy in ten minutes? Fuck ten days*.

"Marcus, I told you I have a million-dollar client to come up with ads for. This is what is important to me. This is what I want. Can't you support that?

"No."

Marcus was honest. If he and Kendra got married, his first order of business would be to switch her birth control pills with placebo pills. He figured a baby would surely slow down Ms. Independent.

Kendra didn't appreciate Marcus's selfish ways at all. It was so confusing. He was all too ready to give in the bedroom, but outside it, he was stingier than a toddler.

"That isn't fair. I love my job."

"You love your job more than you love me then?"

All you could hear now was the sound of crickets.

Shocked, Marcus said, "Wow!"

"Just hear me out," Kendra said, trying to explain, still torn between bettering herself and giving into her compulsive behavior. Like with any other addiction, it was hard to quit.

"No need. I guess a career keeps you warm at night. Moaning too."

"That's another low blow, Marcus."

"I don't even know why I bother. Kick rocks!" He hung up.

Sick and tired of trying to beg her to spend time with him and his son, Marcus was really beginning to feel she wasn't the one for him.

Later that day at the game, Marcus and his son ate popcorn, hot dogs, and super-large sodas at the Red Sox/Orioles baseball game. The entire time, he didn't think of Kendra once. They were having too much fun. He only wished Marquise could stay with him more often. Eight weeks out of the year just wasn't good enough.

"Hey, Dad, I thought you said Kendra was coming."

"She had to work."

"Mom never had to work. Do you like working women?"

"Not really," Marcus said honestly.

"Then why do you like Kendra?"

"Son, sometimes a relationship between a man and a woman is so complicated that they don't even understand it. That is how it is with Kendra."

Marquise shrugged his shoulders. "Well, I know you must love her."

Shocked at his son's intuition, he asked, "How do you know that?"

"Because I hear you and her making love all the time."

Marcus choked on his Diet Coke, spilling some on his clothes. "Excuse me."

"Mom says that noise coming from your room is lovemaking. And that is what married men and women do when they love each other."

"Son, me and you will have that talk soon, but you're not even twelve yet. Let's wait until puberty, son. Please, let's just wait."

Marcus hoped his son didn't bring up sex again. He wasn't prepared for that talk on this trip. *What next?* "Wait a minute, son. Your mom told you this when?"

"When we all lived together. When you were married." Marquise shrugged. "But Mom isn't married yet. No noises come from her room."

Marcus exhaled in relief. He could appreciate that Sheri wasn't bringing home strange men if she was dating. "How's your mom doing?"

"She was sad when I spoke to her. Well, she sounds sad anyway."

"She misses you. And I know you miss her too."

Marquise nodded. "But she wasn't sad today. She actually sounded pretty mad."

"Why?" *What did a hundred-and-fifty-million-dollar woman have to be mad about? Shit, that kind of money could buy you happiness.*

"I dunno." Marquise shrugged. "It happened after I told her you were married."

"You told her what?" Marcus couldn't believe what his son was telling him.

"You two be making love, so you two are married."

The sound of the bat smashing the ball into the crowd muffled Marquise's words. The fans reached and climbed over each other to catch the first foul ball of the game.

Marcus scurried away with his son to protect him from the fans wanting to catch the ball, which landed in a batch of people right next to them.

When the patrons looked to see who caught the ball, this petite-framed woman wearing Betsey Johnson pumps and an off-white skirt suit with the ball in her French manicured hands teased, "Looking for something?"

"What are you doing here?" Marcus asked her in surprise.

Kendra smiled. "Looking for my boys." She changed her mind and decided to come to the game. She felt guilty and wanted to make things up to him. This was her only shot at kicking her addiction and trying to make an honest recovery.

"You look surprised to see me."

"I am." Marcus was never a "think-before-speaking" kind of guy, but he cleaned it up. "But I am happy to see you. Glad you could make it." He smiled a sincere smile.

Kendra signaled the popcorn and beer guy to come over. Then she flipped out her MacBook and proceeded to talk and work at the same time. "So what did I miss?"

Marcus rolled his eyes. "Brought your other lover, I see."

"So what did I miss? Who's winning?"

"Red Sox. My granddad is a big fan. He used to take me to a game every summer when we would visit and he used to . . ."

Blah, blah, blah. Kendra tuned Marquise out. She sipped on her beer and pretended to listen to his endless chatter. She came to the game, so having to entertain and be entertaining and do work was a juggling act she wanted no part of. She wanted to change, but one step at a time please.

Marcus resented the fact that she brought work to an outing he set up for the three of them. *She might as well have kept her ass at the office she loves so much.* Suddenly, he, she, and his son didn't fit so well together. She wasn't his type, but he was so into her, physically, emotionally, and spiritually. How could he have been so wrong?

"So, Kendra, when did you and my dad get married?"

Her low-calorie Miller Lite came flying out of her mouth. "Excuse me?"

"Married people make love," Marquise blurted out. "You two make love."

Kendra laughed. "Boy, you are trying to give a young woman a heart attack, aren't you? Man, you had me going, had me caught in the matrix."

Marquise shrugged his shoulders in bewilderment. He didn't know what was so funny.

Marcus leaned over and whispered in Kendra's ear, "Something his mother told him about the birds and the bees." He moved his index finger across his neck, meaning, "Off with this subject, please."

But sex was one of Kendra's favorite subjects. "So, Marquise, tell me, is your mother married?"

"Kendra, what did I say?"

The boy shrugged his shoulders again. "No, my mom is not married. She's mad."

"Why?"

He shrugged again.

"Boy, if you shrug your shoulders one more time." Marcus was sick of this conversation and sick of his girlfriend on her laptop. "I will talk to your mother when I see her about explaining the birds and the bees to you, son. Now let's drop this subject altogether. I've had enough of it."

"Okay, then you can talk to her today, Daddy." Marquise took a sip from his soda.

"And how do you suppose I do that? Telecom?"

"No. She said she was coming here today after I told her you were married."

What the fuck? The last person he wanted Kendra to meet was Sheri. Not now.

Kendra's thoughts exactly. She packed up her laptop and said good-bye. A current wife or ex-wife coming to town never went over well with her, especially since she was the other woman.

She wasn't anywhere near ready to be meeting Marcus's ex-anything; her twelve steps didn't prepare her for that now. Hell, she had already met his son, which was good enough for her.

"Talk with you later, baby. Gotta get back to the office." She kissed him on his cheeks. "Later, Marquise. Enjoy the game." She threw him the ball she caught.

Marquise marveled at the ball. "I like her, Dad. She makes a cool wife."

Marcus shook his head. *What kind of mess am I about to get into now?*

Chapter 15

"Marcus Leon Hill, I need to talk to you!" Sheri came through his three-bedroom condo like the hell on wheels that she was.

Thanks to his son's warning, Marcus was prepared for the witch's landing on her broomstick. He slowly walked up from his finished basement eating ice cream that was as cool as he was.

"Hello, Sheri. Nice of you to call first. Please do come in. Can I get you something to drink?"

"Don't try to sugarcoat anything. Where's Marquise?"

He smiled. "He's asleep. We took him to a baseball game today. He had a good time."

"We?" Sheri raised one eyebrow and stood there waiting for answers.

He didn't know what she was so worked up about, the idea that he'd moved on, or that some other woman was around her child. "We're not married, Sheri."

She lowered her voice. "Oh, so you're just fucking some random whore while our son sleeps down the hall from you?"

"You're blowing this way out of proportion. What's the problem? All work and no play making you horny?" He stuck his tongue out at her. His intention wasn't to piss her off, just make her feel sore that he had moved on even with half the money he used to have. "Can't stand it, can you?"

"You are absolutely right. I can't. I'm here for my son. He's coming back to Boston with me."

"No, he's not." Marcus was serious now.

"You think I'm not, but I am." She walked toward the steps. "My mother was right about you having my baby—"

"Fuck your mother!"

"Excuse me? What did you say?"

"Fuck your mother, and fuck you! I don't know what kind of heartless woman would take a boy away from his father. Evil, you are. And for what? Because we didn't work out. Because you left. You quit. And now we have to suffer?"

"You best watch your mouth. Don't let this get ugly."

Marcus, starting to see red, paced back and forth. "Sheri, I swear to you on our son's life, if you try to take him away from me again, you're going to make me do something I don't want to do."

"Oh, please. What are you going to do? You can't even tie your own shoe without someone to do it for you."

"I learned. And I would hope you did too. You see every day how unhappy Marquise is without me, but yet you just sit and tell yourself, 'He will get over it.' But he's not. And in a few years, you will be the one he hates for taking his father away from him. You will be the one he resents."

Sheri knew he was right, but didn't want to admit it.

"You really want to do that to your son because of your hatred for me?"

She shook her head. "I don't hate you, Marcus. I despise what you've done to me. Made me so bitter, so jaded, so incapable of letting go." She started to cry.

Feeling for her unexpectedly, Marcus went to hold her. He didn't want to make her cry, but she brought out the beast in him.

She pushed him away. "You don't get it. It's over. It's been over between us way before I left. I had to put distance between us, so I could get over you."

"But why make Marquise suffer? I'm trying to give you your space. I just want to spend time with my son. Is that not allowed? Is that wrong?"

She shook her head. "I gotta go. Tell Marquise I will see him in the morning." She stormed off.

"Wait. I have room here. You can stay."

"It's okay. I told my sister I would be in town. She is putting me up tonight."

"How long will you stay?"

"Not long. Probably come by, see my baby, and then head back to Boston."

"Wish you could stay longer. I'm having a get-together next weekend. Joyce and Jeff will be over and the rest of the gang. It will be like old times."

"But it's not like old times. I'll see you in the morning."

Marcus made sure she got into her rental car safely and closed her door. He signaled for her to call him by placing his imaginary phone to his ear. He mouthed, "Call me."

Sheri nodded.

Marcus was exhausted after he got in from seeing his ex to her car. *What a day! Man, what a day!*

He thought about calling Kendra to let her know things were fine with him and his ex-wife. Instead, he texted her—EX-WIFE IS GONE. WE WORKED THINGS OUT. YOU SHOULD HAVE YOUR DRIVER BRING YOU OVER.

A half an hour went by before he got a response from her. He tried to call her, but his call went straight to voice mail.

Finally, just as Marcus was retiring to bed, his phone chimed with "You're All I Need to Get By," by Method Man and Mary J. Blige. He really thought he could replace Sheri with Kendra in every sense. He picked up his phone and looked down at his LED touch screen on his iPhone. He read her text—SORRY BABE. STILL WORKING. WILL CATCH UP WITH YOU IN THE MORNING. LOVE YOU.

Months ago, when Marcus's feelings didn't run as deep as they did for Kendra, that would have been okay. But now, getting back to him when she felt like it was unacceptable. He wasn't playing games with her anymore. He'd made it clear to her that she was in his plans, but was he in hers?

Chapter 16

One Saturday in late July, Marcus organized a couples' night. He hadn't hosted one in almost two years, mainly because he didn't have anyone he could really show off. Now he had Kendra, and the more she fell in line with his needs, the more he knew he would be showing her off for the rest of his life.

She made her famous spinach lasagna, salad, and meatballs, and Marcus ordered fried chicken, collard greens, macaroni and cheese, and potato salad from his favorite soul food palace in D.C. And every couple was responsible for bringing a dessert.

Marcus fixed his signature frozen piña coladas, which the wives loved, and the husbands raided his fully stocked bar for beers, scotch, Patrón, and cognac.

Meanwhile, Marquise was in his bedroom playing Wii, Uno, and Monopoly, entertaining the other kids whose parents couldn't find a babysitter.

The host was also in charge of picking the game that the couples would play. Marcus always liked throwback games from his day, so he decided they would play old maid with the oversized playing cards.

Kendra thought she could really kick her bad habit and actually consider a life with Marcus. Small wonder, she was nervous meeting all of Marcus's friends for the first time. She was hoping she didn't know any of them from business or, more frighteningly, her past. She was pretty sure she didn't, because Marcus talked about them all to her.

Jeff and Joyce were the closest couple to Marcus. He was truly friends with both of them, and since Joyce's son, Jeffrey, was the same age as Marquise, that made them important in his life as well. If there was a couple to win over to be a part of this crew, it was them. After all, Sheri was the woman of the house for thirteen years, so Kendra had no doubt that Joyce wouldn't take too easy to the new bitch in town.

"Lamant plus one" was Marcus's cousin. His lady was always a different one, so no one could get used to any of his lady friends. They all knew he was too picky with his women, so trying to get used to one was pointless, because they would be gone in a blink. Although, Melinda, his girlfriend of two years, they did buddy up to. And just as they did, she was gone. So Lamant would be easy for Kendra to get along with and win over. Playas were her specialty.

His brother Gregory and his wife of three and a half years, Dawn, were still trying desperately to have their first child. Marcus had warned Kendra to be sensitive about the childbearing challenges, and she agreed not to bring up the subject in any way.

She figured Dawn would be the easiest to win over. Kendra didn't want to mess up her only chance at beating her addiction and staying out of rehab.

Lastly was a new would-be pair to the group. Lamant had convinced Marcus to include Jerome, a friend of his. It didn't take much convincing, seeing that Jerome had spent a few nights hanging out with Marcus at the nightclubs when he was going through his divorce. Marcus had returned the favor, helping Jerome out while he was going through all his legal trouble.

Jerome had been going through some rough times lately, so being around positive people and having a good time would do him some good anyway. He didn't have a lady to bring, so Marcus thought this was a good time for him to meet some of Kendra's friends.

At first Kendra objected, but then she thought, *What harm could it really do anyway?* She called up her best friend, Zahara, who was successful, fabulous, and single. If there was one person Kendra could count on to keep her secrets, it was Zahara. Plus, she needed an air bag, in case Marcus tried to throw her in a lion's den, meeting his friends.

Just before the guests began to arrive, Kendra set up his kitchen buffet-style. She wasn't serving anyone. *Let their women serve them.*

Her friend Zahara had arrived first and helped her with everything.

Gregory and his wife Dawn greeted and hugged Kendra.

"You are wearing that black jumpsuit, girl. I love it," Dawn said to Kendra.

"Thank you. I love your earrings. Where did you get them?"

"This boutique downtown Alexandria. They have a lot of unique pieces."

"Alexandria? That's where I live. We'll have to make a date to go shopping."

"Sounds like a plan. Shopping is one of my favorite things to do."

Zahara chimed in. "*Confessions of a Shopaholic* have nothing on you I bet."

They laughed.

Instant girlfriends, Kendra thought.

As the girls admired each other, Lamant arrived and gave his friends high fives and manly hugs. "What's going on, playa?" Lamant said casually. "So this is the missus I've been hearing so much about?" He extended his arms to hug and greet Kendra. "Nice to finally meet you. You have had my man on lock." He laughed.

"Nice to meet you too. I've heard so much about you as well."

Lamant got caught up in how hot his cousin's girlfriend was, and that her friend was even hotter. He started thinking to himself he should have come by himself and ditched Jerome altogether.

Kendra extended her hand toward his date. "Hi, I'm Kendra. This is my friend, Zahara, and Marcus's sister-in-law, Dawn." Kendra wasted no time playing the lady-of-the-house role. In fact, she was beginning to like it.

Embarrassed, Lamant said, "My apologies. This is my friend Akira."

"Hi. Nice to meet you all."

Akira was gorgeous. At least five foot nine, slim, half-black and half-something else, with buttermilk skin and curly soft hair. Maybe, Puerto Rican. Not sure.

Just as Marcus described, Lamant was sports fishing, and from the way he introduced Akira as his friend, she was definitely a throwback, as opposed to a keeper. Kendra took note, but didn't dare hate the player. She knew the game.

"*Akira*—Is that Latin?"

"No, my mother is black, and my father is Brazilian," she said with a little bit of an attitude.

Kendra chopped it off as her own insecurities, not at all her problem. She didn't feel she insulted her, but whatever, she knew how women worked. And even more, she knew she didn't have to waste her time chumming up to her because she'd be gone in a blink.

"Hey, everybody," Joyce said with her bigger-than-life personality. A social butterfly, if she didn't like you, you couldn't tell.

Kendra knew if there was anyone who would give her trouble, it would be Marcus's best girlfriend. But Kendra sold ads. *Game on*, she thought to herself. She waited for Marcus to bring Joyce over after she hugged the familiar faces.

He introduced her, "Joyce, I would like you to meet my lady, Kendra Black."

Joyce hugged her. "Well, it's nice to finally meet you. So you are the one Marcus can't stop talking about?"

"I hope so," Kendra said honestly. Something about Joyce felt warm, like they really could get along. Like she really could be this other person.

"I see why. I don't know why this is our first time meeting either. I'm starting to think Marcus was purposely keeping us apart."

"I don't know why. He has nothing but good things to say about you." Kendra was a little jealous of the relationship Joyce had with Marcus. They seemed close and brutally honest with each other, the kind of intimacy she'd never shared with a man without sex running her life. She wanted so badly to morph into this other person Marcus thought he was in love with. If only it were that simple.

"He better." Joyce playfully punched him on his arm.

"Where's Jeff?" Marcus asked.

"Slowing around. He's been dragging his feet all night, and moody like a teenager on her period. I don't know what his problem is."

"He knows he's going to get spanked. Hell, everyone is. It's about to be on." Marcus missed hanging out with coupled friends. They always had such a good time together.

Jeff came through the door. "You only wish you had skills like the Standsons." His big smile must have glowed in the dark.

He greeted everyone with a playas'-club hand-
shake and hug, and a kiss on the cheek for the ladies. He wore a beige fitted tee and black slacks,
with black-and-beige Gator shoes to match, and
his chocolate complexion sweetened his muscular six-foot-two frame. He was a gentleman, as
handsome as they come, along with the arrogance to match. Joyce was a lucky woman.

Marcus said, "Kendra Black, this is my longtime friend and former teammate, Jeffrey Standson."

"Nice to finally meet you." He extended his
hand then gave her a hug and a kiss on the cheek.
"Marcus can't stop talking about you. I have to
give him a 'no Kendra' zone warning when he
comes around."

"Nice to meet you too. He's had nothing but
nice things to say about his best friend Jeff."
Kendra smiled. "And, of course, his lovely wife
Joyce," she added, cleaning it up. "I must say, I
was a little intimidated to meet you both. I know
how close you are."

"That, we are. We've been friends, it seems
like forever. Right, champ?" Jeff gave Marcus a
slap on his hand.

"Don't worry, girl. It's not us you have to im-
press. If Marcus loves you, then we love you,"
Joyce said, trying to sound honest.

The truth was, she had no reason not to like Kendra. It was Jeff who always made it seem like she wasn't the one for Marcus, or out of his league. But meeting her, she didn't get the feeling Kendra thought she was better than anyone. The only vibe she got was a nervous one. And she chopped that up to really meeting his friends, which meant he really wanted her to stick around.

Kendra's smile began to hurt. She let it go for a while. She was exhausted pretending. She began to regret even trying.

Jerome was the last to arrive. He was a somber fella, like his spirit had taken off, and the only thing left was the flesh. Kendra introduced him to Zahara, who liked what she saw. Tall, butterscotch skin, and slanted eyes.

Kendra played hostess all night. They won a few rounds of old maid, as did Joyce and Jeff. The rest of the couples struggled to secure a win. It was clear who was dominating the game.

Kendra occupied herself with being the perfect girlfriend, being sociable with the other wives and girlfriends. Her game was always on, neat and tight, despite the fact she intimately knew at least one of the husbands or boyfriends that evening. She played along, as did he, his game just as tight as hers.

The evening was near perfect until Lamant got a phone call. "Slow down, Jeanette," he shouted through his mouthpiece at his older sister. "What happened?" He lowered his head.

"What happened? Is everything all right?" Marcus asked.

"I gotta go." Lamant got up and went for the door.

"Yo, what's going on?

He turned to Marcus. "It's Dad. He had a heart attack. I have to get to D.C. Memorial."

"I'll take you," Marcus said. "Joyce, can you take Marquise back with you tonight so he can stay over?"

"No worries. Kendra, do you need help straightening up?"

"No, I got it. You've done enough. Thank you." Kendra was a little snippy because Marcus chose Joyce to take care of his son. She didn't want to, but the fact that he didn't even ask pissed her off a little.

"Thanks." Marcus rushed out the door with his cousin. Not the night he was expecting, he only prayed his uncle would pull through. He knew Joyce wouldn't have a problem looking after his son. He didn't think to ask Kendra because he really didn't want any more conflict with Sheri. He knew she would understand, or hoped anyway.

Kendra straightened up the kitchen after the guests left. She saw Zahara giving Jerome her number. For a second she wondered where that would go. Jerome was a hottie, she couldn't deny that. Her compulsions wouldn't let her.

Zahara walked over to Kendra to help her clean up. "That was fun. Marcus is such a sweetie."

Kendra nodded, her mind preoccupied. *He could have warned me. Trey wasn't even his real name.* She felt deceived and duped.

"I am so proud of you, girl. You have come a long way." Zahara reminded her, "You never answered my question."

"I'm sorry. What did you say, girl?"

"Has the therapy sessions with Marcus been helping?"

Realizing she was caught in another lie, she said, "Um, yeah. They're great."

"You haven't told him, have you?"

Kendra shooed her off. "Yes, I have. It's all good. We're fine."

"I know when you're lying to me, girl. You told me you were going to tell him. Hell, you running around here like you belong, like you have really changed. Kendra."

"What? I'll tell him. Soon. I promise."

Zahara shook her head. "Kendra, you have to tell him you're a sex addict. How else are you really going to get better if you're not even being honest with yourself?"

Kendra blocked out her friend's concerns. She wasn't ready to tell Marcus. She wasn't sure she was ready to change, for that matter. She wanted to, she needed to, but she didn't know how to stop, didn't know how to control her urges.

She couldn't worry about that now. *He* was more important. Her first order of business was to call him and give him an old-fashioned what-for.

Chapter 17

Marcus was quite impressed with how Kendra doted on him the last couple of weeks since his uncle had passed away. She called him three times a day, texted him, made sure he had meals cooked every day, even on the weekend. She entertained Marquise, showed him how to play blackjack, and how to create a business plan. She would hold Marcus at night after sex, or even if he wasn't in the mood. She was really there for him.

Marcus threw away his doubts about her, and got back on the "making-her-his-wife" plan. He did it. He changed her. He wanted to make it official, so he took his son fishing early Sunday morning to tell him what his plans were.

"Hey, little man. I've noticed you and Kendra have gotten really close. You like her, don't you?" Marcus asked.

"She's great, Dad," Marquise said with enthusiasm. "She shows me a lot of things and talks to me. I see why you like her so much."

"I'm glad you feel that way, son, because I want to make things permanent with her." Marcus put his hand on his son's shoulder to brace him. "I want to ask her to marry me."

Marquise inhaled big enough to take all the world's problems on. Silence went by for a minute or two.

"Is that going to be okay with you?" Marcus really wanted to know how his son felt.

"I guess." He shrugged.

"What's up?" Marcus wanted to make him as on-board as possible.

"I don't know. I guess it's better this way, since you and Mom hate each other."

"We don't hate each other, son. We are both hurt from not being able to be together, so we say hurtful things to each other. I know that is no excuse for how we behave, but it's the truth."

"Whatever. Now that you are marrying Kendra, you are definitely going to fight more."

"You are probably right about that." He smirked. "But listen. When we argue, it's not because we hate each other. It's because the love that we shared is still there. And I will always love your mother, but we can't be together. It doesn't work. I will make a deal with you though. If you give Kendra and I a chance, I will promise to not argue with your mother so much." He held out his hand to shake his son's, to make it a deal.

"Deal. I'm going to hold you to it." Marquise started to breathe a little easier. "Should I call her *Mom*?"

"Not unless you want your mother to kill us both."

Marquise and Marcus laughed. His son knew he was dead right about that.

Later, after catching four clean, filet-worthy fish to put on their plates, Marcus and his son began preparing them. Frying fish was probably the only meal he knew how to prepare. He wanted to do something special for Kendra since she had been awesome to him these last couple of weeks.

He called and left her a message before they left the pond, but he still hadn't heard from her.

Dinner was prepared, no word from Kendra, so Marcus decided to eat without her. He and his son shared a nice evening of eating out on his condo patio and then playing football on his Wii. Still no word from Kendra. He started to get worried, so he called all her numbers, house, office, cell, backup cell. Nothing. This was one of the things he never was able to change about her. He couldn't get in touch with her if she didn't want to be reached. It annoyed him so much, he couldn't describe it. It was like she could always reach him, but he could never get her. It made him feel extremely insecure, wondering what she was doing that was so important that she couldn't answer his calls.

Later that night, after Marquise went to bed, Marcus was up wondering where the hell his future wife was, thinking maybe getting married wasn't such a good idea.

The phone rang in the middle of the night, and Marcus, groggy, answered, thinking it must be bad news again.

"Hey, baby," Kendra said in her sweetest voice. "Did I wake you?"

"Yeah. What time is it?"

"It's late. I'm sorry I didn't get back to you earlier. Me and my team have been pulling an all-nighter for this new client. This deal is crucial to my firm. But I should have texted you. I turned my phone off and told my secretary not to interrupt me unless it was life or death. I'm sorry. Did you and Marquise eat dinner?"

"We fried fish that we caught."

"I'm sorry I missed that." She tried to butter him up and spread him across her bread as much as she could, to right her wrong.

Marcus was used to it by now. Before, he didn't notice, but now he knew when she was trying to get over. He even liked it. The ice queen trying to melt him, the irony of it was appealing to him.

"It's cool. I'm going to get back to sleep. I will call you in the morning."

"Okay, baby. See you tomorrow. Love you."

"I love you too."

That was the first time Kendra had ever said the *L* word. First, last, or anytime really that he could hear clearly. He rolled over and pulled his sheets up closer. In his heart of hearts he knew something about her wasn't right. His intuition screamed at him to look deeper. Instead he fell asleep, saving those concerns for another time.

Chapter 18

Before he went down this road again and made yet another mistake about the woman he was in love with, Marcus decided to do some digging. He called his cousin for advice. As always Lamant had an idea for his problem. They met at the gym, and lifted weights to maintain those muscles, tight and right in all the best places.

Lamant suggested, "You need to find out what she does when she's not with you, not with her girls, and not at work, to put your mind at ease that she really is the one for you. To certify that you really know her."

"So follow her?"

"No, tell her you are going out of town, so she knows you're not around. Then show up at her place on a Saturday night late, like the time when you should be there. You understand?"

Marcus wasn't sure if he wanted to find Kendra with another man. He'd rather just break things off with her. He was sure he would kill them both if he found them.

"That's extreme. Maybe I will talk to her instead. Just ask her point-blank."

Lamant shook his head. "That's a good idea, especially if you want her to lie to your face." He lifted his weight set. "Think if it was you. Would you be honest and up front about sleeping around? No, you wouldn't."

Marcus knew he was right. "Of course not. Deny, deny—That's how we work. But I just don't think I'm ready to find out if she isn't faithful."

"So you would rather wait until after the 'I do's?' Spend another fortune on divorce, not to mention if you have kids involved. That's insane. Always look under the hood before you buy. Hell, I wish there was a CARFAX for women. Better know now than before you've really invested your time, money, and heart." He put down his weights. "Come on, man. You know good and well how tight you are with your money. If you don't want another Sheri on your hands, you better handle that."

Marcus let his cousin's words sink in. He didn't want to do it. He didn't want to believe Kendra could be this other person. Defeated, he knew what he had to do.

"I'm going out of town this weekend, baby. Taking Marquise to Myrtle Beach. We only have a few days left before he goes back to Boston. I would have invited you, but I wanted to—"

Kendra cut him off. "No need. I completely understand. I think it would be good for you two to spend time alone anyway." She smiled with enthusiasm.

"Thanks, baby, for being so understanding. We'll be back Monday afternoon."

"And I will have dinner waiting for my favorite guys. Have a good time. When are you guys leaving? I can take you to the airport."

"Thanks, baby. I've got it. We are leaving tomorrow morning."

"I have a meeting, but I can reschedule if you need me."

Marcus couldn't remember Kendra rescheduling anything to meet his needs. Maybe she had changed. "You're the best, baby, but no worries. I got this. See you tonight. Love you."

"I love you too."

Marcus could hear the excitement in her voice, but he didn't know if it was because she did love him or because she couldn't wait for him to be away.

As planned, Marcus left early that morning with Marquise, their bags packed. He kissed Kendra good-bye and hugged her tight. He drove

Marquise to Joyce's house for the weekend. Jeff was away on business, so it was a perfect time for the boys to have a play date.

Marcus sat around his foundation office, waiting for nightfall. His plans were to drive by Kendra's house around midnight to see if she was spending the weekend alone.

For all he knew, she could have decided to have a girls' night and not get in until five or six in the morning. Yet he waited and waited down the street from her gated property in an SUV he'd rented earlier that day. She never came home. Marcus really was on edge now. Where was she? Earlier when he'd called to tell her they had landed, she said her plans were to go home and relax after a long workweek. He reasoned plans could have changed, but his worry was, *With who did they change?*

Stuck, he didn't know where she could be. It was five thirty, and the sunlight was coming up. True, she was out late who knows where, and with who the fuck knows, but he didn't have all the facts.

On his way home he kicked himself for listening to his cousin's idea. He should have confronted her head-on.

Marcus pulled into his driveway licking his wounds. As tired as he was, he missed the two familiar cars parked across the street. He pressed the off button to his alarm and unlocked his front door. All he wanted was a hot shower, his bed, and to forget about his outlandish ideas about Kendra being with another man. He convinced himself that she wouldn't treat him like that. Out of all her shortcomings, being a whore wasn't one of them. She was too much of a class act to pull something like that.

He opened his bedroom door and began to pull off his clothes. He walked past his bed and into the bathroom. *What the fuck?* He was so exhausted, he'd almost missed it. Marcus walked slowly back into his bedroom and over to his bed. He was in disbelief. The rays of sunlight coming through the window highlighted the truth. There Kendra lay, butt naked, cuddled with another man. In his house. In his bed.

She must've let herself in with the spare key he'd begged her to use more often than she did.

Marcus's veins began to pop, and his fist curled, his heart pumping. He breathed with anticipation, embracing the insanity. He waited for Kendra to open her eyes, and she did.

She covered them from the sun and looked up at her man hovering over her like a hawk. Startled, she screamed, "Marcus!"

Her outburst awoke the man cuddled beside her. Groggy for a second, alert for the next, and afraid thereafter, Jeff looked up at his friend.

Marcus smiled like a sociopath. "Good morning." Without giving Jeff a chance to respond, he grabbed him out of bed by the scruff of his neck and slammed him to the floor.

Kendra screamed, "Marcus, noooo!"

Her outburst awoke the man, cradled beside her. He sat up for a second, then lie down and tried, breathing, Jeff looked up at his friend.

Marcus smiled like a serial killer. "God mercy." Without giving Jeff a chance to respond he grabbed him and squeezed the breath out of his neck and slammed him to the floor.

Kendra screamed, "Marcus, nooo!"

Chapter 19

Marcus's hands gripped Jeff's neck with no intention to let go. Jeff struggled to breathe as he looked into his best friend's eyes with shame and guilt. Marcus stared at him, with raging fury, and gripped tighter and tighter. His painful feelings ran him.

Kendra jumped on his back, yelling, "Marcus, stop it! Stop it! You're killing him! Please!" But her tiny arms were no match for Marcus's.

"Muthafucka!" Marcus spat, foam coming out the side of his mouth like a mad dog.

Jeff's face was turning blue-black. He was almost unconscious and would certainly die soon if Marcus didn't back off his windpipe.

Marcus looked into his fading eyes and shouted, "Fucking bastard!" He let go of his friend and pushed Kendra off his back, to the floor.

On her back, she began to sob, and Jeff rolled over, gasping for air.

Weak and barely able to speak, Jeff managed to curl up to his knees and catch his breath. He put his hand up in surrender. "Man, I'm sorry. I tried to warn you. I tried."

Marcus circled him like a shark. "You tried to warn me?" He shouted. "When? Did you say to me, 'By the way, I'm fucking your girlfriend'?"

He charged Jeff and started throwing blows like a heavyweight—one-two jab to the ribs, the face, the ribs, the face two times. As Jeff's body aimlessly danced around the bedroom like a rag doll, Marcus pulled his arm back like a windmill and smashed his fist with an upper cut to Jeff's chin that sent his body, flying out the bedroom balcony and over the ledge to the ground one story below.

"Jeff! Noooo!" Kendra ran out of the bedroom, grabbing her robe on the way, rushed down the stairwell and flung out the front door.

Marcus walked onto the balcony and looked below, where he saw Jeff spit out blood from his broken facial bones. He watched as Kendra rushed to his aid. The sight of them together made Marcus snap into a psychotic rage. *Still breathing?* He shook his head. "Not for long."

Marcus rumbled through his bedroom closet and pushed a stack of suits to the side. He quickly pushed in his four-digit safe code, 0897, his son's birthday, pulled out his 9 mm silver hand-gun, snapped in the bullet chamber, and clicked off the safety.

He walked downstairs with the weight of a bull on his heart, the steel gripped between his fingers. Jeff was bleeding all over, twitching in and out of consciousness.

Sirens heard from afar got closer. The red and blue lights pulled up in front of his D.C. condo-minium home and into his driveway. Marcus could see the lights but ignored them.

"Drop the weapon, Mr. Hill! You don't want to do this."

"Marcus, please," Kendra begged, "don't do this. I am so sorry. Please, think about your son."

"This is your last warning! Drop the weapon!" the police officer said, his weapon aimed in the direction of his intended target.

Marcus dropped his gun. He refused to go to jail and never see his son again behind this bullshit. He fell to his knees and put his hands behind his head.

The police arrested him and put him in the squad car and called an ambulance for Jeff. The officers, being fans, knew both former players. They shook their heads because they could only deduce what took place after seeing a beaten man on the front lawn and a half-naked woman crying herself silly.

"Mr. Hill, I'm going to have to take you downtown and process you. You will make bail later this afternoon. Is there anyone you want me to call to come bail you out?"

Marcus wanted to tear up. "Joyce. Call Joyce Standson." He dropped his head back into the headrest. *Of all the people to fuck me over, I never imagined it be a man I considered my brother.* He held back his tears. He refused to let anyone see him cry, but inside, he was a waterfall.

Chapter 20

Marcus met Joyce in front of the courthouse. He didn't know what to say to her. From the look on her face, she knew. There was no question.

She hugged him as tears rolled down her face. "How long?"

Marcus shrugged. "That's something you are going to have to ask your husband."

She bawled some more. "This is a fucked-up day."

He patted her back. "I know we're going to get through this."

"Sheri needs you."

"What?"

"It's her sister. She died in a car accident yesterday. She said she's been trying to reach you."

"Oh, no! Who? The youngest?"

"No, the oldest."

"Where is Sheri?" Marcus wanted to be there for his ex-wife and son.

"She's at my house. She flew in early this morning. Come on, I will take you to her."

"And Jeff?" Marcus wasn't sure he was ready to face him again.

"Released an hour ago. I can't say where he is."

"Come on." Marcus could feel the urgency to get to Sheri.

When they reached the Standson's home in Rockville, Maryland, Marcus rushed in and called out, "Sheri, where are you?"

No answer. He searched through their thirty-room mansion.

He got to the finished basement and found her rocking back and forth, almost zombie-like, in front of the projector TV.

Marcus kneeled to the floor. "Sheri, I'm so sorry, baby."

She didn't look at him.

Joyce left them alone and went to tend to Marquise.

"I am here for you. I will help you and our son get through this. I am here for you."

Sheri sniffled. "What did I say to her last? I can't remember. It was something silly, or mindless, probably something about you." She shook her head. "I know it wasn't I love you or I miss you. Or I need you. I appreciate you." Her tears flowed heavier down her cheek. "Why don't we say things like that? We should. We should."

Marcus hugged her tight, a lump in his throat. "I love you. I miss you. I need you. I am sorry. I didn't appreciate you. I never showed you how much you meant to me."

Marcus stroked her hair and rocked with her. He didn't let her go until she was ready. He kept repeating to her, "I am here for you. Whatever you need, I'm here for you and our son."

Sheri wanted to refuse his help, but she knew deep down inside, she needed him desperately. So she temporarily let down her guard and let her ex-husband take care of her needs, the thing she craved most during their marriage and only got now in death.

Marcus didn't let go. He planned to help her out and be there for her until she wanted him to go. He secretly hoped she didn't let him go again.

Chapter 21

After the funeral, Marcus insisted Sheri temporarily move back to D.C. so he could take care of her and Marquise. He saw Sheri was broken, and he wanted to help put her back together, if she would let him. She resisted for a couple of weeks. Not wanting to abandon her niece, but trying to avoid all the drama that was going on with her family and her niece's biological father and the money, she couldn't take it anymore and finally agreed to let Marcus take care of her. He found a therapist for her to talk to and enrolled Marquise into his old private school.

Marcus stopped at the drugstore to pick up some things for the house and some things for Sheri. The one person he didn't want to run into ever again, he did.

"I've wished you dead a thousand times," Marcus said to Jeff, devoid of feeling.

Jeff hung his head low. "Me too." He shrugged. "I fucked up. I fucked up your life. I fucked up my own. I don't even know how it got this far."

Marcus waved him off. "You need to step, before you catch a serious case of whup-ass again."

"One minute," Jeff pleaded. "That's all I am asking for. One minute. Then it's done. You won't see or hear from me again."

Marcus had the urge to ram his cart down Jeff's throat, but he stormed off, leaving his cart of items in the store with his jive-ass best friend.

Jeff chased after him. "Look, hate me all you want, but I tried to tell you the minute I realized she was the same girl."

Marcus turned around. "How long? How long have you been fucking her?"

"I met her almost a year ago at a bar. I told her my name was Trey. One thing led to another, and we ended up sleeping together, and have been ever since." Jeff shook his head. "She knew I was married. I never hid that. She wasn't looking for a relationship anyway. She was something else."

Marcus was steaming. "Something else?"

"I mean, I kept thinking to myself, how can a woman that fine and that well put-together not want anything from me other than sex? How can she be okay with being the other woman? It was exciting. It was like a drug, and I couldn't stop."

"Even after I told you I was in love with her."

He gritted his teeth. "I tried to tell you. I tried to warn you. I even stopped seeing her."

Marcus stormed off.

"I mean, one minute I'm meeting up with her on Tuesdays, and the next, she starts seeing me on the weekend. She never once mentioned you. Never."

"But you knew. You knew she was with me. That is sick." Marcus balled his fist. "So why didn't you tell her?"

"Man, before I knew it, you were trying to get us to meet. I was trying to break it off, once I figured out it was the same Kendra."

"How did you know? Why didn't you say something?"

"It was too late. You were already in love with her, and talking marriage. She didn't know we were best friends. The only way I knew before the couples' night was because the security officer at her building one day said to me, 'Whoa! Two Baltimore Ravens in one day? You just missed Marcus Hill. Are you running a football ad with Blackside'? That's when I knew my Kendra was your Kendra."

"Oh, really?" Marcus didn't believe him.

"I had my suspicions. That's why I tried to steer you off her course. But Marcus always knows best."

"Apparently not. And what about after she found out at the party?"

"She laid my ass out and said it was over."

"So how the fuck did you two end up in my bed then, if it was over?"

Jeff shook his head. "I dunno. She's like a drug. I couldn't get enough of her. I think she enjoyed the game, enjoyed the fact that you didn't know. Or, maybe the fact that she was so close to the fire without getting burned. I don't know. But me, I just couldn't stop, couldn't get enough of her."

"And now look at you. Look at what you've caused."

"If I could take it all back, I would. Now Joyce kicked me out. She's threatening to file for divorce. What am I supposed to do?"

"You'll get everything you deserve and more." Marcus walked off, leaving Jeff with those thoughts. His friendship was done. Years thrown away. Could he forgive him? He didn't have the answer. His main priority was Sheri and their son. Nothing else, including Jeff or his scheming ex-girlfriend, mattered. He couldn't waste any more energy on it.

Jeff called out after him. "I didn't press charges, man. I'm sorry. I really am."

Marcus waved him off.

***

When Marcus got home, he found Sheri in a huff. "What's up? Your family causing trouble?"

She laughed. "On the contrary, it's you who has some housekeeping to do."

Marcus was dumbfounded. Then he thought about it. *Kendra.* "What happened?"

"She came by unannounced, claiming she was coming to get her things." Sheri laughed cynically. "Not in that little black freak-'em dress, she wasn't."

Marcus rolled his eyes.

"She was surprised to see me, didn't know who I was, proceeded to step inside and push by me like I was the next chick."

Marcus shook his head, knowing exactly where this was going, given Sheri's temper.

She mocked Kendra, pretending to walk like her. "'Is Marcus here? I'm his girlfriend, Kendra.'" I couldn't help but laugh at her. "His girlfriend? You mean the one that fucked his best friend Jeff? She halted her stride with that comment. I walked up on her and informed her that I was your ex-wife Sheri. I was living here for now, and she was trespassing, so her things or not, she had to raise the fuck up out of here before she ended up a hot beatdown mess like her man Jeff."

Marcus tried not to laugh. He still loved her fury. "So what about her things?"

"I told her you would tend to those matters personally. In case she was misinformed about who she was to you at this given moment in time and space." Sheri spun around and fell onto the sofa. "And with that, I had a cocktail."

He laughed. "I'll handle it."

"And the phone keeps ringing. I keep answering, and she keeps hanging up. Unless that's another one of your ex-girlfriends." She sipped her cantaloupe martini. "I mean, really, Marcus, is this what life after me looks like? I feel bad for you."

He laughed. "You should."

Marcus made a mental note to take Kendra's things to her, and let her know that her girlfriend title and privileges were permanently revoked.

Chapter 22

Marcus pressed the doorbell to Kendra's estate, determined to end things once and for all with her, period. He was carrying a box with her things in one hand, and in the other, the four-carat canary diamond he'd planned to propose to her with.

Madie opened the door with a look of surprise when she saw him. "Good evening. Mr. Hill. Is the missus expecting you?"

Marcus shrugged his shoulders. "I have no idea. If she is unavailable, I would like to leave her things with you, if you don't mind."

Madie gestured for him to come in. "Please come in. I will tell her you're here."

She seated him in Kendra's great room. "Are you staying for dinner, Mr. Hill? I made your favorite, spinach lasagna."

I know her lies run deep, but the lasagna, come on. Is everything about her fake? "No, thank you, Madie. I won't not be staying for din-

ner. And, by the way, you should put a patent on
that dish. It's really like that. My son and I love
it."

Madie nodded and left the room. She could
be doing better things with her time than taking
care of the missus, but who else would? She'd
been taking care of her since she was a little girl
after her parents were brutally murdered.

In less than two minutes Kendra arrived wearing a black sheer nightgown with the visibility of
a glass window. "Marcus, so glad you could join
me. Can I fix you a drink?"

Marcus waved her off. "No. But how about
some of Madie's spinach lasagna that I love so
much?"

She froze in her "man-trap." "I'm sorry. I just
didn't know how to be who you wanted me to be.
What you wanted from me seemed unnatural. I
wasn't ready. And for that I am sorry. I should
have told you."

"That's it? That's your apology?" He got up.

She chased after him. "Marcus, wait! I have a
problem. It's an addiction. I'm a sex addict."

Marcus halted his exit. He turned around. "A
what?"

"You heard me. I have a disease, and I have
been trying like crazy to kick it. I've gone to therapy, I've gone to rehab several times, but noth-

ing seems to work. And then came you. I wasn't read for your love. I wasn't ready to be who you wanted me to be. I tried. I thought I was, but I was kidding myself. Can you forgive me? Can you give me another chance?

"A sex addict? Kendra, just say it was all a game to you. Just say you are a deceitful, hurtful bitch, and it's done. At least that makes sense, because what you're saying is a bunch of bullshit."

Something about his tone gave her a tingle. She flung her arms around him and kissed him on his lips then his neck."

Marcus stopped her. "Kendra, I see you. I see you now for who you are, and I'm good. I just wanted to bring your things by, so you would really know that we are done, no matter what you say or do."

"You are really going to give all this up?" She ran her hands up her torso and back down to her thighs. "Me? How I make you feel? For what? Her? She's half the woman I am."

Marcus pulled out the ring. He wanted her to feel his pain. "This is what I wanted from you. What I wanted for us."

Kendra shook her head. "I'm not ready. Give me time. I can be a better person."

Marcus smiled. "Our time is up." He put the ring back in his pocket. "And correction—Sheri is one hundred times the woman you will ever be. Why? Because she's honest, true, knows how to act like a lady instead of a lying whore who sleeps with her man's best friend and then says it's an addiction." Marcus laughed like, *Bitch, please* . . .

"Excuse me. What did you call me?"

"I used to think it was you I was after, but it was the chase. If I could change you, then I could change just about anyone. I could have anyone I wanted, marry anyone I wanted. You were the ego trip I needed to help me rebuild myself, to be a better man, father, and husband. I don't think I really ever loved you or wanted to marry you. I'm still in love with Sheri." Marcus couldn't believe he admitted that aloud.

Kendra huffed, "You're a fucking lie! You love me, you're just hurt." She grabbed his face to force a passionate kiss. "Can you really say you don't want me?"

Marcus pulled back. "Baby, I never *not* wanted you, but marry you? You must be out of your damn mind."

"See, that's your problem, Marcus. You think I'm jumping in line for that brass ring. That false security that you hold so high and think really means something. But I'm not dying to be Mrs. Marcus Hill. I just want to be Kendra. I just want to be me. And you just want someone to tote around on your arm that will take care of your every need. Well, I am not that woman, Marcus. I never will be. You better wake up and stop daydreaming 'cause you are living in a fantasy world."

"You're unbelievable." He shouted at her loud and clear, "You are fucking my best friend, and I'm living in a fantasy world? We're done here. Thanks for the good times. I had a ball laying my pipe in you. Thanks for the memories." He stormed off.

All this time, Kendra was fighting being who she really was, fighting her compulsions, wanting to change for a man she thought loved her unconditionally. Someone she thought could be her antidote.

She whirled around and picked up her lamp and threw it at his head, barely missing him. "That's right! Blame me! Blame me because you are too selfish to comprehend what it takes to be a real man. What it takes to stand *by* your woman, not in front of her." She marched after him. "You will never find another woman like me, Marcus. Never!"

He turned around and smiled. "I hope to hell I don't. For your sake and this so-called thing that you have, get some help." He slammed the door behind him and ended his would-be life with the next Mrs. Marcus Hill.

On his way home, he thought, *Am I really so full of myself that there is no room for anyone else? Don't listen to her. Her words are poison. She betrayed you in the worst way.*

Marcus needed to get home. He didn't want to leave Sheri by herself for too long. He was determined to be there for her.

For the first time in a long time Marcus tried to put someone else's needs before his own. Maybe, just maybe, if he could keep his high-maintenance needs in check, he could be the man Sheri deserved from the beginning.

She still will have to take care of a brother, Marcus thought to himself. Here's to hoping anyway.

Part Two

"Mr. Perfect"

Chapter 23

"Laaatricia!" Lamant yelled out in the heat of passion after he shot his loaded sperm into a co-worker, who'd been eyeing him and his corner office. Ejaculating after five minutes of pleasure was unusual for Lamant, but the pussy was so good, he had no say in the matter. *What's done is done.* His only hope now was that the jimmy was still on tight, since his life bore no room for mistakes.

Whew! That felt extremely good! Lamant thought to himself. He rolled over on to his back, worn out, not feeling like snuggling.

Latricia rolled over to her back and wiped off her beaded sweat with the back of her hand. She got what she wanted from him but might just be interested in a little more, if he played his cards right.

Two weeks ago, during the midday rush, always-on-the-go Lamant bumped into Latricia as he was leaving his office, not for lunch, but to catch a courier who didn't deliver to him an important package from an important client he was working with. He almost knocked her off her rocker as his shoulder rammed into her chest. She was strong, though, because she didn't fall to her bottom like the average skinny little paperweight would have.

"I'm so sorry. Are you okay?" Lamant asked her. Yes, he was in a rush, but he wasn't raised by wolves.

Latricia caught the wind back in her sails, shook off the instant agony in her chest and nodded yes. "You really should watch where you are going,"she said, clearly pissed off.

Feeling terrible, but needing to catch that courier, Lamant responded, "Yes, I know. I'm so sorry. I owe you lunch." His eyes darted over her head, looking for the FedEx guy. *Dammit! He's getting in his truck.* "Could you wait right here?"

Latricia looked at this neatly put-together red-boned green-eyed cutie like he'd lost his mind. But before she could help him find it, Lamant ran toward the street like nine-one-one wasn't a joke and the police were hot on his trail.

"Wait! Wait! You didn't deliver my package!"Lamant yelled frantically at the bulky bald-headed brother dressed neatly in his black shorts and black crewneck uniform. His muscles flexed and his panther tattoo arched as he put the truck into gear, taking off.

Lamant's late-afternoon deal would tank if he didn't have the projections for the Water Falls Project his firm was pitching to Mark Tony & Company. But the courier drove off as soon as one of the D.C. natives let him into traffic.

"Goddammit!" Lamant yelled. *All that work for nothing.* The deal wouldn't go through today, and meant more work and aggravation tomorrow. But, more seriously, his chances for being promoted to partner would be diminished.

Lamant watched the truck drive up the street, his hands on top of his head. He contemplated running after it as it slowed for the next traffic light. *What the hell.*

His stride was interrupted by a five-foot six-inch sister dressed in a fitted black striped skirt suit, and heels inched high enough to make Dr. Scholl's scream out in pain.

"Excuse me. You owe me lunch?"

With a courier to catch and his own ass to save, Lamant wasn't in the mood. "What are you talking about?"

"In your haste, you knocked over my chicken Caesar salad. Didn't you notice?"

Lamant hadn't noticed, nor did he notice how attractive she was. Her big light brown eyes peeped out from her bang, and her pouted lips hinted he was about to get told.

"Look, I'm sorry, but I have to catch the courier. Wait here. I promise I will rectify the situation." *I definitely want to* wreck *something, with your fine tail, Ms. New Booty.*

"I'm sure you can call the eight hundred number and have them track your package. It just can't be that serious that you're knocking people over to get your delivery."

"Trust me, it is. I have an important deal to close. Now, if you will excuse me."

"What's your name?"

Lamant wasn't trying to brush her off, but he didn't want to be responsible for a nine-figure-deal screwup either. "Excuse me. I have to go."

"Is it Lamant James?"

"Yeah. How did you know that?"

"I'm Latricia Smith James. For some reason I'm always getting your packages and have to send my assistant to hand-deliver them. When you said big deal, I figured you must work for the firm as well."

"Did you get something from Capitol Permits?"

"Not sure. You knocked me and my lunch over, so I haven't had a chance to check my mail yet."

Oh, if you have my package, you would definitely get this package.

"Come with me to my office. I will check. If it's not there, then you can call the eight hundred number and have them bring it back to you in an hour. Trust me, they foul up all the time, so I know how to get satisfaction. Tell them Ms. Smith James needs it. They know better not to mess with me."

Sophisticated, educated, and motivated on the job. My kind of woman.

On the way up to Latricia's office, Lamant apologized again and again for knocking her over.

"I promise, I can get you fed," he said. "No problem. I can have delivery here in less than ten minutes with one phone call."

"I see you have your connections too, but it's okay. I'll just grab a sandwich from the cafeteria after."

"Well, then I owe you a lunch. I promise, I'm not such a madman all the time. It's just this deal is like air right now. Can't live without it."

"Then I would hate to be you when your boss finds out you might have blown it."

"How do you know I'm not the boss?"

Latricia looked him up and down carefully. She giggled, and then quickly recovered it, placing her hand to her lips.

"What?"

"Nothing. But your fly is open. And I know damn well no boss is running after anything except his secretary. You look like you could use a drink of water."

Lamant laughed. *Comical and witty. Yes, I need you in my bed and in my life. Please.* "You got me there. Now you can understand why I was running the way I was."

"Indeed." She nodded. "I am the only woman—correction, I am the only Black woman in my office who holds the senior title. So I am very familiar with how corporate America works."

When the elevator reached the tenth floor, Latricia hopped off, Lamant on her heels.

Man, I hope it's here.

She walked past Marsha, her assistant, who was eating honey boneless wings from Champions across the street, inside the Marriott Hotel.

"Did the courier drop off a package from—" She turned to Lamant.

"Capitol Permits." Lamant was still hoping and praying.

Marsha wiped her sticky hands and thumbed through the mail. Chewing and swallowing at the same time, she said, "Here it is." She handed it to her. Still chewing, she added, "It's for that Lamant character again. When will they get it straight?"

Latricia attributed Marsha's unprofessional behavior to her being twenty-two, having no assistant experience, and her daddy's friend helping her land a job for her to play at all summer. Latricia longed for a real assistant sometime soon.

"You have no idea how much you are saving me right now. Forget lunch, I owe you lunch *and* dinner. Just say when."

"Glad I could help. Can you do me a favor though?"

"Anything." Lamant would trade favor for flavors any day of the year.

"Watch where you're going next time, and leave the running to the runners."

Latricia didn't crack a smile. Lamant figured his mojo was on low today and she just wasn't feeling him. "Thank you again. And if you change your mind about anything, you know where to find me." He walked away confidently, being the drop-dead "divo" he was. Getting up with Latricia was definitely in the cards.

Oh, but Latricia was feeling him. She just wasn't about to be that easy. He just had to wait a little.

Inside the four meticulous decorated walls of his bedroom that left some wondering hetero-, homo-or bi-sexual, Lamant contemplated if Latricia fit into his program. Work came first then pleasure then creativity. For the past two years he'd tried to turn that order around, but his OCD-like tendencies always seemed to win.

Latricia scooted next to him and placed her hand on his chest, trying to ease into his nook. She kissed the center of his chest. "Another round in five? I gotta be out before dawn."

"Not a problem." *Fine with me. Mr. Stick It could go until dawn, but if you gotta go, you gotta go.*

She placed her hand atop his nipples and massaged them with her thumbs and index fingers.

Lamant gazed at the ceiling, trying to lose himself in the moment. He wondered where this was going. Unfortunately for Mr. Stick It, he was in-between relationships and couldn't be sure when his next series premiere would begin, but he was definitely thinking of picking up Latricia for an episode or two. She knew Mr. Stick It's anatomy inside out.

She licked his nipples up and down as she climbed onto his pelvis, and Lamant ran his hands up her spine, pulling her close and tight to his body. Her eyes caught his, and he stole a kiss from her lips.

She gyrated her childbearing hips rhythmically onto his penis, while he cupped her breasts and tongued her down. "Get hard for momma."

Lamant aimed to please. He slipped on another condom from underneath his pillow. "I want you from behind." He assumed the position.

Latricia had no trouble getting on all fours, one of her favorite positions.

Lamant mounted her and stuck Mr. Stick It deep inside, hoping to get lost in it, and pumped in and out, in and out, like he knew her insides, and Latricia moaned with each thrust, loving every minute of the pleasure he was giving her.

Lamant pounded her kitty, stroking harder, deeper, pressing her lower back down to the sheets and her ass up to the heat. He gave her behind a hard smack. *Wham!*

She moaned, ready for him to give her all he had.

He grabbed her hair and pulled it like she was his pony. He could hear Mr. Stick It shouting, "Ride, Lamant, ride!"

"Give it to me, muthafucka! Give it to me!"

Potty mouth. I got something for that potty mouth. He flew back his head and dug deep inside her, ready to explode again and again. And he did. "Oh, yes!" he shouted. "Yeah!"

Lamant collapsed, convulsing onto her back and holding her breasts. *Whew! That is some mean "punani!" Definitely an episode or two. Shit, she might even get picked up.*

Latricia rolled over to her back and hopped off the bed. She liked what she was receiving and wouldn't mind doing it on a regular basis.

The next morning, Lamant's alarm awoke him precisely at 5:45 A.M., enough time to run around the block, do one thousand push-ups and sit-ups and make him an omelet with wheat bread all before he needed to leave his house at 8:00 A.M. He strived for perfection in every way, his body, his home, his personal life, and, of course, his job.

After exercising, the shower cooled and cleaned him. A flashback of smacking Latricia's behind danced inside his head. *Definitely got to preview that again.*

Latricia had left earlier, around 2:00 A.M. Lamant didn't argue when she protested about him following her home, proclaiming she was an independent '90s woman, and could take care of herself. But the gentleman in him had to at least make sure she was home safe, so he'd called her to make sure she was inside her house safely.

He got out of the shower and prepped his face to shave. Stroke after stroke, he cleaned up the stubbles to leave his usual so fresh and so clean baby face ready for another long day climbing the investment banker ladder.

He reached for his toothbrush and noticed his brush was wet. He recalled Latricia going to the bathroom to freshen up before she left. And her breath was amazingly fresh when she French-kissed him good-bye. Lamant attributed that to a breath mint or some gum, but now he knew the truth. She had used his freaking toothbrush, and for that, she wasn't ever, ever, ever going to get a callback, or ride from Mr. Stick It again. Straight up! *That shit is nasty.*

Chapter 24

Teased by his family for being a pretty boy, Lamant James was a peculiar guy, even though he didn't think of himself that way. Women were more than sport to him. He actually liked their company and didn't mind being in a relationship. It was the women who didn't seem to meet his standards for him to stick around.

For example, his last long-term girlfriend of two years had this awful habit of flossing outside the bathroom, which he thought disgusting. He put up with it for so long, until he went to sit down on his five-thousand-dollar leather sofa and reached under his matching pillows to find his hand covered in plaque-covered floss. He lost it. Before she came home, he packed up her stuff and left it out on the porch with mountains of floss strands covering her boxes. He never heard from her again.

Lamant set his standards so high that the women generally seen on his arm one night would not be seen on the next due to some hang-up, phobia, or violation of his dating rules. Perfection was what he was after, and he was willing to knock over a few bad apples until he found it.

As for his professional life, Lamant was an investment banker who secretly wanted to release his creative side and become a published writer. He worked on it every now and then, but his job kept him so busy, he always put what he really wanted to do on hold.

After a long day's work, he poured himself a glass of Hennessy and fell back into his plush leather sofa. He flipped his HDTV fifty-inch screen to his home station, *ESPN*. He was looking forward to an evening of baseball news and pre-season football coverage, delivered Thai food, and as many shots of Hennessy necessary to mellow out. Thursday evenings had become a ritual relaxation night for him, after working hard all week with only one day of misery to go.

A die-hard New York Jets fan, Lamant was listening to *SportCenter*'s "Tom Brady return-to-the-field update" when his phone buzzed a text message—RUNNING LATE WILL BE THERE IN A HALF AN HOUR. AMANDA

"What the!" Lamant forgot he'd invited his new lady friend over for dinner last week. He wanted to text her back and say, "Can we re-schedule?" but after the week he'd had, a night of passion would surely be the way to go.

Lamant hopped up, freshened up, and ordered Thai food for two instead of one. His three-bed-room condo in Alexandria, Virginia needed no tidying up, since he kept his place spotless at all times. Lamant was able to maintain his sexy in less time than allotted. When his doorbell rang, he buzzed his guest in, grabbed his wallet, and proceeded to open his front door, expecting either Amanda or the Thai food.

"Hey, you." Latricia smiled. "I was in the neighborhood and thought I would drop by." She leaned against his doorway.

Oh, shit! "Hey yourself. How's it going?"

She gave him a look like, "Aren't you going to invite me in?"

Never one to sugarcoat anything, Lamant said, "I'm expecting a guest. You should always call first."

"Well, excuse the shit out of me."

"I didn't call you back. Usually that means there was no connection and one should move on."

"You have some kind of nerve! Well, if you think you can just fuck me and roll over to the next, then you obviously don't know who you are dealing with." She stormed off.

Lamant yelled after her, "Don't be mad. It's nothing personal. It's me. Can't we at least be friends?" he said, meaning it. On one hand he felt he didn't handle that well, and on the other, he felt she deserved it for showing up unannounced. "Oh, well. Blame it on the Henny."

Latricia kept walking and stuck up her middle finger as she disappeared into the night.

Lamant was glad she left before his date arrived; he tried to avoid drama at all cost.

Amanda was sexy, aggressive, smart, and a tomcat in bed. All the things Lamant loved about a woman, she had—curves, attitude, a sense of humor, and knew how to let a man be a man. Lamant thought to himself, he wouldn't mind seeing more of her, at the beginning, a familiar theme he played inside his head about all women he dated.

They'd met while he was waiting for his train downtown D.C. She was engrossed in an *Essence* magazine and didn't notice him. He walked up to her, "Hello. You look awfully beautiful today. It must just be another Wednesday for you though."

She took her attention from her magazine. "My name is Amanda, and yours?"

"It's Lamant. Lamant James."

He had her at hello, and they reveled in light conversation until they reached their stops.

For what Lamant saw so far she was perfect and fit right into his life, all the way down to her pedicured toenails.

The next morning, Lamant got up and freshened up. He laid a new toothbrush out for Amanda, trying to avoid the last incident with Latricia. He climbed back into bed and tapped on her shoulder.

Groggy, she rolled over and said, "Good morning."

Lamant instantly covered his nose. "Good morning." She had the worst dragon breath he had ever smelled.

She began to say something. With his nose still covered, he put his other hand to her lips. "I left a toothbrush for you in the bathroom. Just nod if you like vegetable omelets."

Amanda nodded. She removed his hand from her mouth and proceeded to the bathroom to freshen up.

Lamant couldn't get that smell out of his nostrils. He tried to spray Air Spritz to replace the doggy-poop smell of her breath still lingering in the air.

He made up his bed, and before he could dart downstairs to make breakfast before work, Amanda returned.

"Hey you." She snuggled onto his back and laid her head in the nape of his neck.

Lamant hugged her back. He could smell the mint coming from her lips. He turned around to kiss her. "Hey yourself." He put his lips to hers, and his tongue inside her mouth. *Dammit! I can taste the dragon*. He pulled back.

Confused, Amanda said, "What is the problem now?"

"Your breath. It's still not right. Did you brush your tongue?"

Infuriated. "You're unbelievable." She found her clothes and began to quickly put them on and leave behind this crazy man.

Lamant wanted to apologize, but he couldn't help it. Her breath smelled like shit. Even after she brushed it. "I am sorry, it's just . . . didn't you appreciate it when I got up and you could smell the freshness in my mouth before I kissed you? That is considerate, don't you think?"

Amanda rolled her eyes. She collected her things and walked out.

"Wait. Don't go. Floss. I bet that's all you need."

"You need a shrink because you are fucked up in the head. If you really think every morning your woman should get up, brush her teeth before kissing you, then you are deluded about what being in a relationship is. Now I see why such a so-called catch like yourself is by yourself."

"Hey, I like what I like. Is that wrong?"

"What you like doesn't exist. No one is perfect. Especially you."

"Excuse me? I am the closest thing to it."

She laughed. "You know what you're close to? A bitch ass."

Lamant's been called many things before, but a bitch wasn't one of them. "Okay, you're just upset about your breath."

"I may be imperfect, but I would rather be imperfect than a grown bitch-ass man." She stormed off, shouting. "You couldn't handle a good woman if she put on a blindfold and plugged her ears. Good riddance!" She slammed the door

Lamant shrugged his shoulders like, *Oh, well . . . another one bites the dust.* He caught

a glimpse of himself in the mirror and reaf-
firmed what he already knew. "Bitch ass? She
must be crazy." He blew a kiss at his reflection
and kept it moving.

Chapter 25

Fridays were the worst days at the office. Deal-closing days. Lamant had worked on bringing aboard a major pharmaceutical company for the past month. This deal would surely bring him closer to making partner and leaving his working-like-a-dog days behind him. Maybe start working on his book and really live out his passion. Lamant's life savings could have carried him for at least two years, focusing solely on his book. Why hadn't he taken that plunge? Fear? He enjoyed nice things and the life that came along with it. To give that up and hustle for two years to make ends meet wasn't daunting to him, but he knew he couldn't go on like he'd been.

"Hey, man. Don't forget about the couples' party this weekend. Kendra has been working extra hard to put it together."

"I am glad you reminded me," Lamant said on his way to lunch. "It's blazing out here. What is the temperature like? A hundred degrees?"

"And climbing. Who are you bringing? Amanda?"

"That's a done deal. I will bring someone. Don't worry. Oh, and Jerome is coming through. I don't think he's bringing anyone though." Lamant had planned on asking Akira, a wannabe model that he had on the back burner for a few days.

"Then why is he coming?"

"Come on. The brother has been through a tough couple of months. Last year he brought you to Chocolate City's nightlife, when you were down, looking for women. It's time you return the favor."

"I got him a job and a volunteer gig." Marcus whined in his defense. "Whatever. Let me see if Kendra has any available friends she can invite."

"Cool. Because I already told him you would hook it up."

Marcus laughed. "Premature of you, but I guess that's your nature."

"Step in the ring with me and you'll see a premature ass-whupping."

"Chill, little fella. Wouldn't want you burning unnecessary calories. You're still a growing boy."

"Whatever, soft serve. Just make sure Kendra hooks it up. Peace."

Lamant and his cousin went back and forth like that every day of the week. Why should Friday be any different? He often teased Marcus how quickly he fell for Kendra, knowing it was in his cousin's nature to fall hard and quick. He couldn't stand being alone. From everything Marcus had told him, Kendra didn't strike him as the settling-down kind.

Feeling like the deal with Flush Pharmaceuticals was good as done, Lamant took a long lunch to clear his thoughts. He sat inside Panera Bread, two blocks from his office building, lost in a fantasy world about this male character he'd created almost five years ago. Marvin Drexel. A young talented man who recently found out he had incurable cancer and decided to go on an adventure worth a lifetime.

Lamant flipped open his laptop and started typing in his thoughts. He made it through half a chapter and turned back on his cell phone. It instantly started to buzz. It was his assistant.

"Lamant, where are you? I've left you tons of messages and sent you e-mails."

Lamant had turned his phone off and ignored incoming e-mails to zone out into his fantasy world. "I didn't get them. What's up?"

"More like what's not up. Flush is pulling out, your deal is going down the drain, and you are on an extended lunch break?"

"When I left, they were sending over the signed contract hand-delivered. What the hell happened? That was almost two hours ago. Did you get them?"

"No, I never received them. And Mr. Flush said you sent him back the signed documents with entirely different terms than stated in the deal. He sounds pissed, like you were trying to pull a fast one on him."

"How could I have switched anything when I never received the contract? Have his secretary fax them to me. I'm on my way."

"I don't think it will do any good. But okay."

Lamant was on fire. He couldn't believe his deal he worked so hard at acquiring wasn't going to go through. And even more frustrating was the fact that he was still going to have to put in even more hours to be where he wanted to be to live out his dream.

Distracted, he forgot to save what he had been working on before he logged off. "Dammit! My story!" Things just couldn't get any worse for him today.

By the time he reached his office, his assistant had a copy of the contract on his desk. Mr. Flush was right; everything they'd negotiated was changed. He pressed the call button to Liz, his secretary. "Get Mr. Flush on the phone. There seems to have been some mistake."

"I don't know if it will do any good. He sounded really—"

"Good thing I don't rely on your opinion. Now get him on the phone please."

"Just a minute please."

Lamant couldn't figure out what happened, how did this contract wind up in Mr. Flush's hands if he didn't send them to him? Who would want to mess up his deal? "Fuck!" He knew the answer.

"Mr. James, I have Mr. Flush for you on line one."

"Thank you. Put him through."

"Mr. Flush, let me first apologize for the mix-up. I'm still baffled myself how the contract we drew up for you to sign came back to you with this wording, but let me assure you, the deal we negotiated still stands. I will personally hand-deliver the contract to you, and we both can sign together in your office to prove to you our word is our word."

"That won't be necessary, Mr. James. In fact, I'm in touch with another investment banker at your firm as we speak who can guarantee me, the way she closes a deal involves precision and perfection."

"Mr. Flush, I can assure you, you are speaking to Mr. Perfection and I can—"

"Forget it, Lamant. You got caught with your pants down."

"Excuse me."

"You've been exposed and if this is how you conduct business by switching the terms at the last minute with back-end fees to fatten the pockets of your company, then you're not Mr. Perfection. You are no better than Maddoff. Good day."

Lamant was flabbergasted. *How could she do this? What a conniving little bitch!* He stormed out of his office and made his way down to hers.

Her assistant Marsha tried to stop him. "She's in a meeting, Mr. James, and this will have to wait."

He stormed past her and walked right into her office. "Latricia Smith James, I had no idea what a spineless supercunt you could be."

To his horror, Lamant walked in on Latricia and saw their boss, Mr. Faraday, in the office.

Mr. Faraday never thought that kind of language could come from such a tight-wound individual. "Lamant?"

Embarrassed. "Good afternoon, Mr. Faraday."

Latricia smiled, watching Lamant squirm.

Mr. Faraday ignored his outburst for now but made a mental note to address it later. "Lamant, Latricia tells me she just saved the company from losing a billion-dollar client. One you were supposed to close today, no doubt."

"And did she tell you she intercepted my hand-delivered package from Flush Pharmaceuticals and changed the terms of the contract?"

Astonished, Latricia covered for herself. "I can assure you I've done no such thing. Where is your proof?"

"She's right. Where is your proof, Lamant?"

"I will get all the proof I need. Don't you find it strange that she picks up a major investor in the same hours he pulls out? That seems a bit coincidental."

"Not if you are on top of your game, it isn't," Latricia spat.

Mr. Faraday grinned. "Lamant, you know what my motto is—If it doesn't make money, it doesn't matter. And, right now, what you're saying doesn't matter. I wouldn't waste my time trying to find proof. I would be looking for the next investment to cover the loss of this one." He shook Latricia's hand like one of the big boys at the decision-making table. "Good job, Latricia. I look forward to seeing what other businesses you bring in."

If Lamant didn't know any better, he would swear they were sleeping together.

Mr. Faraday left the office without even so much as a word or eye contact with Lamant.

"This isn't over."

"Yes, it is. If you're lucky, I may not steal any more clients from you." She laughed.

"Bitch! Guess the dick was too much for you to handle."

She burst into an evil laugh like the devil and flung back her head. "How ironic. You try to call me out like a bitch ass to the boss, and now you're leaving with your tail between your legs." She laughed harder. "The only bitch in this office is you. Now get the fuck out!"

That was the second time a woman called him a bitch. Lamant started to wonder, Was it really him who had it wrong. He shrugged it off, stroking his ego and licking his fur on the way.

Chapter 26

Lamant's week had gone from bad to unthinkably worse. How could this happen? His father was a young sixty-eight. Walked, ate healthy foods, and hardly drank. *A heart attack? This is insane.*

Marcus raced into the emergency entrance at D.C. Memorial. "Go. I will park and meet you inside."

Without a word, Lamant jumped out of his car and headed to the check-in desk. "Excuse me. I'm looking for Julian James. He was rushed here by ambulance for a heart"—He looked up and saw his mother hunched over in the waiting room with his oldest sister Jeanette, face dripping with tears, cradling her.

He walked over to them as if he didn't want to know the truth. "Momma. How is Dad?"

She couldn't speak, bawled up in tears, rocking back and forth in her daughter's arms"

"Jeanette, how's Dad? Is he all right?" Lamant questioned, fully knowing the answer.

She pulled herself together and shook her head. "He's gone, baby. He didn't make it." His mother cried harder and yelled out, "Julian!"

Lamant's tears had no say as they strolled down his face. "Where are Nakia and Melody?"

"They are on their way," Jeannette managed to get out between sobs.

"I want to see him."

Marcus slowly walked up behind Lamant and put his hand on his shoulder. "I'm sorry, man. Uncle Julian was a great man."

The anger of loss took over. "I want to see him. I want to see him!" Lamant flung Marcus's hand off of him.

"Okay, okay, man. I will get the doctor." He knew his cousin was upset and tried to help him. Marcus's father had long since past away, and his brother, Lamant's father, looked after him and his mother ever since. Marcus let the sorrow in but knew he was going to have to be the strong one in this situation, to see his family through.

Lamant sat down next to his mother and stroked her back. His other two sisters arrived, and Jeanette braced them.

Nakia fell out in despair, shouting, "Why! Why! This shouldn't have happened."

Melody, a lawyer and rock of the family, proceeded to take charge. She helped Jeannette settle her and then consoled her mother and Lamant. She would grieve later. "I will take care of everything. We will get through this together. Momma, would you like to see Daddy before we go? Lamant?"

They both nodded their heads, as if they couldn't speak. "I'll find the nurse." She found Marcus on the way.

He hugged her. "So sorry, Melody. I am so sorry."

"Thank you. I want Mom and Lamant to see Daddy before we go."

"The nurse is on her way. As soon as they get him ready, they will come and get you."

She nodded.

Marcus knew Melody could handle just about anything, but he wanted to help any way he could. "Lamant is going to take this the hardest, you know."

She nodded. "I know. We just have to stick together." She tried not to cry.

"I will look after him."

"I know, and I know how much Daddy meant to you."

Lamant sat alone watching from afar his family's despair. He was still in shock. The last time he saw his father was over the Fourth of July, when his parents had hosted a barbecue. He couldn't even remember who he'd brought to the cookout, but what he did remember was what his father said to him.

"Son, every time I see you, you are with a different girl. Now I am not dogging you. Hell, I even envy you. But when are you going to realize time doesn't sit still for anyone?"

Lamant nodded. "I know, Daddy. But she's fine, isn't she?"

His father gave him a nod, and they tapped closed fists.

"It's all good, son. I can't disagree with you there. But one day you are going to wake up and look around and wonder, Did I really just waste my life on fine? Figure out what you want out of this life, son, and take it."

Lamant nodded. "I am trying, Daddy."

Lamant got lost inside his head. His tears got heavier as he reeked regret. He'd been meaning to pick up the phone or go by to visit his father, but work, women, and himself got in the way.

Chapter 27

Melinda, Lamant's girlfriend of two years, his longest relationship to date, stretched out across his sofa. She was exhausted from the weeklong inauguration celebration of the first African-American president, Barack Obama.

Three months and two days of cohabitating, Lamant couldn't find one thing on his list of no-nos. He started thinking she might actually be the one, minus the flossing outside the bathroom, which he'd made every attempt to stop.

It wasn't a big deal to her, the flossing; in fact her college roommate also told her it was nasty. If that was the only thing holding Lamant back from marrying her, then she definitely would try to quit.

After the dinner he had prepared for the two, she rubbed his stomach, and he rubbed hers as they watched *Late Night with David Letterman* together.

"Is there some reason every comic book or cartoon I grew up watching is now a flipping movie? GI Joe, come on now." Melinda gave her two cents.

"They're running out of material. Sometimes I think the Writers Guild is still on strike." Lamant joked.

"You need to stop lollygagging and submit your work. I would go see it, blog it, rent the DVD, and then buy it too. You have talent."

"You're absolutely right. It seems I purposely let things distract me. What is that?"

"Procrastination, afraid to fail, fear of the unknown . . . I could go on." She rolled her eyes at the frustration of having this conversation over and over with her man. She loved Lamant and wanted him to succeed at whatever he did, but his constant need for everything to be perfect had soon become a drag.

Lamant couldn't help it though. His high-maintenance behavior was a bit daunting at first, but overall women found themselves jumping through hoops to please him. But, to him, that was how he rolled. Melinda was on board, he convinced himself. And she didn't do things he couldn't bear. He nicknamed her Bonita Apple-bum, because her apple-bottom shape attracted him the most, secondary to her almost being perfect.

"You're right. I can't even remember the last time I wrote something in my journal," Lamant said, feeling like life was passing him by.

"Well, then stop wasting time. Get up now and go write until your eyes squint."

He loved it when she acted like his drill sergeant. It turned him on. "I was thinking you could give me some new material first." He stroked her long black natural set hair and stared into her dark brown, gumdrop-shaped eyes.

"I've always got new material," she whispered. She kissed his bottom lip.

"Show me." Lamant kissed her back.

Not much of writing got done that night, or thereafter.

Her words followed him wherever he went. *Stop wasting time*. Lamant reminisced. His father's death was a shocking blow. Everything seemed meaningless now. Everything seemed hopeless. He stared at a picture of his family taken last November during Thanksgiving. During that dinner, he and his father sat on the porch of the home his parents raised him and his sisters in and chitchatted about life.

Julian asked his son, "Are you living, son, or are you just existing? You work at this high-in-the-sky firm, but are you happy? Is this what you really want to do?"

"No. Not really."

"Then what? What do you want to do?"

"I've been thinking about writing, I dunno, a novel, a play. Something I can call my own."

"A man needs that, son, something he can be proud of. I've worked my whole life on someone else's dream. Someone else's to call his or her own. I look back and say, 'Where did the time go? How come I didn't make my own mark?' " He shook his head. "Don't make that mistake. Carve your own, son."

Lamant shook his head. He agreed with everything his father was saying.

"So what happens when you live with only regrets? Like you, Dad, how do you find happiness?"

"By realizing you are where you are supposed to be. I am where I am supposed to be right now, giving my only son advice. This is what I was meant to do, be a father, pass on my legacy. That is and will always be my dream."

Confused, Lamant said, "But you just said you regretted not building something of your own."

"Oh, but I did, son. I built a home, a life, a family of my own. That is worth any sacrifice I may have made in following any dream. This was my ultimate dream. This is what defines me as a man. What defines you?"

Lamant shrugged. "I don't know."

"Well, you better find out before it's too late."

Lamant shook his head. Tears welled up. He regretted not having more time to show his father what defined him as a man. He took the family photograph off the ledge and tucked it under his arm. He closed the door to his father's study and walked toward picking up the pieces of his life.

Chapter 28

Lamant rummaged through his thoughts. Inspiration was hard to come by. He didn't know where to start. He would write down an idea in his journal and then cross it off in a millisecond. "Why can't I get focused?" he yelled at himself.

His bereavement time would be ending soon at his job, and he would be forced to put back on his uniform and fall in line. He found himself detached and uninvested in his career as an investment banker long before his father had passed away. It just now seemed more amplified, and the urgency to make his dream a reality made the idea of work unattractive and depressing. He hadn't a clue how he would pay his bills, the thought of becoming this starving artist didn't appeal to him much. Never a multitasker, he had no solution to his problem.

He lay back on his bed and tried to concentrate on a direction, on a thought. He rolled over and pulled the covers over him. Exhausted, he retreated and let thoughts of "would-be writer" dreams rock him to sleep.

The next day wasn't quite different from the day before and so forth. Lamant was beginning to understand why he never gave up his day job.

"I suck!" Self-loathing wasn't going to get him anywhere, so he decided to get some much-needed attention.

He yanked out his cell phone from his night-stand and searched through his contacts for the number. He hit send and the receiver began to ring.

"Hello," a woman's voice answered. "Mahogany's."

"Hi. This is Mr. James. I would like to make an appointment today for three o'clock, preferably with Jen."

"Hold on, Mr. James. Let me check her availability."

It seemed like forever went by. All Lamant could think about was that he needed a fix and badly, sooner rather than much later. He felt like he'd seriously caught a case of the Jones, like Pookie from *New Jack City*.

About a split second before he hit the end button, the woman returned to the phone. "Mr.

James, I'm sorry. She's booked today. She has an opening first thing in the morning."

"No good. I need to see her today. Is someone else available?"

"Sorry, sir. We're booked for this afternoon."

"So if you knew that, then why did you put me on hold for so long? I need to be seen today. Can you tell Jen it's an emergency. A code blue. Something."

"Hold on a minute."

Another uncomfortable doomed minute went by. Lamant was on edge if he couldn't get to Mahogany's today.

"Mr. James."

"Yes."

"Jen said she could squeeze you in for an hour, not a minute longer. Be here by three fifteen."

"No problem. I'll take it. Be there at three."

He hung up, darted into the shower, got dressed, splashed on some cologne, and sprinted out the door. He had to get serviced immediately.

After forty-five minutes of fighting D.C. traffic, Lamant rushed into the front door of Mahogany's, as if taking advantage of a "doorbuster" on Black Friday. He walked up to the receptionist. "Three o'clock with Jen," he blurted out in a nervous, jittery way. "Mr. James."

"Have a seat, Mr. James. Jen will be right with you."

He looked at his watch. It was five minutes to the hour. He didn't budge from the desk. "It's almost three. I can't be late, and she said I only have an hour."

"I am aware of that. Mr. James. We spoke on the phone. Your appointment, like I told you, is at three fifteen." She was even more annoyed with him in person.

He nodded his head. And sat down and waited.

Although Lamant had showered and lathered up, he still needed a shave, and his clothes were wrinkled, a far cry from the Lamant of yesterday, who wouldn't dare step out of his house unless he was dressed to the nines.

When the clock hit three fifteen, he shot up and headed toward the receptionist. Before he could rip her a new one, he saw her out of the corner of his eye.

"Good afternoon, Mr. James."

His heart slowed its race. "Jen. Thank you, thank you."

She lifted one eyebrow at his appearance. "If I knew you needed me this bad, I would have cleared my schedule."

Give a man an inch, he'll take a mile. "Can you?"

She grinned. "I will see what I can do."

Lamant exhaled. Finally he would get taken care of.

Jen led him back to her room, where she dimmed the lights and played the jazz he liked. She lit her candles and scented the room with his favorite incense. "Undress and lie down, Mr. James."

Lamant obeyed his Asian-American goddess. "Anything you say. Be gentle. A brother needs some TLC."

She smiled and nodded. "Of course."

Lamant lay on his back butt naked, awaiting her soft touch. He closed his eyes and tried to imagine absolutely nothing. Jen went to work and began to massage his upper, middle, and lower body. She told him to turn over and massaged him from head to toe.

Lamant got extreme pleasure and relaxation simultaneously. He bit his lip as she massaged his feet. The toes were his spot. "Ooh! Girl, be gentle. Be gentle."

"I'll try. Now roll over again."

Lamant did as he was told, but this time his appendage got a little longer and harder. Unembarrassed, he smiled. "I told you to be gentle."

She smiled. "And I told you you only have one hour."

"That's all I need."

She shook her head. "Such a macho man. Wait here. Let me give you a mani and pedi."

"I thought you said—" Lamant was surprised.

"And then I said *maybe*."

She placed her hands on his rocket ship and massaged it until takeoff. Then she told him to get dressed and go to her nail station. "You look like you really could use this, Mr. James. What's wrong, work?"

"I wish it was that simple to solve."

"Well, relax and sit back. Put your troubled mind to rest. The problems will still be there when you leave, but in here at least you can escape for a little while. Have some peace."

He dropped his head against the headrest of the salon chair. Jen was absolutely right. He relaxed, rested his mind, and for once in a long time, felt tranquil.

"Melinda."

"Who?"

"That's the answer. She always supported me and always believed in my dream. I have to find her."

Jen was intrigued. "And then what?"

"Right a wrong. It's overdue."

Lamant convinced himself that finding Melinda and trying to get back together with her would lift his writer's block and help him find his passion again. She was the closest any woman ever got to him, and he honestly believed there was a reason for that.

Chapter 29

Lamant's workday was overloaded with client demands to reallocate funds into more secure interest bearing accounts. In this economy, even Lamant's knack for creative financial projections in the gloomiest of times was being challenged. His boss, Neil Faraday, appreciated Lamant's hard work but offered him no break even after his father's passing. Especially since his last deal fell through. This was a business, and in business, personal matters were checked at the door, emotions were obsolete, and capital gains took precedence over family matters, even death.

For the most part Lamant could appreciate an office where men outnumbered the women. The less emotions he had to deal with, the better. And he had no problem meeting his deadlines. Up until now, his job felt somewhat rewarding. Lamant found himself staring off into space or out his window, completely ignoring the mounds of work he needed to get done, the deadlines he had pushed back, and his boss's nagging e-mails regarding his current losses versus gains. Lately, Lamant felt that the total amount of money he brought into the company was never going to be enough for Neil to see what an asset he really was. His profits equaled around 1% gains for the company, so Lamant was easily expendable.

At this point though, he didn't seem to care. He was only interested in finding Melinda. Since he'd kicked her out, she'd changed her number, blocked his e-mails and IM, and switched jobs. She held the key to his future as a writer. She was his muse.

Instead of googling recent foreclosed properties to finance a neighborhood takeover for his client's convention center they wanted to build, he looked for Melinda. And, sure enough, he found Facebook, a place for friends. He signed up, and a half an hour later he searched for Melinda Devoe, age twenty-seven, in Washington, D.C. As easy as it seemed, he found her. He looked through her page, and enjoyed viewing her photos and reading her wall posts. He learned she finished her masters in nursing and would begin a new job this fall as a nurse practitioner. She belonged to the Democratic Party and joined groups like Black Nurses in D.C., Obama for Change, and Old School Hip-Hop. She was in Cocoa City Network, and Howard University Network.

An hour went by, and Lamant was still engaged in looking up what his ex-girlfriend had been up to for the past seven months. He felt a wave of emotion surge. He missed her and wanted her back.

Another e-mail popped up from Lamant's boss, reminding him that he had deadlines to meet that day. Lamant looked at the time. He was too smitten with thoughts of Melinda to care. He figured out how and decided to send her an e-mail, hoping he would get one back. He wrote on her wall, "Long time no see. Congratulations on your recent accomplishments. I knew you would always succeed."

He was about to close out of her page until he paid closer attention to the left side of the Web site under her picture. Her relationship status read, "Engaged to Mitchell Walker."

What the fuck? Lamant was devastated. Who was this guy? And how the hell could she have moved on so fast? It hadn't even been a year.

Lamant looked through her events page, waiting for a return e-mail. He wanted to know where she was going to be tonight. She'd replied yes to an event called Fashionable Late Thursdays this week. He marked his calendar and made a plan to ambush her and really see if, one, she was over him, and two, if he could win her back before she gave what he believed was his to another man.

Lamant knew he had to step up his game entirely to approach her after all this time. He plotted out his strategy and planned to use all tactics known to man, except the one that for sure would win her back—the promise to marry. He shook that thought out of his mind, convinced he could get around that. Maybe a trip to an exotic island, like Fiji.

Chapter 30

Lamant walked into the downtown D.C. lounge on New York Avenue and Tenth Street on a mission. It didn't bother him that the setting was covered with women wall to wall. Only a handful of guys attended the event, and most of them played for the other team. Lamant examined the scene, hoping to find who he was looking for. He walked through the crowded lounge twice and didn't see her. Feeling defeated, he made his way to the bathroom, thinking she changed her mind and decided not to come.

In the bathroom, a gentleman wearing a dark purple fitted shirt tucked into his off-white slacks asked, "How are you doing, partner?"

"Good." Lamant gave him a look like, *Don't even go there, partner. The sign on my ass says, "Do not enter."*

He got the nonverbal message and said, "No hard feelings. Can't blame a guy for trying. Loving those Gucci shades though. Work it." He snapped his fingers, and off he went.

Lamant had been feeling low lately and hadn't tried to meet anyone new. Maybe this all happened for a reason. Maybe, instead of trying to convince himself and Melinda that they belonged together, he was supposed to get back on his grind and start flipping over single ladies until he found Ms. Perfect.

He checked himself in the mirror. Without question, he knew who he was, what he should be doing, and how much he was going to make. He needed to be tightened up in the worst way, and it just might be some lucky lady other than Melinda who could get it.

He marched out of the bathroom with the confidence of a lion in the jungle. His confidence quickly jolted to the left when he saw her coming out of the bathroom.

"There you are," Lamant said.

Caught off guard, she responded, "Here I am."

He leaned in to give her a hug, and she gave him the church-girl pat on the back and not-too-close-body-contact kind of hug.

"I've been looking for you for a while now. Can we talk?"

Coldly she said, "I'm with my girlfriends. I really don't want to leave them hanging. Send me an e-mail or something." She began to walk off.

He grabbed her hand. "I did, Melinda. You've made it clear you don't want to talk to me. I know you got my last e-mail on Facebook, and I know you can figure out this is not a coincidental meeting. I wanted to see you."

"So now you see me, I can go, and you can go on with your pretentious, stuffy, live-by-the-rules life."

"I'm doing it. Melinda, I'm writing, and it's all because of you. Won't you give me two minutes of your time please?"

"Two minutes and a watermelon martini. Nothing more, nothing less."

"Cool. I have a spot in the corner." Lamant led her over to the table he'd reserved, and signaled the waitress to come over. "I've been thinking a lot about you. Us anyway. And I owe you an apology. What I did to you was foul, and I'm sorry. It's me. It's always been me. And you didn't deserve that."

She nodded.

"I didn't track you down to waste your time. I love you and want to make things work between us. I miss you."

The waitress interrupted the long, awkward silence between them. Melinda picked up her drink and sipped it slowly. This was too much for her to process.

"Do I ever cross your mind anytime, Melinda?"

She took another sip. "Look, there is something you should know. I am—"

"I know. Engaged. I saw that on your page. But I just can't believe you've fallen in love with someone else that quick. You may call it arrogance, but I call it confidence. I know you still have feelings for me. Or else you wouldn't have shut me off the way you did."

Melinda tried not to cave. "I do love you, Lamant, but I'm going to marry someone else. I'm in love with him."

"No, you're not."

"If I break off my engagement, then what am I supposed to do? Marry you?"

Lamant got stage fright all of a sudden and sweated with anxiety. He stuttered, "Um, no, I'm not saying that. I'm not saying we won't. I just need you back in my life. Don't you need me?"

"As your girlfriend, you need me. But when are you going to be ready to be something else?"

"I don't know. We will see. Let's take it one step at a time."

"One step at a time?"

"Yeah. What's wrong with that? I need you."

"Oh, so I should drop my life and run back into yours?" Furious, Melinda threw her drink in his face. "Fuck you, Lamant! You are the same selfish muthafucka who didn't have the balls to tell me it's over. Instead you packed up my shit and left me a Dear John note. Well, here is my response. Fuck off!" She got up from the table.

Lamant quickly wiped the flavored vodka off him, and off his shirt before it stained. "What the fuck?"

"You need me to be there for you and only you, cater to your needs, and maybe, maybe one day we will get to mine. No, thank you, Lamant. I've found someone to meet my needs, and if I don't hear from you again, that will be just fine with me." She stormed off into the crowd, never looking back.

Lamant barged out of there, pissed, wet, and smelling fruity. He couldn't believe Melinda treated him that way. So much for his muse. *This night couldn't be any worse.* Without looking where he was going, he darted out into the street, and the next thing he knew, he was flat on his back from a parked car pulling out.

Dazed, he looked into the bright stars and wondered, *Is this it?*

The stars were replaced by a woman's face. She screamed, "Oh my God! Are you all right? Oh my God! Somebody help!"

Her screams worsened his concussion, made him want to be dead, but her long eyelashes and voluptuous lips made him want to stay a little while longer.

Chapter 31

"I'm so sorry. I didn't see you. I was backing up, and when I turned around to put the car in drive and take off, I pulled off, and you walked in front of my car. What are the odds of that?" She smiled, her cutie pie routine on overdrive. She was driving her cousin's Mustang, even though her license was suspended.

Lamant sat upright and rubbed his head.

She had scored an ice pack from the car's built-in emergency aid kit. Her hands nervously pressed onto his head where he'd been holding, and onlookers started dialing their cell phones, calling for an ambulance.

Lamant's head felt like there were little chirping birds circling it. Dazed, he looked at his assailant. "I'm going to need license and registration."

Quick on her feet, she said, "No problem. It's in my car. Why don't you sit in the passenger seat until the ambulance arrives? Come on, I'll help you up."

He gave her his hand reluctantly because he didn't know if she had washed them. "I'm okay," he said, still feeling dizzy and disoriented. "I don't think I'm going to need an ambulance. Just give me your information, and I will call someone to pick me up."

"Nonsense. You need to see a doctor. I have my papers in the car." She gestured for him to sit in the plush leather seats of the Mustang convertible. She seated him and closed his door, and quickly ran around to her side, hopped in, and slammed her door.

Lamant rested his head on the headrest. "Okay, I'm good. License and registration please." He thought to himself, *I might have to sue.*

"No problem." She started up the car and pulled off, looking both ways this time for a pedestrian and the police.

Lamant put his hands on the dashboard. "Whoa! Whoa! Stop the car. Where are you going?"

"Okay, here is the thing. This is my cousin's car, my license is suspended, and I am in-between jobs, so I can't give you that information. But I can drop you off at the hospital and get you checked out, if you promise not to sue me."

Lamant's head began to spin even more. She was a lunatic. "You must be out your goddamn mind! Pull this shit over!" Usually he was polite with the ladies and did not use profanity. Whoever she was, a lady was the farthest thing from it. *Who pulls a hit-and-run and kidnaps the victim?* She had to be nuts.

"I can't do that. I am sorry. Look, I will pay for your co-pay. I can do that. How much is it? Fifty, seventy-five, a hundred dollars?"

Lamant vehemently shook his head. "No, no, and no. You will pull this car over now. I'm not fucking kidding with you. You must be from another planet."

"Look, just help me out. I have no money and no assets, so you will be suing me for absolutely nothing." She picked up speed. "Really, this is a better deal."

Lamant rubbed his head. He was caught in the twilight zone. "You're crazy. Your cousin has insurance. It will be his problem. I could have broken something. I could need serious therapy. More than your pocket change. There are rules. When you get into an accident, you get the driver's license, registration, and insurance information, call the police, and, if need be, an ambulance. You are completely off the grid."

"I know, I know, and I am so sorry. But I just can't go that route. Won't you please consider what I am saying to you? You aren't even hurt. Nothing is broken." She jabbed him in the arm.

"What the fuck!" Lamant yelled.

"See . . . nothing is broken. Come on. Let me pay your co-pay."

"Oh my God! You are crazy. I could have a concussion. Slow down. You are going to get into another accident with your crazy no-license ass. Just slow down."

"So it's a deal then? Emergency room or bust?"

In no position to argue, hell, he was trapped and he knew it. So he agreed for now. "Just take me to the damn ER, please."

"My pleasure."

"And you can keep your money and go buy some sense. Because I don't think you're playing with a full deck, sweetheart." Lamant held the ice pack to his head. "Seriously."

"I know this is unorthodox. But you are really helping me out here. I won't forget it."

"I plan to." Lamant closed his eyes and prayed his assailant would get him to the emergency room quickly, and as far away from her madness as possible.

Through his aggravation he managed to notice she was a little hottie. Long black hair, almond-shaped eyes, and peanut butter skin. Her noticeable thighs glistened as she pressed the gas and pumped the brakes, wearing white short shorts and a white-and-gold-striped tank top, captivating her real charmer, the cleavage from her succulent breasts.

Lamant was guessing, as crazy as she was beautiful, she got her way in and out of a few tight jams like this one, quite often. Forgetting her would be impossible.

Chapter 32

"Thank you again. I'm so sorry this happened to you. Really, I am," the woman said. She was so grateful and ecstatic she was able to convince him not to press charges as she pulled up to the ER entrance.

Lamant nodded his pain-stricken head as he climbed out of her cousin's convertible, still icing his injury. "Just watch where you are going next time, please."

"I will. Sorry again."

Lamant waved her off and made his way to the ER entranceway. He knew he would probably have to wait an eternity. He could see the entranceway to the ER getting fuzzier and darker by the second until it was gone. He felt as if everything was slowing down and he couldn't keep his eyes open. His legs buckled, and his body fell to the concrete.

"Oh my God! Someone, help!" was the last thing he heard.

***

Lamant grabbed his head as he came to. He felt like dwarfs were mining inside it. He pressed the nurse button, expecting to get some answers.

A few seconds later, the nurse came into his room. "How are you feeling, Mr. James? You took a nasty fall." She adjusted his blue and white gown. "How many fingers do I have up?"

"Three." He grabbed his head. "Where am I? How did I get here?" He was still groggy.

"You're at Washington General Hospital. You were admitted after suffering a concussion from a fall. The doctor wants to keep you overnight. Can you tell me your name and date of birth?"

The nurse went on and on with a host of questions, trying to assess his mental status, and Lamant answered her questions.

"When can I go home?"

"Probably by morning. Your MRI showed a mild concussion, but that is it. The doctor will see you in the morning again and most likely release you."

He nodded. "Okay. Thank you."

"Your girlfriend will be so glad you're awake. She was so worried, poor thing."

"My girlfriend?"

The nurse opened the door and gestured for someone to come in.

Lamant thought he had dreamed it all, but to his dismay, it was her.

"I will leave you two alone. He will be fine, sweetie. Don't worry."

Lamant grimaced. "So you *are* real."

"I'm sorry. I just couldn't leave after you passed out. I felt so bad. I might be a little flaky about where I am in life, but I know it wasn't right to leave you like that. I'm sorry, again."

"You should be."

"Good thing I took you to the hospital."

"Good thing. How about, you should have never left the scene of the crime in the first place?" Still grieving his father, lost in his career, rejected by Melinda, and now run over by a mental patient, Lamant was on his last leg.

She ignored him. "I think you need a massage."

"No. Please don't touch me. I have had enough of you for one day. Thanks for staying to make sure I'm okay, but I am fine. You can leave. Please just leave." He pulled his covers over his body and turned away from her.

She ignored his request and climbed into his hospital bed. "You're so tense and uptight, Lamant." She placed her hands on his neck. "You should relax more."

"Get out of my bed. Just leave me alone. Damn!" He pulled away. "You're like a nagging cockroach."

She laughed. "Ha-ha! I've been called a lot of things, but a cockroach is the first. You're so stuffy, so rigid. Just relax. You know, I went to school for massage therapy."

"You don't say. And what happened? Let me guess—You quit and moved on to becoming a photographer. No, wait, a teacher. Or is it a chef?"

She pinched his neck.

"Ouch!" He flinched. "Where is my call button?

She grabbed it. "Stop being such a baby. Just let me do this for you. Why do you have to be so difficult?"

"Why do you have to be so annoying? Don't you just disappear?" He tried to get the call bell from her.

She smiled and put it tightly behind her back. "You really want me to disappear?"

Lamant tried to reach around her and went for it.

She blocked him and locked eyes with him. "Lamant, you really want me gone?"

"I don't even know your name," he said, his arms wrapped around her back.

"It's Keke." She extended her hand with the call bell in it, out of his reach. "Nice to meet you."

Lamant looked at the call button and looked back at her. Then again and again. "Fuck it!" He grabbed her face and stuck his tongue down her throat.

Keke fell back onto the hospital pillow and wrapped her arms and legs around him.

He pulled off his hospital gown and fused his lips with hers. He stopped and gazed into her eyes. "Nice to meet you." He smiled.

Keke giggled and rolled him onto his back. She pulled off her tank top and unhooked her bra.

Lamant ran his hands up her abdomen and cupped her breasts. He pulled himself up and took one into his mouth.

Keke could feel his penis stand at attention, ready to salute her. She pushed him back onto the bed and pulled off her shorts and bikini brief panties. She kissed his neck and his nipples, working her way down.

Is she doing this? Lamant couldn't remember the last time he received head on the first date. Hell, this wasn't even a date. He didn't know her from a hole in the wall. He relaxed and enjoyed being a hospital patient, thinking, he should get run over more often.

Keke pulsed her lips and tongue rhythmically alongside his shaft. She massaged his nipples with both her hands as she continued giving him something he could feel. Lamant left his troubles behind, moaning every time her mouth suctioned his head.

Keke came up for air and continued caressing his penis. She whispered, "Do you have a condom?"

Lamant nodded as if he couldn't speak. He pointed to the "patients' belongings" bag on the nearby table.

She pulled the table closer and rummaged through his things and found a gold Magnum in his wallet.

Lamant lay on his back as if helpless, willing to let Keke have her way with him.

She ripped open the package and placed the condom in her mouth. She made her way back down to his woody and slipped the condom on it with her tongue. She teased him and tongued his head with her teeth and massaged his scrotum between her hands, as if milking a cow.

Lamant roared gently, "Don't stop!"

And she didn't.

Keke placed his hands inside her and guided their flow. Lamant eagerly took over, proving he knew the route. Then she sucked her way up to his chin, moving his prying hands from her warm, juicy peach pie and replacing them with his shielded, rock-hard penis.

Keke worked him. She buried her face in the nape of his neck and gyrated her hips and pelvis like a super wash cycle. Deeper she wanted him. Deeper. Lamant sweated heavily with pleasure. He wanted to come. He was almost there.

Keke stopped. She dismounted and turned her body, her back facing him. She guided him back in her and braced herself on her arms and hands. She rocked back and forth with her torso parallel to his. She could feel her G-spot being rubbed in all the right ways. She moaned with anticipation.

Lamant could feel her rupture. He couldn't hold it. "I'm about to come. Damn! I'm coming!" he growled, sweat pouring down his head.

Keke collapsed on top of his naked body. After she caught her breath, she said, "I bet you're relaxed now."

Lamant smiled. He kissed the back of her neck. *I am more than relaxed.*

By morning, Keke was gone. Lamant rolled over onto his back and recapped what had transpired over the last twenty-four. He grabbed a pen and hospital notepad and began to write. It was his first time writing in months. He didn't stop to analyze a thing. He wrote what he was feeling, no inhibitions or rules. He had already broken so many.

Chapter 33

Keke was more unpredictable than a hurricane, and when she hit, man, did she leave a mess. An afternoon-at-work quickie was the last thing Lamant wanted today, but Keke always, always had her way with him. Lamant could never refuse.

So instead of going over last-minute details to closing his deal, he was going over Keke's clitoris with his tongue. She brought the bona fide freak out in him.

It didn't help either that Liz walked in on him. "Oh dear. So sorry, Mr. James. I just wanted to leave these projections with you. Oh my. Sorry." Flushed, she dropped off the paperwork on the nearby chair and scurried back out the doorway.

Caught with his tongue in the cookie jar, Lamant stuttered, "Oh, okay. Thanks." She was already gone. He didn't have the nerve to face her. He was just glad it was her and not his boss.

"Don't stop, baby," Keke muttered, her backside on his desk and her legs bent to form a perfect *V*.

And he didn't.

A few minutes later, Lamant tried to regain his professionalism by refocusing his attention on work.

"Hey, you. I have an interview later. After that, I will be at Rendezvous down Adams Morgan. You want to meet me?"

"That sounds like a plan. But I really need to get back to work."

"All work and no play," Keke teased. "You've got to live in the moment."

"You're absolutely right. And in this very moment I have work to do." He kissed her on her forehead. "And a secretary to find before she runs off at the mouth."

Keke giggled. "I am sure she has a mouthful to say about you."

Lamant mocked her. "Hearty *ha-ha*."

He started wiping his desk down and putting everything back in its rightful place. He didn't know what it was about her that he couldn't refuse. They had been seeing each other since the accident a month ago.

Keke shook her head. "It must get exhausting."

"What? Sex? Never." Lamant grinned harder than his dick was a few minutes ago. "Sorry if you can't hang."

"Oh, I can hang. I was referring to you. It must be exhausting trying to be perfect."

Lamant continued his obsessive involuntary tasks. *It is*, he thought to himself. He wanted to open up to her, but for some reason, he held back. Even though he felt a vibe that he hadn't felt with anyone, he still couldn't break down all his walls. Not yet anyway.

"Really, I have to get back to work." He finished his fixing. "I will see you later."

"You better. No call, no show is a deal-breaker for me," she said, meaning it, yet trying to sound as if she was keeping their relationship light.

"Oh, so now you have rules. Imagine that. The girl that can't follow rules has the nerve to come up with some." He snapped his fingers and neck, and sucked his teeth. "Don't get it twisted, girlfriend."

"Don't do that again," Keke said with a straight face. She kissed him on the lips. "Hearty *ha-ha-ha*!"

Keke didn't know why she was feeling what she was feeling in only a matter of a month, but it was something. Like their souls knew each other before, but all their day-to-day life got in the way of them really reuniting. Lamant was so stuffy and uptight at times. She couldn't stand him. But in the same breath, she loved to unwind him and get him looser.

Lamant adored her freedom to do her. She was bat-shit crazy at times, even manic, but that's what he loved most. Fearless, she wasn't afraid to do what made her happy. He hoped, being around her, that energy would pass to him.

Lamant daydreamed about Keke later that day and well into his meeting later that afternoon. So much that he couldn't figure out why everyone was looking at him. *Shit! I don't have a woody, do I?* He looked down into his lap.

Mr. Faraday was furious. "Lamant? Didn't you hear me? Why do these projections show losses? Aetna Mae will not invest their money if they stand to lose eighty-five percent of their capital. Is this a joke?"

Lamant snapped out of it. "Excuse me. What were you saying?"

"I'm sorry, Lamant, if we are boring you with our mindless mongering about how to close a multi-million dollar deal with Aetna Mae, the biggest deal this company has seen in months, especially in this economy. Or is it that your Ivy

League education skipped the part about what it means to be a seller versus a shit-for-brains buyer?"

Lamant took the high road. "Excuse me. I can assure you, I am up for any challenge you throw at me and more than capable of closing this deal. It is as vital to me as it is to this company."

"Really? I was under the impression your face was in other places." Mr. Faraday remarked, aware of this afternoon's fiasco in Lamant's office.

Leave it to these gossiping heiffas at work.

Lamant avoided his boss's deliberate sucker punch again. "I can assure you my head is where it needs to be. I will fix these projections tonight and have them ready way before dawn and for tomorrow's meeting with Aetna Mae."

"I want a hard copy in my office first thing in the morning and an e-mail file by tonight. This deal is way too important for mistakes. I want one hundred and fifty percent perfection tomorrow and nothing else."

"And you will have it," Lamant assured him.

"Meeting adjourned." Mr. Faraday pulled Lamant aside. "Mr. James, may I have a word?"

Lamant nodded. *WTF?*

After everyone cleared the boardroom, Mr. Faraday said, "Lamant, I'm concerned about your work ethic lately. I don't like it. I don't have the tolerance for it. If you're going to work here, mistakes like this can't happen. Consider yourself notified."

Lamant attempted to comment, but his boss walked out.

Lamant can't say he didn't see this coming, but to try to castrate him in front of everyone at work was unforgivable. He knew his head wasn't into the job, but he figured, he could lay low until he figured out his next move. Every day at the office seemed more stressful than the last, and he couldn't help but long for the day his bullshit, nine-to-five nightmare of a job would end.

Later that night, Lamant worked feverishly to fix the projections. It was a technical error with his Excel program that caused a mismatch of formulas. Figures were in data cells that didn't belong there. Four hours later, he finished. Upon request, Lamant e-mailed them to his boss and printed out a hard copy and placed it on his desk.

Lamant drove home, half-awake. He barely had the energy to get undressed. He tucked himself in and rolled over. The clock read quarter to three o'clock in the morning.

He closed his eyes. "Keke." He forgot he had to meet her. He checked his phone. She didn't call him, send him a text, or e-mail.

He felt bad, so he got up, got dressed, and burned rubber twenty minutes to Rendezvous' lounge. He pulled up and jumped out of his car. No sign of her. He tried calling her. No answer. He sent her a text. No reply. He left her a voice mail. *Hope she gets it.*

Lamant drove off and headed home. Before he got in bed, he left Keke another message. "Hey, sorry about tonight. Got caught up at work. Plan to make it up to you. Take care." Whether she believed him or not, Lamant didn't know why it was important to let her know he didn't stand her up.

Chapter 34

"Lamant, great work on the projections. I'm confident this sealed the deal."

"No problem, Mr. Faraday." Lamant's light suddenly came on. "Excuse me, did you say *sealed*, as in past tense? The meeting is this afternoon. Aren't you being a little overconfident?"

"Never that. Oh, and yes, the meeting was rescheduled for nine o'clock this morning. You didn't get an e-mail?"

"No. Did you send me an e-mail?" Lamant knew he hadn't. "My secretary sure as hell didn't."

Mr. Faraday smirked. "No wonder you weren't there. Guess it's just one of those things, Lamant. Communication, you know. Oh well, what are you going to do?"

"'One of those things'? That was my deal!"

"Correction, that was the firm's deal. It's a team—"

"Really. So I imagine the usual commission will go to me then?"

"Well, you didn't sign off on it today. I did, so it's kind of like finders keepers."

"Or larceny."

"I don't think I like your tone. Face it, you haven't been on your game lately. And I couldn't risk you fucking this up. It's too important. There'll be other deals. Don't be sour about this, chalk it up as a loss."

"Fuck you!"

His boss was totally steamed-rolled by that one. "Excuse me?"

"I am pretty sure there will be more deals for you to screw me over on. Let me do all the heavy lifting and you take the credit. I am so glad this happened though. I'm good. You can take that deal and this job and shove them up your back-stabbing ass. I quit."

"Always dramatic. There is no need to get girly on me, Lamant, with your emotions. It's business. Be a man, suck it up."

"*You* suck it up! I'm a man. I know who I am, what the fuck I do, and how much I fuck-ing make, and how much I am worth." Lamant walked out of his boss's office. Then he turned and said calmly, "Thank you, Mr. Faraday, for making this easier for me to walk away from."

"Well, I guess you can take a poor kid from the ghetto, but you—"

"I have never been a poor kid in my life. I have always been rich. Rich with my values, instilled from one of the wisest men on earth. So don't pass your stereotypical judgment on me. You planned this all along and will continue to do the same when I leave. I'm just not going to be your statistic anymore. This is your dream, and it's high time I start putting in the kind of work I do here, for myself, for my dreams."

Mr. Faraday rolled his eyes. "Here we go with the dramatics again."

Lamant left him and any nosy spectators standing there in his office doorway. He didn't care. He was free. And it felt incredibly good. He owed it to Keke, for getting his mind right. It was in that moment he knew what he was supposed to be doing. He was clear and finally ready to live. Now, his next step was finding her.

Chapter 35

Two weeks and two days, and no sign of her. It was near impossible to find a girl who lived like a ghost. She had cut him off since he'd stood her up. She never went to the same spot twice, never showed him where she lived, and he didn't know her last name. If only she would call him or show up at his front door.

Lamant was devastated and heart sick. He had written and poured his emotions onto paper. He'd finished his first draft in less than ten days. His freedom took his mind places that the old stuffy, responsible Lamant wouldn't go. He was doing everything he felt passionate about. Lamant could have found someone to share his bed, maybe even made them what he needed them to be, but he only wanted one woman, Keke, flaws and all.

A month of hoping to find her and shopping around for an agent to solicit his untitled manuscript, Lamant finally went to catch up with his boy Jerome and his cousin Marcus at the golf club. His cousin Marcus was planning a re-proposal to his ex-wife Sheri and seemed happier than ever.

"Are you sure she's going to say yes this time?" Lamant asked. "Isn't she still grieving?"

"I don't see how she couldn't. She admitted she still loved me and has noticed how much I've changed for the better. It's just different now. In a good way. It's right."

"Hey, I'm not knocking you." Lamant put up his hands. "I'm not saying she's a gold digger, but she ain't messing with no broke nigga." Lamant chanted and bopped his head to an imaginary beat, reciting a verse from Kanye West's *"Gold Digger. Holla, we want pre-nup, we want pre-nup, yeah!"*

Marcus laughed and playfully jabbed him then put him in a headlock. "Some little lady will come along and you will be singing a different song, my man. Trust me."

"She did, but I lost her."

Shocked his cousin could step outside his tight, neatly fitted relationship box, Marcus probed him, "What? Who? When? Where? Are you talking about Melinda? That's right. Last year around this time you and her moved in together. That was foul how you ended it. Even for you."

"No, it's not Melinda. She wasn't for me." Lamant shook his head, feeling hopeless. "Man, it doesn't even matter. She's gone."

"What's her name?"

"It's Ke—" Lamant's heart skipped a beat as he watched a black Ford Mustang convertible pull up. He was sure, almost positive, it was her.

He stood up and made his way to the doors to catch her. When he got outside, it wasn't her. It was Jerome. He snapped out of his wishful thinking and gave Jerome dap and a manly hug. "What up, man?"

"Good to see you. Your man here?"

"Yeah, in the clubhouse, chilling, ready to tee up. He's talking one hundred a hole. You game?"

"You know it," Jerome said, overconfident about his stroking skills.

Lamant eyeballed his car, still thinking Keke might magically appear from it. "Nice ride. Is it new?"

"Yeah. Bought it a few months ago. But will probably have to trade it in, if all things go well. And, don't you know, I'd only had it for a hot second, and I let my cousin borrow it, and she got into an accident two months ago. She's lucky I owe her a favor or else." Jerome shook his head thinking about his irresponsible cousin. "She's a mess. Flaky as hell, always in trouble, but somehow finds her way out."

"What's your cousin's name?"

"Shakela. But we call her Keke."

Lamant's heart began to pump quickly. "I need to holla at you, playa."

Chapter 36

Lamant wasted no time in tracking Keke down. He walked into the Hooters, hoping this would be his night.

Keri Hilson's "Knock You Down" played overhead as the mixed crowd of young and old, men and women, enjoyed fried chicken wings, beer, and black short shorts. Lamant was seated in a booth alone. He planned to wait there all night if he had to.

Three hours later and three orders of hot wings later, his persistence paid off. A pair of black short shorts strutted by, and Lamant recognized the bounty they carried. He seized his opportunity. "Shakela Hart," he shouted.

She reluctantly turned around, not sure if she should run, duck, or hide. She wasn't aware of any warrant for her arrest, but hell, it wouldn't be the first time. Her fear rebounded to anger when she saw him. "Oh, it's you." She turned to walk away.

Lamant grabbed her arm, not willing to let her go again. "Marry me."

"Excuse me?" She knew he couldn't be serious. This must be a joke.

He shouted louder, "Marry me!"

Suddenly the rowdy noise silenced. Lamant bent down on his knees. "I don't ever want to lose you again. Marry me."

"You are crazier than I thought." She dismissed him.

"And so are you. Probably even crazier. You show up when, where, and however, at the most inconvenient times. You move around more than the earth's axis. You put things out of place and don't put them back. You eat anywhere besides the kitchen, you never heard of a coaster, and you snore. You drive me crazy. And I love that about you."

"Ah!" the crowd crooned collectively.

"With you, rules are meaningless, trivial and meant to be broken to fit your needs. So I am throwing out my rulebook, because you are what I need. I love you. It doesn't make sense, but I love you." He stood up and took her hand as he pressed his body against hers. "You more than knocked me down. You ran my ass over," he whispered gently in her ear.

She could feel his heartbeat as his body poetically rubbed against hers. She shook her head. "This is crazy. You are crazy, you know that?"

"So what's it going to be?"

Keke felt completely ambushed. She was still mad at him. He'd stood her up. But her heart begged her to give him a second chance. "I get off at—"

He put his fingers to her lips. "What's it going to be? Yes or no?" He placed his fingers on her chin and smiled, waiting for whatever she threw at him. Ready to jump through her hoops to be with her. Ready to meet her needs. He stared into her eyes, pressing his forehead against hers and asked again. "So what's it going to be?"

Keke took a deep breath, as her head and heart argued, and the crowd waited with bated breath for her answer. She looked into her lover's eyes and said, "Maybe."

Part Three

"Mr. Costly"

Chapter 37

Jerome pimp-walked to Ying Yang Twins' "The Whisper Song" through Love Nightclub, one of D.C.'s hottest spots for careless men and promiscuous women. This was Jerome's usual routine, clubbing Thursday through Sunday, picking up chicks, as he called them, sometimes a number in his cell phone, a naked body in his bed. Jerome preferred the latter. This was how he got down and wasn't ashamed of it.

Working nine to five, sometimes ten to seven, or twelve to nine, whenever and wherever construction work was available, he was up on it. He made a few thousand after taxes, and that made him feel rich. He worked hard but played harder. On occasion he would drag his longtime buddy along, Lamant, only if he wasn't in one of his jive-ass relationships. And even sometimes, Lamant's cousin, Marcus, recently divorced and ready to scratch and sniff, if you get the drift, would join the all-night party. Jerome preferred, however, to do his hunting alone.

Jerome drove a 2008 BMW 7 Series, upgraded from his four-year 2004 lease. He bought expensive shoes and jewelry but always bargain-shopped at Marshall's or Macy's to buy his discounted polo shirts and white polo wife-beaters. His Jean Paul Gaultier cologne kept him smelling edible, and he frequented the barbershop every seven days to keep his goatee and low-cut deep wave Caesar prim and proper.

Six foot two inches tall, chocolate chip cookie skin complexion, with Morris Chestnut pearly white teeth, Jerome knew he was fly. His eyes got narrower every time he licked his bubblegum lips and smiled at the ladies. His women mistook him for half Asian and black, but his family was from Trinidad, and he was full-bred Washington, D.C.-born and raised. But, hey, to Jerome, if thinking he was mixed got him the digits and the Vickie's, then a PGA Championship-Tiger Woods muthafucka he was going to be for that evening.

Jerome would tell any tale to get those panties, as he would say. It didn't bother him one bit that he was thirty-five, irregularly employed, and living at home with his momma. Outsiders looking in would declare Jerome was living foul, but to him that was the only way to live.

Choosy with his women, he had standards
and all. Right now his standards had him creep-
ing across the dance floor to somebody he would
come to know as Shana.

Jerome moved his pelvis in a rhythmic motion
like he was doing the Brazilian samba, snapping
his fingers and two-stepping closer and closer to
her.

Shana pretended she didn't notice him and
continued to sip her White Russian and move
her hips to "The Whisper Song."

Jerome got closer and closer as he circled
around her, not saying a word, just staring at
her, mind-sexing her down. He was so close, he
could smell Chanel N°. 5.

Shana took another sip and imagined Jerome
sucking her lips. But she still stood strong and
continued in her own world, dancing by herself.
She could smell Jean Paul, her favorite, and her
id was beginning to send signals to her ego. *Hold
out, girl. Make him chase it.* That was her ego.
Damn! He's fine as hell, though. I wouldn't back
down.

Without a word or eye contact, Jerome could
tell she wanted him. Her body language was
loud and clear. He moved in for the kill, dancing
around her and making his way behind her. He
slowly grinded up against Shana's booty, barely

touching it. He wanted to tease her first. Then he moved his hips as Shana moved hers, their bodies connecting without touching.

Shana didn't want to give in, but then he did it. Jerome without permission gently grabbed her unoccupied hand and led her to the dance floor. Shana loved a brother who took charge. *Grrrr!* Id shouted like a tiger inside.

Jerome turned around and took her White Russian out of her hand and placed it on a nearby table without saying a word. Shana wasn't worried. He would be buying her another. That, she was sure of. She let him take the lead.

Jerome placed both his hands on her waist and pulled her into his nook, and they rumbaed to the music like old bedroom buddies.

The brother's got skills on the dance floor. But how does the booty work? Shana fantasized riding him like a racehorse, fast and hard, eagerly trying to get to the finish line. She was holding back though, wanting him to chase her more, but didn't know how much longer she could keep up her antics. He moved like a Latin stallion, and she couldn't ignore his dark, smooth, clean-cut good looks.

Kanye West's song, "Gold Digger," came on. That was Jerome's song. He couldn't let Shana go now, not until he sewed up his game so tight that her punani would be his at the end of the night and well into the wee hours of the morning. He made a mental note that she couldn't stay longer than that because he had to take his momma to church by eleven a.m.

Jerome bumped, did the slow grind, and the dipped-down-and-back-up front grind. He whispered in Shana's ear, "What's your name, beautiful?"

"Shana Harding." She turned her head toward his ear and asked, "And yours?"

"Jerome Hart." He grinned. "Well, Ms. Harding, would you like a drink?" He rubbed his fingers down her shoulders. "Sorry, I didn't mean to get you all sweaty and wet."

Shana coughed, almost choking on her own saliva. "Yes. White Russian, please."

Jerome led her off the dance floor as if they were coupled. At the bar they chopped it up. He discovered she was a hairstylist and owned a salon. Jerome didn't pass up the opportunity to flash his BMW car key as he searched through his pockets for his wallet to pay for the drinks.

He ordered a Diet Coke and could see Shana's judgmental facial expression through the corner of his eye. Drinking wasn't something Jerome ever got into. He would drink and fall asleep, or get so pissy drunk, he couldn't stand himself. He worked out, ate a healthy 3,000-calories-a-day diet and took care of his body. So alcohol didn't fit in his "body-is-my-temple" way of life. Now, on the other hand, smoking purple haze marijuana was his recreational activity. After all, it was from the earth, so how could it be bad for his body? Besides, haze always made his game tighter.

He was banking that he would be able to book this chick tonight. And so he began, "You have a beautiful smile, Shana."

Shana giggled like a schoolgirl. "Thank you."

Jerome could see her defense withering. She was a pretty tight package. Prime rib off the menu. Caramel complexion, her thick thighs led to her fat backside, and her tiny waist anchored two cantaloupe breasts set nicely below her neck. She rocked a blondish hair rinse and shoulder-length crimped curls, and her dimples pierced her cheeks with every grin. Jerome wanted to smack her momma for laying out all that beauty.

Whoo-hoo! he thought as he envisioned doggy-styling her behind all night long and into the morning.

"What are your plans this morning? I would love to take you to breakfast." He smiled and then licked his lips. "I would love to feed you."

Shana recognized game, and she liked what Jerome was selling. *But what kind of man is he really?* she wondered. "Going home to bed. I have to get up for church."

"Really? Me too. I have to bring my momma by eleven A.M."

Shana's id and ego conversed. *Loves his momma and the Lord. Takes care of his momma, treats himself well too. Oh, not to mention, he's fine.*

"Did you ride here alone, or come with a friend?"

"Yes, I rode with my girlfriends over there." She pointed to her two closest friends, Suzette and Felicia.

"I would love to see you again, especially get a chance to dance with you again. You've got some kind of moves on you, girl." He tapped her shoulder playfully then gazed seriously into her eyes. "Do you think that would be possible?"

Shana wanted to say, "Right now, honey dip," but was trying to change her bed-hopping ways. She pulled out her cell phone. "What's your number, Jerome? So I can make that a possibility."

After they exchanged numbers, Jerome played his last hand. He looked at his watch. "It's almost two. I better make my way to my car. I hate getting caught up in parking lot pimping, so I better make my exit now. It was nice to meet you, Shana." He leaned in and kissed her cheek. Playing hard to get was almost a winner in his book.

Shana couldn't tell if it was the cologne or the White Russian, but she wanted to taste his lips, so she did. And that led to the tongue-down jump-off.

Chapter 38

Back at Jerome's place, he and Shana tore each other's clothes off without interruption. Boots flew, condoms ripped, and they sexed each other until eight a.m. the next morning. They both fell asleep, exhausted by each other.

Jerome was tired. He'd worked extra hard to stay up, literally. Shana was a wildcat who knew how to break a brother off.

Beep! Beep! His alarm buzzed. It was ten in the morning. Jerome had to shower, get dressed and get this chick out of the house before his Momma got up and was ready for church.

He shook Shana up after he got out of the shower and dressed. She was still sleeping. He grinned to himself. *Big Dig strikes again.* He shook her again, "Shana." Keeping the names of his ladies straight was his specialty, even after a long night of hot sex, drugs, and very little sleep.

Shana opened her eyes and was greeted by grogginess and a sharp headache. "What time is it?"

"It's after ten. I have to bring my momma to church, love. Don't you have to go to?" he said, trying his best to get her motivated and the hell out of his room.

She yawned. "Don't think I'm going to make it. I have a wicked hangover."

"Cool. Can you be up and dressed in ten minutes? I can drop you by the Metro or call you a cab."

Shana must've still been groggy because she knew this muthafucka wasn't trying to get rid of her like that.

She shook it off, because she smelled the bacon. *Okay, maybe he's not a beast. He's cooking breakfast for me. Dang! He must've got up with the roosters. When did he have time for all this?*

She got up and slipped into last night's little black tube-top dress. She searched for her black thongs and shoes, feeling the walk of shame coming. Last night in the club, her plan was to call Jerome, not go home with him. Mad at herself for backsliding into her old ways, she began to give up any chance of getting to know him better. What's done is done.

Jerome kept checking his watch. *Can you move any slower? Damn!*

"Where's your restroom?"

Oh, hell no! Jerome pointed to his master bathroom inside his master suite, which he'd built two years ago inside his mother's three-bedroom condo. He was so busy getting dressed and getting Shana out of his room, he didn't realize his mother had started fixing breakfast. When he smelled the familiar aroma, he became even more annoyed. "Great. Now I would have to bypass her to get to the front door," he said out loud to himself.

Roberta Hart knew her son was promiscuous. She prayed that her son would get it together and settle down with the right woman.

She appreciated all the work he did around the house and his driving her to church every Sunday, Bible study on Wednesday, and choir practice on Friday, but she prayed for the day he would get out of her house, get married, and have her some grandbabies. She figured she must've breastfed him too long, because he still wouldn't get off the boob.

Shana fixed her hair and cleaned her face to freshen up. She met an impatient Jerome outside his bathroom door, already dressed in his Sunday-suit best.

"You ready?"

"Yeah, but I'm not taking the Metro, and I don't have enough cash for a cab. You're going to have to take me home." Shana wasn't going to let Jerome treat her like a one-night stand. "I know you have to bring your momma to church. I live by Howard University, so it's not far from here. Does your momma live close?"

Before Jerome could answer, his mother knocked on the door. "Fifteen minutes, baby. I have your breakfast ready. We've gots to get to stepping. I can't be late."

"Wait. You live with your momma?" she asked in a "get-yo'-shit-together, nigga" kind of way.

"Yeah. Is that a problem?"

Shana laughed out loud, no regard for his feelings. "Why am I not surprised? You were sucking on my breast like a newborn. That should have been a telltale that you've never left the nest."

"Excuse me?" Jerome just knew his selection from the fast food late-night takeout menu wasn't trying to carry him.

"Never mind. Cab fare will be fine," she said, still giggling as she held out her hand.

At first Jerome wanted to tell her to kick rocks, but after thinking about it for a split second, her leaving any which way was the best thing she'd said all morning.

"Cool. Here you go. I'll call you one." He gave her a fifty-dollar bill.

Jerome's mother knocked again. "Come on here, boy, and offer that girl a plate to eat too."

"Excuse me?"

"You heard me. Always sending these gals home hungry, like they don't have an appetite, except for you."

"Momma!" Jerome was embarrassed, like he was a child again.

"Let's go. I can't be late now."

Shana couldn't believe it.

But then again all the hell she'd been through waking up next to a momma's boy was far better than waking up in an alley of D.C., no money, no shoes, and no panties after a night of clubbing and leaving with an asshole who'd slipped her a date rape drug. She had no clue who had been in her that night. It was all a blur. A blur that only the Good Lord could get her through. She left her careless, party-hopping ways behind her that night, vowing to be a better person. Well, she tried anyway.

Shana swallowed up that thought again, trying to forgive herself for who she used to be. She sat down at the breakfast table with Jerome and his mother in her nightclub dress and ate Sunday breakfast.

"Good morning. My name is Shana. Thank you so kindly for the food. I appreciate it, Mrs.—"

Jerome's mother couldn't get over how polite and well-mannered this gal was. *Maybe she's not just another hot one.* "Ms. Roberta."

"Well, thank you again, Ms. Roberta, for a lovely breakfast. It was nice to meet you."

"The same here, Shana."

Parents were Shana's specialty. She could get along with anyone's. Now, men, that was something she just couldn't get right.

Jerome called her a cab, and as Shana waited, his mother tried to convince her to let them take her home.

"No, that's okay, really, Ms. Roberta. I've held you up enough this morning. I would hate for you to be late for church. If I hurry, I can make the early-afternoon service."

Roberta liked her son's hottie even more. "What is it you do for a living, honey?"

"I'm a hairstylist. I own Shay's Spot over on F Street NW."

"Is that so?" *A businesswoman too.*

"If you are ever in the neighborhood, come by. The least I can do is get you a wash and doobie for all the hospitality you've shown me."

"Cancel that cab, Jerome. We're taking her home."

Jerome did as he was told, and Roberta and Shana chatted on the way like schoolgirls.

Jerome wondered how a booty call worked her way into his mother's good graces. He knew he would never hear the end of Shana now. He imagined his mother nagging him with, *"What happened to that nice girl?"* He was worried sick that Shana might turn out to be her regular hair-stylist too. *Oh Lord. It would be another Terri situation, all over again.* He fumed inside at the thought. *Dammit! Next time gotta get 'em out right after I come. No more sleepovers. Hit it and quit it, that's how I gets down. No attachments.*

Women would know, had to know, he was a hard man to keep and didn't want to be kept. Only high-end, career chicks, and stuck-up undercover hoes, he would entertain and introduce to his "man-man." Then that's it. That's all he wanted from them. *Beat it.*

He would give up his right rib not to meet another woman like Terri. Relationship and commitment, he wanted no part of that. Oh no, he wouldn't put his heart on the line again. Never.

As the two new best friends chatted it up, Jerome remained quiet. *Now why can't I find a chick who's down with my program?*

Chapter 39

February 2007

Jerome loved women and women loved him. His handsome smile and bedroom eyes never failed him with the ladies. When he'd met Terri at Honolulu International Airport for the first time, he felt she was out of his league.

"So were you here for the game?" Terri asked, sitting close enough for Jerome to sniff her scent and preview her cleavage.

What does she know about the Pro Bowl. "Yes, I come every year. It's my little getaway." Jerome was in disbelief. He didn't think a woman like her was this easy. "And you, business or pleasure?"

"Business. I attended a conference."

"And now you're heading home to D.C.?" Jerome was intrigued. In fact, her scent had him open at her first hello.

"Yes," Terri said. His eyes attracted her most.

"Must be nice. What kind of conference was it? What do you do?"

"I'm a sex therapist." She smiled, knowing she always got the same response.

"Interesting." Jerome imagined her dark peachy skin rubbing against his. "So you . . ." He got lost in his fantasy and just smiled.

"You were saying?"

"Sorry. Lost my train of thought. You say you're a sex therapist, and I can only imagine what men say when you tell them that. I was trying not to sound like another jerk-off."

"Does that take effort?" Terri giggled.

Jerome smiled. He was smitten with her and became enthralled by her pink lips and long black eyelashes to match her long black hair. Her thighs seemed juicy and well nourished. He wanted to lick between them, so anxious to get a taste of her.

"Jerome, do you ever ask yourself, are you living, or are you existing?"

"No." He took a quick minute to reflect on what she said. He was so into her already. "You got me thinking. I love life and all its unpredictability." He paused. "Like meeting you." He decided to play his hand. For some reason he didn't want to play games with her. "I know you saw me watching you. You must have seen something you liked."

Terri thought, *Direct. No bullshit. I like it.* "Well, aren't we cocky today."

Jerome smirked. "Fine choice of words."

Terri smiled. She liked him.

They continued their conversation like old lovers. To onlookers, they carried on like a couple.

The plane began to board. Jerome didn't want to miss his chance to hook up with Terri in D.C. He pulled out his cell phone. "What's your telephone number, in case I'm in need of therapy?"

Terri smiled. "I don't have a cell phone." She leaned in and whispered in his ear, "Maybe destiny will bring us together again." Then she softly kissed his cheek, got up, and boarded the plane.

That kiss lasted longer for Jerome, her scent still there, her touch still felt. He had to have her, destiny or not. Her body called him.

When Jerome boarded the airplane, he looked for her and when he spotted her in the middle row of first class, her eyes caught his. He smiled. Her return smile was gentle, her eyes delicate.

The flight was loaded. Jerome found his seat in the back row of first class, strapped himself in, and leaned to the side to get another glimpse of her.

After the aircraft took off, and the passengers were free to roam around the airplane, he slowly walked toward her seat, but she wasn't there. He didn't see her get up. *Where did she go?*

He excused himself down the aisle, but other passengers were waiting in line for the bathroom. He tried to flex his muscles to get by them but was unsuccessful. Not giving up, he waited, looking for her over the shoulders of passengers waiting to use the restroom.

He was about to look down the other end of the aircraft when the bathroom door opened. His eyes met hers again. This time he wasn't going to let go. He pushed her into the bathroom stall and wrapped his large arms around her back. He kissed her passionately, moving his hands down to her butt cheeks. He lifted her up, and she wrapped her legs around him. With one hand, he pulled her curly hair back and suckled her neck like a vampire.

Terri moaned. She wanted him just as bad. The thrill of doing the forbidden dance and the electricity of their bodies touching made her vagina throb. There was no turning back now.

Jerome made his way down to her breasts and bit them through her pink camisole. He let go of her hair and snatched her breasts out of her shirt and into his mouth.

The sucking made Terri hotter. Jerome could feel her body quivering. He dug both his hands inside her pants and found her vagina. Jerome slipped down his pants, put her legs to the ground, quickly slipped down her thong and raised himself up, along with her pelvis, legs, and his dick all in one seamless motion.

Jerome squeezed her back tighter and plunged deeper and deeper, while Terri braced herself and squeezed his back, moaning with every thrust. His man-man veins popped tightly with pleasure as her inner walls suctioned his shaft. The moans got louder and heavier as Jerome and Terri pleasured their way to seven minutes of heaven.

Jerome released and pulled out, his heart beating a thousand times a minute against Terri's chest. Before he could say anything, a loud banging came across the bathroom door.

Terri smirked. "I guess they can't hold it either."

Jerome laughed. He handed her pants with the thong still inside to her. He slipped on his pants and handed her his number he previously wrote down for her.

"Use this anytime you want. I would love to finish our conversation." He grinned and kissed her lips softly.

Terri didn't say anything. She watched him dart out of the bathroom and close the door. She fixed her clothes and hair, but the smell of sex stayed on her. When she opened the door, she wasn't the least embarrassed when she saw a long line of people in first class waiting to use the lavatory. They looked her up and down, and she politely said, "Excuse me," with a smile that could kill misery.

She sat back in her middle seat and later ordered a glass of Pinot Grigio. She never once glimpsed back at Jerome for she was uncertain if pursuing him was a good idea, given her current situation. She contemplated this the entire way to D.C., wondering what life would be like if she stopped pretending and actually found a man she loved. What was love but a four-letter word to her anyway? She tucked his number in her wicker beach bag. Maybe she would use it, maybe she wouldn't.

Chapter 40

Jerome stared at himself naked in his bedroom mirror as he brushed his hair to perfection. Another Saturday night of club-hopping was on his agenda. His destination for whore-hunting was H_2O. This time Marcus, who wasn't having any luck meeting someone on his own, planned to tag along. Evidently, he needed Jerome's help.

Jerome's only objective for the night was to find her, fuck her, and leave her. Relationships were a thing of the past; he wanted to be single forever. He pitied Marcus. Finding a good woman to make his wife was like trying to find an honest politician. There simply weren't any.

Jerome lathered up and lightly dipped his body in Jean Paul. He pulled open his top drawer to put on his underclothes, forgetting about the little black box he'd concealed. Disillusioned that the sting wasn't gone every time he saw it even after five months, Jerome, a secret "cutter," could feel the instant pain. He tried to shake it off, but couldn't. He opened the black box and began to stare at the two-carat princess cut diamond he'd planned to propose to Terri with. He began to get lost in his thoughts.

Jerome loved to watch Terri slip on her pantyhose just as much as he loved watching her slip them off. He lay stretched across the bed, in no particular hurry to make it to Marcus' and Sheri's New Year's Eve party that night. He'd much rather spend the night home alone with his girlfriend.

"Let's not go tonight, baby."

Terri caught his gaze. "And what would you rather do?"

His naughty grin answered her. Terri returned the gesture. "I am putting you into therapy," she joked.

"Fine with me. When can I start?"

She walked over to him and climbed on top of his back. She kissed the back of his neck and then nibbled on his ear.

Jerome rolled over and grabbed her hips. "I must confess, I am a Terri addict. Is there anything you can do for me, doctor?"

She giggled. He could always make her laugh, and she, him. They seemed perfect for each other.

She kissed his lips and grinded her hips slowly. "I am afraid, you are a hopeless cause." She hopped up. "Now get dressed. We're going to be late."

Jerome rolled back over to his stomach, not wanting to go anywhere. He wanted to show her the ring now; he didn't want to wait until the ball dropped. He wanted her to be his forever now. "Terri, I have something for you."

"Well, give it to me." She grinned and slipped on her short black cocktail dress. She patted her back, gesturing for him to zip her up.

Jerome obliged and whispered in her ear, his arms wrapped around her, "I could never imagine a life without you in it. I love you, Terri Sarkasian." His words were honest.

She turned around and hugged him tight. "I love you too, Jerome Hart."

Never in a million years did he think he would fall this hard, and for someone of a different race. As luck would have it, he ran into her at a Starbucks on U Street as the rain began to pour down. He didn't think he would ever see her again. Jerome didn't want to wonder what-if.

He took a chance and grabbed her by the waist the instant their eyes connected. He kissed passionately, and she didn't pull back. When they came up for air, he said, "Destiny has spoken."

He reluctantly let go, so he could ask her to marry him. "Terri," he said nervously.

Her pager began to buzz. "Wait one second, baby. That's the office calling."

Jerome didn't want to wait.

"Dammit!"

"What's the matter?"

"I have to go in. One of my patients is in a crisis."

"Yeah, you're looking at him."

"Seriously, baby, I have to go. Tell Marcus and Sheri I am sorry."

"Are you kidding me? It's New Year's Eve? There is something important I—"

She kissed him softly. "Tell me next year, baby. You know I can't abandon my patients. They need me."

"So do I."

She smiled. "If I finish before the ball drops, I will call you. I promise."

He grabbed her waist, pulling her in one last time. "You better." He kissed her again, not wanting to let go.

"I love you." She gently pried herself free. "Happy New Year, baby." Just like that she left him alone inside their two-bedroom apartment on the downtown D.C. waterfront.

Jerome wanted to call it a night but instead

decided to go to Marcus's without Terri. He got
dressed and was making his way out the door
when he heard a buzzing noise coming from underneath their bed.

It was Terri's pager. *She must have dropped
it.* Jerome picked it and pressed the green button
to read her last message:

> WHERE THE HELL ARE YOU? THE PARTY STARTED OVER
> AN HOUR AGO.
>
> ROBERT

Jerome was dumbfounded and in denial. No
way, she could be seeing another man. No way.
He scrolled through her messages for that day.

> HONEY, BE THERE AT 7 P.M., I AM RUNNING BEHIND.
>
> LOVE ROBERT
>
> SORRY ABOUT THIS MORNING, HONEY. I LOVE YOU.
>
> ROBERT

The blood vessels in Jerome's head constricted
more and more. He couldn't believe what he was
reading. *She left in the middle of the night last
night. Said her client was in a crisis. Liar!*

He scrolled through message after message:

> HONEY, DON'T BE LATE TONIGHT. I NEED YOU THERE
> WITH ME. IT'S IMPORTANT. NATIONAL PORTRAIT
> GALLERY, 6:30 P.M. LOVE ROBERT

Jerome flew from his apartment and drove
down to F Street to confirm what he already knew.
Terri had been unfaithful. *How long? Who was
he? How could I have been so blind?*

He didn't know what he was going to do once inside the gallery. Heart on his sleeve, he looked for her. Two security guards caught up with him before he reached the private party. They stopped him, but he'd already seen her.

"Excuse me, sir. This is a private function. Do you have an invitation?"

He went deaf momentarily as he saw Terri arm in arm with a tall, frumpy, hairy son of a bitch dressed in a black suit and white bow tie. He watched from afar as they laughed with each other and entertained the couple they were conversing with. The man rubbed Terri's belly, sending Jerome into temporary psychosis.

"Sir, if you don't have an invitation, I am going to have to ask you to leave." The security guard began to usher Jerome out.

"Terri!" he shouted from afar.

She looked over, and her grin evaporated. She looked frozen in time.

"Terri, you need to talk to me!" Jerome shouted. He tried to hold in his rage, but he wasn't making any promises.

The hairy man whispered in her ear without taking his eyes off the man shouting her name, and she whispered back and politely excused herself. Terri smiled at the security guards and gave them a nod.

Jerome watched the hairy man. He didn't take his eyes off Terri.

She nervously began, "Jerome—"

"Who is he?" Jerome only planned to ask once.

"Jerome, I—"

He could tell she was afraid. "Who is—"

"My husband," she blurted out. "Please leave. I am so . . ."

Jerome took that blade to his heart. It wasn't enough to kill him yet. "And you're preg—"

She tried to get him out before her husband made his way over. "Pregnant."

Still standing after the second dagger, he said, "And it's—"

"His." She looked away. "You have to go, please. He thinks you are one of my patients."

"Oh, so he thinks I am crazy?"

"Jerome, please, you have to—"

"Shut the fuck up! You lying cunt bitch!" He planned to show her crazy. He charged for her, wanting to wrap his hands around her neck.

The security guards rushed over and hemmed him up. A voice yelled, "Someone, call the police."

Jerome could see the hairy husband coming toward them. He wanted to fuck him up too. The security guards managed to push Jerome toward the door, but he broke free and, with a one-two combination, knocked both security guards to the ground.

Jerome didn't want to run. He wanted to ruin Terri's life as she did his. But he ran as far away from her as possible.

Chapter 41

"Before this goes any further, I gotta warn you, I'm not looking for anything special, sugar," Westina informed Jerome. She was like Samantha in *Sex and the City*, not wanting to be tied down to one guy.

Jerome was happy to hear that. *Finally, a woman down with my program.* "That's cool with me."

Westina smiled and pushed Jerome back onto her Sealy queen-sized foam mattress. Before his back could rebound from the spring, she pressed her body on top of him, and wrapped her arms and legs around him like an octopus. Her tongue charged his, and she locked, loaded, and passionately kissed him. Her tongue moved to his cheek, and she took a bite out of his brown sweetness.

Then she followed the perfect scent of Jean Paul Gaultier to his neck. It was calling her, and she couldn't resist. She nibbled on his neck and pressed her breasts on his chest. He grabbed them and caressed them nipple to breast, breast to nipple, pinching and cupping them.

Westina, loving his touch, started grinding her pelvis onto his, aching to feel the familiar hardness. Her lips and tongue made their way to his chest, and she buried her face into his ripe, hairless chest and licked her way down.

She stopped at his navel and unbuckled his belt then ripped his jeans and boxers off. Without hesitation, she took him into her mouth and stroked his penis with her lips and mouth. She teased him at first by only putting the head in, licking it slowly, like an ice cream cone.

Jerome wiggled. He opened his eyes to guide her head with his hand, to show her the way, but Westina, familiar with the route, proceeded to take the rest of him in, to her throat, and almost gagging.

A newbie, she was not; she had a Ph.D. in deep throat, and Jerome was happy to be a recipient of her expertise. He could have his dick sucked for hours, but he didn't have that kind of time, nor did he want to spend it with this freak he'd just met at H_2O Nightclub. But if time could stand still, he would like to make getting head an official Groundhog Day.

He flipped her over to her stomach, not wanting to explode in her mouth.

She giggled, enjoying how rough he was being with her. "That's it, daddy. Give it to me from behind. Don't fuck around!" She poked out her behind, peeking out from her black dress.

Jerome was beginning to like this "nothing special." He slipped on his condom and ripped her "like it rough" thongs off. Her slightly hairy ass cheeks almost turned him off, but a hole was a hole, and when he slipped into her butthole, man, was he glad he went to H_2O that night. Stroke after stroke, he plunged deeper; he wanted her to feel like she was splitting in two.

Westina liked it rough and hard. She groaned, "Don't stop, muthafucka! Don't even think about coming!"

Jerome liked her smart mouth. He smacked her hairy ass hard; he wanted to see his handprint. He began to drill into her like a brick building. He wanted to come so bad, he was losing his mind. Hearing voices, sweating like a marathon man, he couldn't believe she was letting him do this. It was too good to be true.

"Anal on the first—Hell, it wasn't even a date. Damn! You're the fucking best!"

"Don't you fucking cum yet! Don't even think about it!" Westina shouted out in passion. She loved it; the deeper he penetrated, the more she couldn't stand for him to stop.

Jerome was ready. *Fuck that! I'm primed.* He pushed Westina's cheeks, down to the mattress and stroked faster and harder. He would break his back if he had to.

"Dammit! I said not for you toooo—Oooh! Oooh!" Westina moaned.

"Shit! Yeah! Ooh shit! Yeah!" Jerome yelled out in ecstasy, as he made it home. He collapsed next to Westina as he convulsed, breathless. "Whew!"

She rolled over to her back. "Don't act like you've done something," she said with an attitude. "I've had better."

Jerome wiped his wet brow. "Yeah, right." He was full of himself and didn't care.

"Don't even think about going to sleep. Put your clothes on and leave if you're done."

She's a bossy bitch. Not wanting his ego to get bruised, he geared up for another round. His appetite was insatiable when he got stroked that good.

He rolled over onto her body and massaged her augmented breasts. He could tell the real from the fake with one touch. The real were soft tissue and, when pressed, felt like water balloons. The fake, when pressed, felt like hot air balloons.

He began to pull up her black dress and slid his way down to her belly, biting her stomach through the black dress. *Guess I will return the favor and shut another one up with my clit-licking skills.* He grabbed the inside of both her thighs and forcefully lifted them up to her shoulders, with the rest of her black dress.

His lips felt a light tap upward as he reconnected his eyes to what he thought was her vagina. *What the fuck was that?* He jumped off the bed, like Jaws was after his penis. "What the fuck is that?"

Westina looked confused, as if she didn't speak English. "What?"

"That fucking thing between your legs?"

Afraid something was there that shouldn't be, Westina looked between her legs. Then she said, "Don't even start tripping now. As if you didn't know I was pre-op." She sucked her teeth and rolled her eyes.

"Arggh!" Jerome lost it. He pulled at his short hair, spitting and cursing. He pulled Westina by her two legs off the bed and kicked her in her stomach so hard, she curled into a fetal position.

He kept kicking her and kicking her with his barefoot until blood ejected from her mouth. Westina couldn't even speak or groan in agony, the blood choking her.

He kicked her in her face and began to stomp her on the back. He wanted to shove his foot up her ass, but kicked her in it instead.

Infuriated, disgraced and disgusted, he got dressed and "he-manned" his way to his car. He didn't care if Westina was alive or dead. He hoped she was dead, 'cause he could never ever ever see her, him, or it again.

He cursed his entire way home. "Fucking shit! Muthafucka! That shit better be dead. Better be dead. Why me? Damn! Fucking shit!" He raced through red light after red light, speeding against the sun, trying to get home so he could dowse his dick in fire and burn his tongue and lips with alcohol. "Fuck! Goddammit!"

Chapter 42

I've been here before, Shana kept telling her-self. No matter how many times she'd visited the OB/GYN doctor's office, she could never get use to the hard cold steel of the speculum inside her vagina, or the uncomfortable skin pressure on her feet from pushing her weight into the stirrups. True, this was the ninth time going through this exam, not counting annual vaginal exams. She had gone through five spontaneous abortions and four therapeutic abortions since she was thirteen years old. But the nerves she felt when lying on that table, looking into the white light, never felt routine.

She'd taken an Ativan before arriving for her appointment, and hoped it would have kicked in by now. Not feeling the full effects of her anxiety, but still feeling like she was going to jump out of her own skin, her OB/GYN constantly telling her to relax as he examined her pelvic cavity with a lubricated ultrasonic imaging device wasn't helping.

Shana had been experiencing some bleeding for the last week, along with cramping. At first, she'd thought for sure it was her menstrual cycle taking over her body as usual, but then something in the back of her mind told her it was something else. Something unexpected.

After her stressful exam, Shana popped another Ativan pill to calm her nerves. She had just quit smoking earlier in the year, along with another bad habit, bed-hopping. That was until she met and slept with Jerome. For five months, she had been drama free, leaving her destructive behavior behind her, trying to start over. She'd stopped taking ecstasy, until recently, stopped sleeping with strangers, only drank socially, and didn't club as much as she used to.

To compound matters, Timothy, a computer engineer she'd met two months ago online, had proposed to her. He'd treated her like a queen, sweeping her right off her feet. *And now this*, Shana thought.

She fought the urge to grab a cigarette from the CVS pharmacy as she picked up her prescription for prenatal vitamins and folic acid. She shoved the pills into her oversized pocketbook, not sure what she was really doing. Her thoughts from her office visit pushed their way back into her head again.

***

"Well, Ms. Harding, ultrasound confirms it. You are twelve weeks pregnant."

Shana lay silent to the news she had been expecting for weeks.

"You really need to start taking your prenatal vitamins and folic acid for healthy development of your baby. I'm going to prescribe them for you."

Shana was paying attention, but not really. This wasn't what she wanted to hear right now.

"Ms. Harding, you need to make a follow-up appointment next month, and we will also need to draw some labs on you today. After that, you can schedule a second trimester ultrasound, to get a full image of the baby and, if you desire, learn the sex of the baby."

Realizing Shana wasn't prepared for this news, he put his hand on her shoulder. "Was this a planned pregnancy?"

Shana snapped back into this world. "What?"

"I noticed you look surprised."

"Unplanned."

"Well, is the father of the baby involved?"

"Yes," she lied, knowing the truth would lead to more questions, which she wasn't sure she had the answers to yet.

"Well, it would be nice if both of you were present for visits."

"Sure," Shana said. *Physicians try to fix all your problems in one sitting, but they know they really can't. No use in spilling my life story to him now.*

She pressed the keyless button to her Acura SUV, opened the door, and threw her prescription in the backseat. She turned the ignition, and her truck sped out of the CVS parking lot in Laurel, Maryland, with no clear plan. She couldn't tell Jerome, although she kept in regular contact with his mother, who was a client.

And Timothy wouldn't be so happy that she was carrying another man's baby. They'd only started sleeping together last month, so there was no way mathematically she could even think of passing this baby off as his. *Maybe love could be blind*, she pondered.

She came back to reality. *Another abortion. You're thirty-six years old, Shana. It's time to face up to your responsibilities.* She wanted children, and swore if God gave her another chance, she would take it. But was this His way of being funny?

With still no answers to her problem, she returned to her salon, where she had four relaxers, two doobies, and one sewn-in weave to do before her day was done. That was enough to keep her thoughts clear.

After getting her third client rinsed, roller-set, and under the dryer, Shana went into the back and grabbed a bottle of Evian water. She was exhausted and nauseous as usual. Her morning sickness was an overall sickness.

Trying to forget about her pregnancy, she called her sister in Boston, to get a double dose of her teenage drama. Jasmine, at seventeen, knew everything there was to know about life, or so she thought. Boyfriends were just that, boy friends, and her focus was on college and making money. Shana wished she was as driven as her younger sister when she was that age. Beautiful, skinny, and tall, she surely could have been on *America's Next Top Model*. But again, money and college were the only things on her mind.

"Please listen to the music while your party is reached," the automated voice commanded. Shana hoped Jasmine would pick up before she heard that exhausted Kelly Rowland song, "Like This," which D.C. radio stations were killing.

Jasmine picked up. "What up, sis? Tired of making 'Ugly Betty' pretty?"

"Smart lips don't make money."

"Oh, don't worry. I knows how to be a house nigga and a field nigga when I wants."

"We're not using that word anymore, remember?"

"Well, until President Obama officially bans the word, then a nigga like me is just going to keep saying it."

"I swear, you are so ignorant sometimes, Jasmine." Shana laughed. Her sister was a pistol.

"Whatever. So what john has got you down now?" Jasmine knew her sister better than she thought.

"Surprisingly, Timothy has been good to me. Can't complain one word about him."

"Oh, really? Y'all must not have done it yet."

Shana spat out her water. "You are a hot mess, you know that?"

"Enough about you. Did you know the boy is still making a play for homegirl?"

"Stop it! Didn't she take him to the cleaners?"

"Naw, son got more money than Jesus. Sis did well for herself."

"Listen to you . . . all about the dollars."

"'Cause nothing else makes sense. Check it."

Jasmine continued to school Shana about why marrying rich, or being rich herself was her only goal in life. She was never going to be broke like her parents.

For a second, Shana's mind was taken off her drama, until she peeked through her office door and saw Jerome's mother walking in.

"Hey, sis, sorry to cut you off, but I have to go."

Roberta wasn't scheduled for an appointment, and they didn't have a lunch date, so why was she here?

Shana tried to act normal. "Hey, girl. What you doing here? I don't have you down for today. Well, nice to see you all the same."

They kissed and hugged.

Roberta so wanted things to work out with Jerome and Shana, who was already like a daughter-in-law to her. She could tell Shana had seen life and was living in the light of God now because of it, just like when she'd given birth to Jerome and was left to raise him after his father skipped out on her.

"I know I don't have an appointment, but I was down by the convention center for a conference today with Reverend T.D. Jakes and thought I would stop by and say hello."

"You are too sweet. Can I get you anything?"

"No, honey, I'm good. You were just on my mind this morning for some reason, and as chance would have it, I was in your neighborhood."

Shana was nervous. *Oh, lawd, Sixth Sense is about to find me out.* "How's Jerome?"

"Well, now that you asked, he doesn't seem himself lately. Not that I'm complaining, but he hasn't come home in the wee hours of the morning for some time now."

"Oh, really? He's stopped clubbing?"

"He's been going with me to church, doing things before I ask him, and been polite to my sisters in church even."

"You don't say."

"Thought he might have called you and you two might have—"

Shana put up her hands. "Sorry. Can't take credit. I haven't spoken to him since we last saw each other."

Disappointed, Roberta said, "I was really hoping you were behind this new leaf."

"That's wonderful, if he is growing up." Shana thought, *Maybe people do change.* She started to picture a life with Jerome and the baby, and her decision was becoming clearer.

Chapter 43

Friday came around like it always did, slow, painful, and agonizing. T.G.I. Friday's couldn't be here soon enough for Jerome. He hadn't been club-hopping in months since he'd met that "thing" he wished was dead because, one, he didn't want to run into "it" and, two, he didn't want any witnesses around in case he went crazy again.

It was homecoming weekend at Howard University, where he was sure there would be enough fast, hot asses and more freaks than his man-man could stand. But he was saddled with his last "freakazoid" encounter. Jerome shook his body every time he thought about it and knew he would never be able to forgive himself. After all, before he realized she was a he, he'd rated the sex in his top five, but now he could never admit that to himself. He looked at it as he had his man-man in some hot, sticky, tight-as-a-mutha punani, instead of some man's ass.

He cursed out loud, "Goddammit, mutha-fucka!"

"What did you say, boy?" Roberta said as she came through the front door of her condo. "I know you're not in here cursing the Good Lord's name?"

"Good morning, Mama. How is everyone down at the Inn?" Jerome couldn't care less about his mother feeding the homeless.

"They're just fine. Now what is all this ruckus for in here?" Roberta was sharper than her son thought and had a memory like a hard drive.

"Nothing. I have to go to work on a hot day like this in October."

"Well, sitting around chasing those fast women don't pay the bills, son."

Jerome flinched. *Don't I know it. Freak!*

"Speaking of women, I saw Shana the other day. I still think you have a chance with her. Why don't you call her?"

"I don't have her number."

"You ain't saying anything but a word." Roberta pulled out her address book from her console table behind the sofa. She thumbed through it and found the names under *S*. "Here it is, son."

"No, thanks, Mama. I wouldn't want to ruin y'all friendship."

"Boy, what are you talking about? Trust me, Mama knows what Mama knows, and when I mentioned you, she lit up. She looked so pretty the other day, just radiant. You really should—"

"Thanks, but no, thanks. I can find my own woman, Mama."

"Don't cut me off again, boy. And if you could find your own woman, you wouldn't be running around here with these hookers."

Jerome smirked. "I'm so fly, I don't ever have to pay for no women, Mama."

She slapped him on his back playfully. "You don't have a clue, boy, not a clue. God has a plan for you though. You wait and see."

As usual, Jerome shrugged off his mother's advice, grabbed his key ring, and left for the job site.

He took out a piece of torn paper from an address book in his pocket. With Shana's phone number. His mother must have slipped it in his pocket that quick. *Mama had to be a pickpocket in her former life*, he thought.

Just as he knew his name was Jerome Scott Hart, he cruised to work in his "get 'im, girl" ride down New York Avenue to work on these redeveloped row houses he had been contracted for. A day's work was just that, and he especially noticed how his pockets were a lot deeper without spending it on clubbing.

The foreman for the work crew was the strict Italian type, always ready to dock a brother's pay if he was two seconds late. Jerome knew the game and had no intentions of letting some mozzarella-eating punk take anything from him.

"When is this heat going to end?" Darien asked Jerome. He was from Providence, Rhode Island, where the weather was fall-like around this time. He wasn't used to the constant scorching from the sun.

"Damn! What are you? A penguin? This heat feels good." Jerome couldn't stand people from the North for some reason. He thought they looked down on him.

Terri had grown up in Boston after her family had migrated from Armenia, and all she did was turn his life upside down with her endless deception. He pushed her out of his mind quickly, not wanting her anywhere near his thoughts.

Jerome noticed two officers walk up to his foreman Mike. Next thing he knew, Mike looked in his direction, and so did the officers.

What da! Freak! He wanted to run, but it was too late.

Mike yelled, "Jerome!" and motioned for him to come closer.

Jerome slowly walked to the officers, who introduced themselves. Officer Sampson handed him a picture. "Do you know this woman?"

Jerome was shaken with fear. If the woman in the picture was who he thought it was, he was a goner for sure. He fixed his face as his eyes crept down to the picture. "Terri?"

"She was reported missing two weeks ago by her husband. We did some checking, and it turns out she rented an apartment on the waterfront back in December two thousand seven, same address as yours back then. Is that right, Mr. Hart?"

"She's my ex-girlfriend. I haven't seen her since January."

"When did you two last speak?"

"That would be January, officer," Jerome said in a sarcastic tone.

"How long were you two together?"

Jerome did the math inside his head. "Let's see . . . we met in February two thousand seven . . . so almost a year then."

"And did you know she was married?"

Knowing where this was going, Jerome stopped himself. "You said she's been missing for two weeks. I suggest you check with her husband then. I haven't seen her since we broke up. Now, if you will excuse me, I have to get back to work."

"Well, if you think of anything else, be sure to give me a call." Officer Sampson handed Jerome his card.

Jerome looked down at it and for sure wanted to toss it to the pavement, but he put it in his back pocket. He didn't want to think about her, but couldn't get her face out of his mind. *What if he found out about us and murdered her? What if he came after me?*

Chapter 44

Jerome drove back to his house after a long day's work. He wanted to shower and check his sexy before going to T.G.I. Friday's in Greenbelt. He wasn't exhausted from work, but more from reminiscing about Terri. Why, today of all days, did he have to hear her name, see her picture?

How could he have been so stupid to think she was in love with him and wanted to marry him and have a family? He kicked his ass several times for falling for her tricks, since he couldn't kick hers. "Bitch!" he yelled out while in the shower.

Jerome got dressed. Doting in front of the mirror, he winked at himself. "You are one sexy muthafucka." He spritzed his neck and wrists with Jean Paul Gaultier and made his way out of his mother's house to throw back a few and hopefully watch the preseason matchup between the Washington Wizards and the Los Angeles Lakers at the bar that evening.

Just then, his doorbell rang. His mother was at her Bible study that evening, so he couldn't imagine who was at his door. To his surprise, it was Shana.

"Hi, Jerome. I didn't mean to pop up like this. I've tried calling you several times, but you don't return my calls," she quickly blurted out. Jerome wasn't in the mood to see her. Annoyed, he asked, "What's up?"

"Can I come in for a minute?" Shana wasn't surprised he didn't offer, but was hoping he had changed. "I need to talk to you."

Jerome wanted to avoid the awkward "why-haven't-I-heard-from-you" moment, so he was hesitant to extend an invitation to come in. "I was on my way out."

"It will only take a second."

"Fine." Cornered, Jerome gestured, opening the door wider so Shana could pass. As she walked in, he noticed a squad car pulling up in front of his house. *Not this again.*

Shana made her way to the nearby sofa and sat down while Jerome was still at the door. She struggled with how she was going to tell him she was pregnant with his child, that she intended on keeping the baby. She was hoping he would want to be involved but knew the odds were against her.

She turned around. "I don't quite know how to say this, but I'm—" She stopped when she saw Jerome put his hands in a halt motion toward the two officers nearing his front door.

"I have already spoken to two officers earlier today. I don't know where she is, but if I find out, I'll be sure to—"

The fair-skinned officer said, "Are you Jerome Hart?"

Not sure if he should answer, Jerome said, "Yes."

"You are under the arrest for the assault of one Westina Clarkson."

"What? Wait! I didn't—"

"You have the right to remain silent. Anything you say or do will be held against you in a court of law . . ." The officer read Jerome his rights, while his banana nut-skinned partner cuffed him.

Jerome struggled and tried to plead his case. "You've got it wrong, she attacked me."

The arresting officer smirked carelessly, "don't you me he?"

Frantically, Shana ran up to the fair skin officer and questioned. "What is this about? What has he done?"

"We are taking him in for assault, ma'am, of a Westina Clarkson, aka Wesley Clarkson."

Both officers giggled.

Shocked, Shana said, "Wait . . . you're gay?"

"What? No. There has been a mistake. Do I look like I'm gay?"

"Well, you do work out a lot, dress to the nines, and wear that cologne pretty heavily. There's nothing wrong with being gay or bi, or what have you."

"What?" Jerome was furious. "Get me away from this crazy bitch! Talking that bullshit. I'm not gay. Was I gay when I had you screaming my name?"

"Fuck you!" Shana stormed off and gave Jerome the finger, shouting back at him, "With your gay ass!"

The officers giggled again. "Let's go, lover boy."

Defeated, Jerome hung his head low and reluctantly went off to jail.

Shana slammed her car door as the tears rolled down her face. "Fuck this shit and fuck that loser! Forgive me, dear Lord." She was a mess. She touched her belly and whispered to her unborn child, "Mommy screwed up, but I'm going to make it up to you, I promise."

Chapter 45

After two long days and very long nights, Jerome gladly collected his personal items from the lockup cage and walked out of the police station in downtown D.C.

His cousin Keke sat outside in her sky-blue Toyota Scion, impatiently waiting for her troublesome cousin.

Jerome hopped in her ride, feeling like an uncaged bird. "Hey, Kee. Thanks for bailing a brother out. What took so long? I was in there forever." Jerome was irate; he called his mother several times from the holding jail and left her messages because he couldn't get a hold of her. "Where's Momma?"

Keke rolled her eyes and drove off. "First off, you're welcome. Secondly, you know damn well your mother don't give a flying fuck if you land yourself in prison. She's just evil that way."

Jerome knew his mother's tolerance for his indiscretions and screwups over the years had faded, but he counted on her to be there when he needed her, regardless of what the Good Lord told her to do. He shifted in his seat. "Whatever. Don't be talking about my momma."

Years ago after he'd finished serving a two-year sentence for assault, Jerome had promised himself he would never see the inside of a jail cell again. Furious at himself for letting his temper get the better of him, he thought about the past two days. He tried to power up his cell but the battery was dead. "Hey, Kee. Let me hold your cell for a minute. I need to check my messages and call my job."

Keke reached behind Jerome's seat and dug for her cell phone in her bag. She handed him the phone. "Make it quick. Don't waste my roll-over minutes."

Keke was sharp on the little things, but clueless when it came to finding a career and settling down with someone. Always on the go—in D.C. this month, Las Vegas the next—she couldn't keep still and hadn't met anyone to stand still for.

Jerome ignored his cousin's pettiness. He had to find out what was up with his job, his case, and his Momma. His first voice message sounded: *"Jerome, this is Mike down at the site. Where are you?"*

Second message: *"Jerome, you haven't been to work in two days. I'm starting to get the idea you don't plan on coming back."*

Third message: *"Jerome, Mike here. I called your mother, and she told me."* Then he paused for half a second. *"Well, anyway, you're fired."*

What the Fuck! Jerome's blood pressure skyrocketed. "Goddammit! Fucking bitch!"

Keke shot him a look, fully aware of his past with loose women and rapid consequences. She didn't want to feed into her cousin's never-ending drama, but against her better judgment, she asked, "What woman done fucked you this time?"

Jerome was boiling. He'd been locked up, fired, and might possibly do some time. *What next?* "Kee, listen to your older cousin when I tell you this. No piece of pussy is worth this shit, you hear me?"

"Well, okay, but I am strictly dick'ng, you feel me?" She snapped her neck. "Mmm-hmm. I might have tried that 'bi shit' when I was younger, but I'm all set. I love meat—You get what I am saying? Shoot!"

Jerome tuned her out after the word *dick'ng*. He couldn't bring himself to tell anyone that he beat up a "he pretending to be a she" after he'd fucked him. He shivered at the thought. "Just get me home."

"Whatever." Keke sensed he wasn't in the mood to chitchat, but she went on anyway. "I need to hurry and get home anyway. I have a date with this new guy I met at the bookstore, suit-wearing you know what. Them the type to fool you, though. They be gay, bi, or overconfident, thinking I am supposed to be so aggressive, while they lay back and count the female-to-male ratio. It makes me sick sometimes. But I keep dating. I keep at it. I guess I just love the chase. Or maybe I just love the hunger. You know?"

Jerome had stopped listening a very, very long time ago. He was giving her a nod here and there, but now he was just staring off into the atmosphere, searching for an easy answer to his problems, which weren't going away overnight.

For the last two days all he could think about was how stupid he was and how he will never date again. He chuckled at the last thought. *Yeah, right. I love the pussy, and the pussy loves me!* Irresponsible and deluded, Jerome continued to think of a way to get him off, find and afford a lawyer since he was unemployed, and not get hard every time his dick reminisced about how tight that "he-she's" ass was.

Keke pulled up to her aunt's house, still chatting away about life lessons and love.

"Thanks again, cousin. I owe you."

"Oh, I intend to collect today."

Jerome looked at his cousin and couldn't believe it. *My week just keeps sucking.* "Ain't this about a bitch!"

Keke rolled her eyes. "Look, money doesn't grow on trees. You said you would reimburse me, so go inside and cough it up. You got issues, Jerome and I—"

Jerome hopped out of her car. "Kee, I will get it to you today. Please, I need to handle something. Talk to you later." He slammed her door, not waiting for her response.

His eyes and attention were on her. Terri, the bitch that stole his heart, was alive and well after all.

Chapter 46

Jerome walked toward his house. The sight of Terri made him rethink prison life. He would gladly turn himself in after murdering her for what she had done to him.

"Please can we go inside and talk. I promise, I can explain everything."

Jerome turned away from her. Her scent reached his nostrils and his hatred and heartbreak for her went hand in hand. He walked toward the front door, ignoring her, trying to get away.

Terri followed him. "Please, Jerome, I am begging you. I am sorry for any pain I caused you. But if you don't help me, I'm dead."

Jerome stopped and slowly turned around. "What really makes you think I give a fuck?" He shrugged his shoulders.

"I deserved that. But, baby—"

Jerome put his hand up to stop her. "Don't you *baby* me. You ruin my whole life, and now you just show up here in front of my momma's house? Get the fuck on before I get locked up again please."

"Jerome, I'm sorry, but I had nowhere else to go."

"Oh, well, good luck." He got out his keys and opened the door, ready to slam it in her face.

"I still love you, baby, even if you hate me. I never meant to hurt you. Please just let me—"

Roberta came to the door. She was fed up with her son and his reckless lifestyle. "What is all this cussing and carrying on in front of my house? Oh no, I won't tolerate it, not now, not ever."

"Oh, Momma, there you are," Jerome said, as if his momma had some explaining to do. "I was thinking something happened to you, since you left me to rot in jail."

"Don't take that tone with me. I will slap the black off ya, so Lord help me Jesus." Her stance in the doorway meant business. She was only four foot eleven inches tall, but the Trinidadian in her made her way taller. "I'm done, Jerome. I'm done, you hear me?"

Handling all he could for the day, he turned around and brushed past Terri. He needed solitude and sanity before he snapped even further.

Roberta stared Terri down with a look of death. "Terri."

Terri smiled. "Mrs. Hart, you look well."

She gestured, to give Roberta a hug, but Roberta intercepted her arms and held them down, grabbing her wrists tight. "I better never see you anywhere near my house or my son again. You hear me?" She pulled her down, to be eye level with her. "I've seen your kind many times before. You are not an original. Unlike your words, I mean exactly what I am saying to you. Don't let this old body fool you. If I ever see you again, you will only wish you were already dead." Roberta pulled her wrists tight and then pushed her hard from her porch.

Terri chased after Jerome and was on his heels again. "I left him."

"No shit." Jerome turned around. "And the baby?"

She moved up closer to him and lifted up her shirt, revealing a long scar down the middle of her stomach. "Gone. Robert killed him." She began to tear up.

Truth be told, a part of him was glad to see her. She still took his breath away. Torn, he said, "What happened?"

Terri shrugged her shoulders. "He found out. I was seven months pregnant when he came home in a fit of rage. He found out about our apartment together. He figured out you were the guy at the gallery, and convinced himself I was carrying your baby." She stopped herself, as if the memory was too hard to relive. "My husband can be a cruel man. I've tried to leave several times, but he won't let go."

"He hits you?"

"He calls it something else. He thinks I belong to him. I have to get away from him. I will never forgive him for killing my baby." She began to sob.

Jerome didn't know what to believe. *Who knows if she is telling the truth.*

"He came home that day. He wouldn't listen to reason. He hit me so hard, I fell down several stairs. He rushed me to the hospital, but it was too late. He killed my baby."

Terri was crying so pitifully, Jerome consoled her and wrapped his arms around her, even though he didn't want to get sucked in. A part of him wanted to kill Robert for hurting her, but he tried to keep his old feelings in check.

"What do you need me to do?"

"I need money. Robert has emptied out my bank accounts, and he's closed out all my credit cards. I have nothing."

"How much?"

"Just enough to leave and start over somewhere, a couple of thousand. I know it's asking a lot—"

"Wait here."

Jerome ran inside his house. By the time he returned, Terri had stopped crying.

"Here. This belongs to you anyway." Jerome gave her the little black box.

Terri looked confused. "What's this?" She opened it. "Jerome, is this—"

"It should be worth at least ten thousand. I have no use for it anymore."

"Jerome, I don't know how I can repay you after the horrible things I've done to you." She began to weep again.

He tried to shut down emotionally. "Take care of yourself, Terri."

She nodded and began to walk away. Then she turned around and said, "You could come with me. I still love you and want us to be together. I just didn't know how to tell you."

"I believe you, Terri." Jerome shook his head. "As crazy as it sounds, I believe you, but that was a long time ago. I could never forgive you. Never trust you. You have no idea what you've done to me."

She nodded again. "I am sorry. You won't hear from me again." And she walked away and out of his life for good.

Or so Jerome thought anyway.

Chapter 47

Jerome dropped off the money he owed his cousin and went to a local bar to mellow out. Hours later, he reached his front door and pulled out his key. Only, he couldn't understand why it wasn't turning the lock. He banged on the door. "Momma, could you let me in. My key's not working." Realizing how late it was, he said, "Sorry. Don't mean to wake you." Feeling like a jerk, he said under his breath, "I sure am a sorry excuse right now. Lord, help me."

Roberta unlocked her bedroom window and pulled it up. "Boy, it's after midnight."

"I'm sorry, Momma. Something's wrong with my key. Can you let me in?"

"No."

"Momma, I know it's late, and I know I've been acting like an SOB lately, and I am sorry for all the pain and embarrassment I've caused you. I will try to do better, I promise."

"No."

"Momma, come on, it's late. Can we discuss this in the morning."

"No, Jerome, there is nothing wrong with your key."

"Momma, I can't get in. Do you want me to sit out here all night? It's not working. Come on."

"Jerome, your key is fine. I changed the locks."

"What are you talking about? You did what?" Jerome, ashamed to look at his mother before, looked up at her. Her face was cold as an igloo. She really was done with him.

"I packed up your clothes and put them in your trunk. I can't lift all that electronic mess in your room, so you will have to come back and get it sometime this week. Daylight hours, I would prefer. I know you lost your job and you're down on your luck, but you brought this all on yourself, chasing after those loose women, turning your back on the Lord, turning your back on yourself."

Jerome knew his mother was speaking the truth. He balled up his fist, trying to fight his emotion, trying to fight how alone and abandoned he was feeling right now.

"Trust me, son, this is for the best. You can't stay here anymore. You need to get your life together, and you can't do it here. I would say I am sorry, but I am not. Now go on before you wake the neighbors." Roberta disappeared from the window.

As Jerome started to walk away from the front porch, his momma appeared in the window again. "Oh, Jerome, don't forget to pick me up early Sunday for church. I'm teaching Sunday school this week." She closed and locked the window, to finally retire for what had seemed like the longest day in her life.

Jerome shook his head. What was he going to do? Even though he felt she sent him up the river without a paddle, he knew, just as the sun rose, that he better be there on Sunday to take her to church.

Jerome reached his car, distracted by his inner gloom, and didn't notice two black men approaching him.

A tall, round man with a beard, gold teeth, and matching gold chains and rings got close to Jerome. "You Jerome Hart?"

Jerome never took his eye off either one of them, sizing them up, imagining how he was going to knock the fat one out and run before the slender one pulled out a piece. "What's up?"

The fat one looked at the slender one, who was wearing a wife-beater and dark blue jeans. His muscles were on the moderate size, but not as robust as Jerome's. Their eyes confirmed whatever they needed to.

"Where is Terri Sarkasian?" the fat one asked, as if he had authority over Jerome.

"Excuse me, I think you got me confused with someone else." Jerome wasn't going to let the slender one close in on him; he kept his distance, awaiting the opportunity to make his escape. Apparently Terri's husband couldn't face him and sent his dogs he instead.

"Naw, you're Jerome. Now tell us where Terri is."

Jerome shook his head. "I don't know anyone named Terri."

"I won't ask again, playa."

Definitely not D.C. dudes, Jerome figured. *New York or New Jersey.* Their clothes and slang were dead giveaways.

"How much did Robert Sarkasian pay you? Does it bother you that you're out here doing the white man's work?"

"Money has no color where I am from, homie, you feel me? So, again, where is she?"

"Yo, playa, you can ask all you want, but I ain't telling you shit." Jerome could see the slender one getting closer, reaching. He was the one holding, the one he had to get to first. "If your boss wants to know where his wife is, then tell him to come ask me hisself," he said, buying time.

Clearly not the brains of the operation, the slender one said, "What ya wanna do, Scottie?"

"Muthafucka, what did I say about that?"

Jerome now knew one of them by name.

"My bag, dude, my bag."

Jerome was inches away from the slender one now, the supposed muscle. "So how about it, Scottie?" he teased.

"How about this, nigga!" Scottie charged Jerome, pushed him up against his car, and started bashing his flesh repeatedly with his gold rings.

Jerome fell to the ground, caught off guard by Scottie's blows. He'd underestimated him, figuring a dude that size couldn't bring his arm to his nose to sneeze, let alone have energy to hit like that.

He shook it off, ready to get up and uppercut the semi-sumo, but then he noticed the slender one pulling out his piece.

Scottie slammed another fist to Jerome's head. Then he started kicking him in his face and head with his Tims.

Bang! A humongous gunshot went off in the air. It sounded like it came from a duck hunter's barrel. *Click-clack!*

The slender one put his hands and his gun up in surrender, and Scottie looked up at a double-barreled shotgun aimed between his eyes.

Roberta, wearing her housecoat, head wrap and slippers, yelled in a thick Trinidad accent, "Ah done call de police! Gimme one good reason not to shoot yuh ass before dey reach!"

The slender one didn't stick around to give her an answer. He took off in the opposite direction.

Roberta let off a shot in his direction, missing him and blowing off the stop sign at the corner. *Click-clack!* She pointed the cannon back to Scottie and began to pray as she moved closer, "Dear Lord, forgive me for I have sinned . . ."

Scottie nearly wet himself, he could hear the police sirens, and he could see the death in this old woman's eyes. He froze. His last wish was for the police to reach him before Roberta did.

His prayers were answered.

As Roberta lowered her weapon, Scottie took off, but the first officers on the scene snatched him up mid-air. Where did a man his size think he was running off to anyway?

Roberta rushed to an unconscious Jerome and prayed for his life to be spared.

Chapter 48

"I can't believe this is happening! I can't believe it!" Shana was more excited than she'd been in a long time, as both her sisters, Sheri and Jasmine, helped her slip into her off-white wedding gown.

"Who you telling? I didn't think you were the marrying kind." Jasmine lovingly joked.

"Trust me, I had my doubts. But the Good Lord has been good to me." After all Shana had been through her entire life, she was finally getting it right, even if it was predicated on a lie.

Shana had accepted Timothy's proposal the day after she found out she was pregnant with Jerome's baby. She wanted to tell him the truth, but seeing Jerome hauled off to jail showed her what life would be like with him.

"Who knew love could be found on the Internet?" Sheri said, excited for her sister. "And I am going to be an auntie. Yay!" She rubbed her sister's belly playfully.

Jasmine smirked. "You sure don't waste any time."

"You should have seen his face when I told him I was pregnant. He was so enchanted."

"No need to brag." Sheri smiled. "I can tell he makes you happy, sis."

Shana recapped the proposal in her mind, as if she was really living a fairytale. In her hair salon in front of clients and fellow beauticians, Timothy, on one knee, asked, "Will you marry me?"

Completed blindsided and unsure of what to saying, she said, "Can I give you an answer tomorrow?"

And a disappointed Timothy said, "Sure."

A few days later, she drove up to his condo in Silver Springs and knocked on his door, hoping she would get the nerve to back out and come clean.

After all Timothy hadn't been completely honest with her when they'd met. First off, he looked nothing like his photo taken fifteen years earlier. Shana was annoyed that the offline Timothy had a gut and a receding hairline. His virtual conversation was good, so she felt she owed it to herself to give him a try.

Timothy came to the door. "What's it going to be, Shana?"

She bent on one knee, holding an ultrasound in her hand. "Yes, Daddy."

Timothy scooped her up in a bear hug. He was in love even more now than before. Shana was to be the mother of his firstborn.

Wrought with guilt for keeping the truth from him, Shana sentenced herself to life with Timothy and the baby. This was her happy ending.

Shana behaved like a beautiful gushing bride should before, during, and after their nuptials. To onlookers, it was a fairytale wedding, and she had everyone fooled. Except her younger sister.

"Shana, every time I see you by yourself, you look like you are going to cry. What's up? Is it the hormones?"

"Yeah. You know how that is."

Sheri nodded.

Later on, while they were inside the bride's dressing room at the function hall, Sheri said, "I'm just worried about you. Something doesn't feel right. Are you worried Timothy just married you because you're pregnant?"

Shana shook her head. "No, it's nothing like that. I'm just emotional. I'm so happy."

"I wish I could believe that, but I know something's wrong. When you're ready to tell me, I'm here. You know I am here for you, right?"

Shana tried to hold back the tears but she couldn't. She wailed, "I know, I know. It's just . . ."

"It's just what?"

But she couldn't. It was her secret to bear. A secret she would take to the grave. She sucked it up and put on her "happy bride" makeup. "You didn't feel unsure when you married Marcus? As if you weren't all the way invested and he was."

"Honey, that is the best kind of marriage. Find a husband that loves you more than you love him. I think I loved Marcus just as much as he loved me. Now see where we are. Divorced."

Sheri smirked. "So, see, you are off to the perfect union." She smiled.

Shana smiled too. She knew her sister was lying to make her feel better, but she was lying as well to make everything better. "That does make sense. Anyone who can put up with me deserves all the love and devotion I can give."

"Correction, any man who can put up with your family deserves a medal."

They laughed.

Sheri told her, "Please tell me Momma don't know anything about that man's finances. And from one sister to another, keep them out of your business, especially when it comes to money."

"Now you know damn well Momma done already looked up everything there is to know about Timothy, his family, and his credit score. Hell, she already had life insurance policies for him to sign."

Sheri belted out a huge laugh. "No, she didn't."

Shana giggled.

"How much? And who is the beneficiary? Momma?"

They hollered.

A knock came on the door. It was Jasmine.

"Would you two old ladies come join the party? You promised to introduce me to some of Timothy's fraternity brothers. Come on, Shana."

"Jasmine, you sound like Momma. Those men are too old for you."

"Their money ain't."

"Yup. just like Momma. Go on. We'll be out in a minute," Shana yelled through the door.

"Come on, girl."

"Sheri."

"What?"

"Can you promise me something?"

"Anything."

"If something were to happen to me, could you make sure Momma doesn't raise my baby. Please keep her as far away from my baby as possible."

"No worries. I will raise her myself, I promise." Sheri hugged her older sister. They were more like best friends. She'd never judged Shana when she was living foul and seemed headed for prison or the grave. She just prayed she would find her way.

Chapter 49

Jerome flipped through the channels in his hospital bed, suffering from a concussion and broken ribs courtesy of Terri's husband.

Scottie squealed like a pig and told the police that Robert Sarkasian had hired him and his buddy Doo-Doo—Yes, that was his name—to rough up Jerome and find out where his wife was hiding.

Jerome cooperated with the police and told them everything about their affair and her visit. They no longer considered her a missing person, arrested Robert, and closed the case.

The social worker met with Jerome to assess his need for shelter, food, and assistance.

"I have nowhere to live, no income, and if I don't have that, then I guess I won't eat. But you can't help me. I don't want your help," Jerome said, wallowing in his own self-pity.

The social worker said, "Jerome, the hospital is going to release you whether you have somewhere to live or not. I'm just trying to help you get what you need."

"He will be fine," a man's voice said from the hospital doorway.

The social worker turned around. "I'm sorry, and you are?"

"Excuse me, I didn't mean to interrupt." He extended his hand. "I'm Deacon Mitchell Hart, Jerome's brother."

Jerome rolled his eyes. "This is all I need."

"Well, we were just about finished here anyway. I will let you two visit." She turned to Jerome. "I will come back tomorrow, and we can discuss this further."

"I look forward to it, Rachel." Jerome waved good-bye. *Good riddance.*

Jerome sulked like a two-year-old. The last person he wanted to see was his perfect brother, Mitchell. With an attitude, he questioned, "What are you doing here?"

"I'm here to help. That's it. No judgment." Mitchell pulled up a chair beside his brother's hospital bed."

Not buying it, Jerome retorted, "I don't need your help. I'll be fine."

Mitchell shook his head. "No, you won't. The life you live has only one destination. Death."

Jerome sucked his teeth. "Here we go."

"My destination is the same. And so is every-one else's. Including Momma. It's what you do with the time you're given that you have control over. Your journey, the road you take to reach your destination." He put his hands up. "I swear, I didn't come here to preach to you. I just want to help. Momma is worried sick about you. Do you really want her spending her time before she reaches her destination worried about you every day? How you live your life? Who's coming for you next?"

Jerome kept silent.

"You've put Momma through so much pain, so much hurt. Isn't it time for you to be a man? Move on with your life without causing so much pain on the way."

"I am a man," Jerome said angrily.

"Well, then act like one. If not now, then get on the path, brother. Please, get on the right path."

"I didn't ask you to come down here. I didn't ask for your help."

Mitchell laughed. "You never do. But, funny, you seem to always need something, Jerome. And, whatever it is, usually it's costly. I am be-ing proactive this time and giving you something you really need. Guidance."

"Thanks, but no, thanks." Jerome put up his hands.

"In this envelope is a name. This person will help you get back on your feet, find you a place to stay, some work, and help you find your way back to righteousness."

"I said, 'No, thanks'."

Mitchell got up and dropped the envelope on his bed. He moved closer to him. "I love you, man. Whatever has gone down between us, I love you. I will always protect you and fight anyone who means you harm, even if that someone is you." He hugged Jerome.

Jerome held back his tears. He used to look up to his brother so much. They'd fallen out after Jerome went to prison years ago.

Mitchell felt guilty, as if he didn't look after him like he promised he would. Shortly after, he joined the church and traded in his life to serve the Lord.

Jerome had always thought that Mitchell had abandoned him, making him feel inadequate and tarnished. He didn't want his help or anyone else's. Feeling withdrawn and depressed, he resented even the gesture.

Chapter 50

Nine Months Later

Jerome stood before the judge during his hearing for the assault charges brought against him by Westina. Disgusted and embarrassed, he didn't have the heart to get anyone to defend him; he was hoping it would all just go away. He rationalized that Westina pretended to be a woman, knowing full well she was a man, which was identity theft, a criminal offense that made him go "ape shit."

Jerome had fired two of his public defenders, believing they were out to get him, so his case was starting to run out of continuances. That bought him time to find odd jobs and a stable home, instead of bouncing from one friend's house to the next, or sleeping in his car.

The first lawyer he'd fired had suggested that he volunteer somewhere, to improve perception of his character. Marcus, who'd hooked him up with a job working on his foundation center earlier that year, came through again and let him work with the boys at the foundation center.

Jerome's family had tried to reach out, but he turned his back on them. He'd never even opened the envelope Mitchell had given him either. Jerome was so lost, without the slightest idea of how he was going to find his way back.

"The Honorable Judge Gooden residing," the bailiff called out.

"The court is now in session." The judge sat down and looked over the motions in front of him. He gave Jerome a look of ponderance. "Mr. Hart, it says here you would like to represent yourself. *Pro se?*"

"Yes, Your Honor," Jerome said, his mind made up.

The judge lowered his eyeglasses and made eye contact with Jerome. "Are you aware of the charges you're facing, Mr. Hart?"

"Yes, Your Honor."

"Nine counts of assault and battery, one count of kidnapping . . . " The judge went on and on.

Jerome was stern. "Yes, Your Honor."

"I won't help you during the trial. You understand that? You will be on your own."

"Yes, Your Honor."

"You do know that the jury will not take into consideration that you are representing yourself?"

"Yes, Your Honor."

"You understand, that if it goes to trial, you will have to prove without a shadow of a doubt, your case?"

"Yes, Your Honor." *How many freaking times do I have to answer yes?* Thereafter, Jerome shook his head and said yes, as if the judge's questions were meaningless.

"And you do understand, if found guilty of said charges, your decision to defend yourself will not be taken into consideration during an appeal?"

OMG! "Yes." Jerome nodded. He was prepared. No one was going to fight like he would for his freedom, or tell him what for. He was in charge of his destiny. He knew how public defenders worked. He knew the system, and he refused to be a statistic. He wanted to shout from the top of his lungs, "Yes, sir! Goddammit!

"And, Mr. Hart, you do know that if found guilty you face up to twenty years imprisonment?"

Jerome's involuntary head gestures and redundant response of *yes* screeched to a halt like a Lamborghini at a sudden red light. "Excuse me?" he said, his eyes wide.

"Just as I thought. Motion denied." Judge Gooden slammed his gavel on the sounding block. "Mr. Hart, if you cannot afford an attorney, the court will appoint you one."

With no job, how would Jerome be able to afford a decent attorney? Twenty years? Hell, if he had to beg, borrow, or sell his body, he had to hire someone.

Jerome walked out of the courtroom without a game plan.

"Jerome?" Zahara hadn't seen him since game night at Marcus's house.

Distracted by his own predicament, Jerome had walked right by her. He looked up and jogged his memory quickly. "Hey. How are you?" Jerome never forgot a pretty face, and Zahara should have been permanently stamped in his "hottie" Rolodex. *What's happened to me?*

"We met at Marcus and Kendra's party a week ago." *Ding-dong. Anybody home? Too bad.* She felt sorry for him.

"Oh yeah, that's right. I'm sorry. Just going through it."

"You looked the same at the party. Anything I can do to help?"

"Unless you can put me in the right direction of an affordable criminal attorney whose price reflects his stamp of courtroom ass-kicking, then no."

"I might be able to help you with that." She reached into her purse and pulled out her card. "Give me a call."

Jerome took the card and barely looked at it. Once upon a time he used to get a thrill from receiving a woman's number. "Thank you. I appreciate that."

"No problem. Give me a call." She smiled. "Stay strong, brother. Hang in there. It will work out." Zahara had given him her number at the party. *Either he doesn't remember, or he's playing games.*

At Joe's Bar later that night, Jerome sat alone. Feeling sociable wasn't in him tonight. It seemed like the root of his problem was women anyway.

He was so caught up in self-pity, he didn't remember what day it was. "Fuck!" he said out loud. It was his mother's birthday.

He took out his cell phone. Ten minutes to eleven o'clock. The day was almost over. He felt even worse now. He knew she was probably asleep but called anyway. She picked up on the first ring.

"Momma?"

"Jerome?" Her voice was groggy.

"Happy birthday."

"Dear Lord," she said, awashed with relief. "I'm so glad to hear from you. I thought . . ." She paused. "Well, never mind what I thought. I'm just glad you called."

"I am sorry. I will bring your present by first thing in the morning."

"Baby, the only gift you could give me is to get your life together. I'm so worried about you. I pray every night for your safety and that you will find your way back to the path of righteousness. Get right with God, son."

At the end of his rope, Jerome didn't tune her out this time. He indeed needed a blessing. "I will, Momma."

"I pray you do. Now if you're coming by, do you mind picking me up a few things from the store?"

Jerome giggled to himself. Someone needed him. "Sure, Momma. Hold up. Let me grab a pen to take your list." He reached in his pocket for the card Zahara had given him. He flipped it to the blank side. "Go ahead, Momma." He took her list and said good night.

Out of curiosity Jerome flipped the card over and read it—*Zahara Washington, attorney-at-law. Oh, shit!* He'd received his blessing yet almost missed it. He made a mental note to call her first thing in the morning.

Chapter 51

Zahara had agreed to meet Jerome the following week, and now they were discussing his case. "I'm not going to sugarcoat things. You are facing some serious charges."

"It's not that simple." Jerome didn't want anyone to know Westina was really a dude.

"Jerome, I can't help you if you're not being honest with me. I have a friend who can represent you, but you have to be willing to cooperate. My specialty is family law."

"What's his number?"

Zahara shook her head. "Okay, have it your way." She wrote down the lawyer's number.

Jerome thanked her, and since he was having such good luck, he decided to play his hand. "Would you like to go out for lunch, you know, so I can repay you for your help?"

"I'm flattered, but it's okay. No need to thank me. I wanted to help."

"But you don't want to go out with me?"

"Can I be honest with you?"

"Sure."

"You seem like a fun guy, very pretty to look at physically, but you're work."

"Excuse me?" *I'll work you in the bedroom.*

"You're like a Mercedes-Benz, fully loaded, the ultimate ride. The envious duly take notice. I could open you up on the freeway in seconds and take off without a care in the world, but if you malfunction or require service, it will cost me an arm and a leg to keep you looking and operating as fine as you do. You're high maintenance. Get it?"

"Not really. What's wrong with that?"

"You're not the right investment for me. If I invest my time, money, and emotion in you, I'm pretty sure I will end up with a hefty invoice for service rendered."

Jerome looked at her like, *Child, please.* She couldn't handle him. He waved her off. "I was trying to feed you. You're looking too far into it."

"Is that all, really?" Zahara asked, playing along.

"Yeah," Jerome said, lying through his teeth.

"Okay, so let me say it to you in a language you understand. I am not a throwback, someone you can catch and throw back once you've had your fun with me. I am a certified keeper. You and I both know you want to sleep with me, but I'm not looking for a good time and to be tossed aside."

"So this was just a favor?"

"I saw you were in need. I wanted to help. That's it. You seem like a decent guy, just having a difficult time. It doesn't mean I want to sleep with you."

"And I appreciate that. I was just trying to show my appreciation."

"And I appreciate that."

"Well, if you change your mind, here is my number. I still would really like to show you my appreciation."

"I am so sure." Zahara knew he was flirting.

Jerome smiled and took defeat for now, but a challenge always built endurance, and he could use some of that. He turned before he left and said, "Zahara, I'm fully aware that you're definitely not a throwback." He closed the door.

She thought, *Game On.*

Chapter 52

Zahara's friend wasn't as cheap as Jerome needed him to be, but a shark and "slickster" he was. He got Jerome off with probation, pending his enrollment in anger management therapy, performing 300 hours of community service, and getting a full-time job. Looking forward to a second chance, Jerome was happy to put his past behind him.

Jerome's therapist, Donika, made it hard for him to focus. Thick in the hips, small in the waist, top- and bottom-heavy, her eyes pierced through her glasses, and her lips glittered glossy enough to give him all kinds of naughty ideas. The sessions were impossible day after day. Nothing good could come of this. Here he was trying to behave, and they assigned him this *Maxim* 100 hottie.

"Jerome, we can sit here silent all day if you want. It's your time. But keep in mind, I report your progress to the courts." She flipped her leg over to cross them.

Jerome couldn't hear anything she was saying, visualizing her riding his man-man. For the past year he'd been semi-celibate, and his man-man was on the picket line. But in just a short time, two women were calling on him to break the strike, first Zahara, and now Donika.

"Jerome, did you hear what I said?"

"I am sorry. What was the question?"

"Why are you so angry?"

"I'm not angry. I just have made some poor decisions." He smiled.

"So beating up a woman was a poor decision?"

"Look, that wasn't a woman. We both know that. And I have tried to make amends for my actions." He smiled. "Fuck it! Do you know how fine you are? It's very distracting."

"Do you know why you're so angry?"

"Oh, we're going to play that game?"

"Like I said, it's your time here." Donika smiled. "What you make of it is up to you."

"What?"

"I know why you're angry."

Jerome was intrigued. "Why?"

"You're sexually frustrated."

"Oh, really? Is that it?" Jerome thought that was funny.

"Jerome, let me be frank with you. I know you want to fuck me. So let's get on with it, so I can assign you someone else who can help you sort through your issues."

Jerome was shocked to shit. "Okay."

Donika laughed. "You really thought it was going to be that easy, didn't you?"

She leaned in closer, her scent hypnotizing.

"Doesn't it make you angry to want something so bad you can't have? Does it make you want to hit me?"

Jerome was sure Donika was some kind of dominatrix, a controlling freak. *Looks like I'm not the only one not working with a full deck.* "From behind. I would love to hit that."

Donika got up and wrote down a name and number. She gave it to Jerome. "His name is Frank Beranger. You can seek counseling with him. I plan to transfer your case to him."

"Cool," Jerome said, relieved. He knew where he wanted this to go, but a part of him knew it would have consequences, like always.

She stared at him. "Good-bye, Jerome."

"Good-bye." He got up and made his way to the door. *She's nuts,* he kept thinking to himself.

"Oh, and one more thing, Jerome."

He reluctantly turned around. "What's that?"

She ran up on him and kissed him. Then out of nowhere, she slapped the juice out of him.

"You're crazy!" Jerome spat out.

"Oh, shut up, you big baby, and just fuck me."

Fuck it! Redemption can start tomorrow.

Jerome was trying to behave, but all that went out the window, and he ravaged her like she was his last meal.

Chapter 53

Roberta congratulated Shana on her baby girl. It had been months since she was able to catch up with her. If Roberta didn't know any better, she would've thought Shana was trying to avoid her.

"Girl, where are the pictures? How old is she now? What's her name?"

"Her name is Tamia, and she's five months now. I can't believe how much she's changed. She is my little angel."

"Oh, I can remember, the first time I held Jerome in my arms, he had the eyes of an angel. Who would've known he would have turned out to be the devil?" She shook her head. "He's trying, though. You know, he's going back to school. I think he is taking up graphic design or something like that. I'm not sure."

Shana was too surprised to hear Jerome was actually growing up. *Maybe I misjudged him after all.* "That's wonderful. I know you must be proud."

"I am. He's finally turning his life around."

"Oh, really?"

"Well, enough about me. How's your husband? I'm so happy for you."

"He's another angel. I've been blessed, Roberta. I am in favor with the Lord."

"Amen to that."

Shana swallowed hard and mentally prayed that Jesus would forgive her lies and deceit.

After Shana finished curling Roberta's hair, she combed and brushed it out for her the way she liked it.

"Almost through. Where are you off too now? For a seasoned woman, you sure do get around."

"Humph. Best believe. Momma has got to have a life too. Been waiting so long for a grandchild. I figured Jerome would have knocked up one of his gal pals by now. And, my oldest son, he's been married for almost seven years and still no grandbabies."

Shana felt so bad that the very grandchild she was so desperately craving for lived two blocks away. She pushed aside those feelings. "All done."

Roberta looked in the mirror and smiled. "I am bringing sexy back!" She bounced her head in a rhythmic motion.

"You are too crazy. Did you make your appointments for the next month?"

"Sure didn't. Where is your book?"

When Shana went to grab it, a 4x6 picture of her daughter fell to the floor.

"Oh, is that her? Let me see."

Shana tried her best to hide her baby from Roberta, changing the subject every time to avoid the unforgivable awkwardness she planned to take to her grave. She reluctantly showed Roberta the picture, hoping it wouldn't go there.

Roberta eyed the baby girl. "Oooh, she is so beautiful, and big too for her age. How old did you say she was?"

"Five months." Shana gave birth in January, but had lied to Roberta to make her baby seem younger than she was.

"Oh, she has your nose and mouth. Her eyes look familiar though." Roberta dug deeper. "She must have her father's eyes."

"She does." Shana extended her hand to take the picture from Roberta before she got a clue.

"Well, she is so beautiful. Congratulations."

"Thank you. All right, well, I will see you in two weeks." Shana marked her appointment in the book and Roberta left. But Shana's daughter's eyes still weighed on her mind.

***

After choir practice that Wednesday, still unable to scratch the itch she had, Roberta began looking through photographs of her children. She picked up her oldest son's baby picture and smiled. He was so thoughtful, so loving. He turned out well. She looked at Jerome's baby pictures and sighed to herself. "Where did I go wrong? Lord help him, please."

She reminisced for an hour and then began to put her old memories of her boys growing up away. She came across a photo of Jerome in a diaper, sitting up on their dark yellow funkadelic sofa with the matching pattern pillows. "My dear Lord."

Shana's daughter resembled baby Jerome as if it was him in that picture today instead of her. Roberta couldn't believe it. After all this time, why would Shana do this?

Furious, she picked up the phone and dialed her cell phone number. Straight to voice mail. Roberta hung up. She rocked back and forth in her chair thinking what she should do next. She had to confront Shana, but if she continued this lie, then what could she do? She just prayed Shana would come clean and right the wrong.

Chapter 54

Jerome enjoyed his community service duty working with the young boys at Marcus's sports foundation. He grew to enjoy being a mentor to young men going down the wrong path like him. To make ends meet, he was self-employed as a general contractor, refinishing basements, painting, remodeling kitchens and so forth. Lamant and Marcus were very helpful in making referrals.

Anger management therapy proved to be useful in helping Jerome, almost forty and nowhere in life, seeing what was really bothering him, instead of blaming it on being raised by a single mother, or being an inner city D.C. native not knowing any better. Not knowing that there was more to life than what he'd grown up doing.

And then there was Zahara, his friend. Jerome never had a female friend who really didn't want anything from him. He still wanted to sleep with her, but just being around her was enough. Her energy made him do things he never thought he could do. Like going back to school to get a degree.

Jerome spent less time in the club, and more of it working, going to school, and volunteering at the youth club. He was getting his shit together. Taking his therapist's advice, he tried to mend his relationship with his family, spending every Sunday dropping his mother off to church. Then one day he heard the altar call and came forth for his blessings.

And now this.

Jerome sat in front of his mother's house as the firefighters tried to explain what happened.

"I don't know if it was an electrical wire or one of those electrical space heaters that caused it. I am sorry for your loss."

Jerome could see the firefighter talking to him but couldn't hear him. It all seemed so surreal, like he was in a dream.

"Mr. Hart, is there anyone I can call for you?"

Jerome seemed to not understand English. *Why is this happening? How could this happen?*

The fireman left Jerome alone. He could tell he needed his space.

Jerome sat outside his mother's house as the flames simmered and the smoke overshadowed what once was. The coroner jackets could be seen from a mile away, with their bright white letters written on the back. The two of them hurried to their truck to wheel the body quickly into and away from the scene. They almost got by Jerome, but he snapped out of his trance and ran over to them.

The police and fireman tried to hold him back for his own good.

"Just let me see her. Just let me see. Please. Please, I need to see her." Jerome shouted as he fought his way to the back of the truck.

The officer reluctantly signaled. "Go ahead."

The coroner pulled back the sheet and laid bare Roberta lying lifeless on the metal gurney.

"Momma?" A ball of tears began to well up. He touched her icy-cold forehead. "Momma?" He bent his face closer to hers and whispered in her ear, "Momma, I am so sorry. I am so sorry. Please forgive me." Jerome erupted in tears.

The coroner quickly covered her up and wheeled her away.

"Why? Why did this have to happen?" He pulled himself together and made his way to his car.

"Mr. Hart, is there someone we can call? Can we give you a ride somewhere?"

Jerome waved them off and shook his head. He couldn't wrap his head around why, of all the people he could think of whose number should be called, it was his mother's. Why?

Jerome drove off in his new black Ford Mustang convertible, the one his mother called "boss." She was getting to be so proud of him lately. He could tell. He still had so much making up do to, and now it was too late. She was gone.

Chapter 55

Shana, grief-stricken and guilt-ridden, curled the newspaper up in a ball and wept. Why didn't he call her? Shana felt sick.

Ananda, one of her stylists, walked by the break room in the back of the salon and caught her crying. "What's wrong, girl?"

Shana tried to compose herself. She shook her head. "One of my clients passed away the other day."

"Oh, no. Who?" She patted her back gently, to console her.

"Roberta Hart, the older woman."

"The one you got into an argument with a couple of days ago? Last I saw her, she marched out of here hopping mad."

Shana cried harder. "Dammit! That was the last time I saw her." She shook her head and began to pray.

"What were you two arguing about?"

"I don't want to talk about it. Can you cover me? I want to try to make it to her services today."

"No problem."

Shana drove down New York Avenue with regret and dismay. The last time she saw Roberta, they parted on bad terms. She'd wanted to tell her about Jerome's daughter, and now she was dead. What did this all mean? Tears welled in her eyes as she vividly recalled their argument.

Roberta stormed into Shana's salon. "Shana, I need to talk to you."

Caught off guard, Shana quietly told her client to excuse her for a minute.

"I was thinking we could talk in your office. In private." Roberta demanded.

Knowing that her baby was in her office napping in her Pack 'n Play, Shana tried to avoid that. "We can go out front. It's a nice, sunny day."

"Shana, I know, okay. I know. So stop hiding her from me. I know."

Shana tried to convince herself Roberta was misinformed.

"You're a good person, Shana. Let's just go to the back and talk."

Defeated, Shana agreed, holding back the tears. Once in her office, she turned to give Roberta the signal to talk, placing her finger to her lips.

Roberta couldn't help being overwhelmed by her first grandchild lying sound asleep inches away from her. She stuck out her chest with pride and went over to her and gently patted her back. "There, there, little angel. Rest easy." She began to hum a church hymn.

Shana whispered, "Shh."

"Shana, on my way over here, I was so angry with you, so upset at what you have done, but the minute I saw her, I realized it doesn't even matter."

"Look, Roberta, I don't know what you're talking about."

Roberta put up her hand. "Save it, child. I know why you did what you did, but enough is enough already. I know. And soon Jerome is going to know."

"What? You have lost your mind!" she shouted.

"Shana, you are a good person. A good woman. I know you are. And I know you struggled with this. I know you have. That is why you made sure I never saw a picture of her or kept rescheduling my appointments. You knew, once I saw her, I would know the truth. And I do. So stop this foolishness. You are a good person. You just made a bad decision, that's all."

Shana began to weep. "I don't know how this happened."

"I do. I should know. I raised him." She laughed. "You got scared, honey, like we all do."

Shana wept harder.

"Now it's time to do what's right, honey." Roberta hugged her tight. "You are going to have to tell Jerome he's the father."

Shana knew it was the right thing to do, especially now since someone finally shared her burden. *But how do I face my husband? How would Jerome react? Would my marriage end?* These thoughts played in her mind like a sky banner. Shana wasn't ready to risk her husband leaving her. She couldn't do it.

She broke from Roberta's embrace. "I can't. I can't tell him. It would ruin my marriage. My life. Our life. I will make a deal with you. If you don't tell Jerome, I'll let you visit with her from time to time. Be the grandmother you always wanted to be."

As tempting as that offer was, Roberta knew she wouldn't be happy unless she was a permanent fixture in her grandchild's life. She especially didn't want to be around when the truth hit the fan. Because it always does. Both the child and Jerome would resent her forever.

No way. Roberta shook her head. "No, no, my dear. Tell Jerome the truth, or else I will." Roberta walked off leaving Shana with that.

Shana yelled after her, "Roberta, that will be a big mistake! You know it! It's better this way, you'll see."

Roberta left feeling renewed. She indeed planned on telling her son, whether or not Shana came to her senses.

Shana couldn't shake her last time seeing Roberta. She had always thought of her as a mother-in-law and hated it when they fought. Of course she died with Shana's secret, unless she had a chance to tell Jerome before she died. Now what was she to do?

Her plans to pay her respects were motivated by the desperation to keep her secret safe.

Chapter 56

Jerome had held up the entire day, even at the burial, while his brother Mitchell sat quietly alone, unable to eat or sleep, feeling guilty for not giving his mother any grandchildren.

Jerome played host, while his family and close friends celebrated his mother's homegoing with a huge feast. That was the culture of Caribbean people, to celebrate life as if it was a big fat Caribbean wedding.

He made his way to each table to greet everyone and thank them for coming. He played host while he slowly ached inside. He did a double take when he saw Shana sitting at a table with Marcus and Lamant. "Hey! Thank you, guys, for coming."

"No problem. How are you holding up ?" Lamant had gone through the same thing losing his father last month. He knew how his friend was feeling.

"I'm holding. What are you going to do? At least she's at peace." Jerome continued his grieving-appropriate behavior. He turned to Shana. "I am sorry I didn't call to tell you myself. I know you and my mother were close. Even when we—"

"That is okay. You have enough to deal with. I will miss her dearly. She was a wonderful woman and friend to me."

Jerome nodded.

"Can I talk to you for a moment?" Shana had to know what and if he knew.

"Sure." He turned to his friends. "Excuse me for a second, would you."

His boys gave him the nod.

He pulled Shana in a corner of his brother's hallway, intrigued to hear what she had to say. "So what's up?"

Shana cleared her throat. "It's about your mother. The last time I saw her we left on bad terms. We had an argument about her hair. Did she mention it to you?"

"No. She did say she wanted to talk to me about something important, but I guess I will never know what that was. Do you?"

Shana felt heartless. "I wish I could tell you. Sorry."

"Well, thanks for coming by again. Sorry we had to see each other again under these circumstances."

"Me too." Shana gave Jerome a long, hard hug. She felt relieved, he didn't know a thing. A part of her thought she should tell him. It would probably make his loss heal quicker. But how could she ruin a life with a man that loved her unconditionally? She planned to take her secret to the grave.

"By the way, congratulations on the wedding and the new baby. What's her name?"

Shana turned and smiled. "It's Tamia. She is the light of our lives."

"Momma always wanted grandchildren." Jerome began to tear up. He fought them off. Not ready to let go. He changed the subject "And the lucky man?"

"Timothy Ellworth. I've really been blessed to have him in my life. When that day comes for you, Jerome, I am sure your mother will be shining down on you, looking after her grandchildren." Now Shana was teary.

Jerome watched her scurry off. He appreciated her coming by to pay her respects.

After all the guests left, Mitchell sat Jerome down to discuss their mother's estate.

"Can this wait until the morning? I just want to go home and go to sleep."

"Momma put me in charge of her assets if anything were to happen to her. She said she had a life insurance policy worth over one million dollars. The house, she wanted you to have, and the money, we were to split between the two of us."

"Then there is nothing to discuss. She planned ahead."

"But there is a problem with the life insurance policy."

"What? She didn't pay the premium? I can cover the funeral. Don't worry."

"The premium is paid in full. In fact, she doubled up her life insurance the day before her passing."

"So, again, what is the problem? Get on with it."

"We're not listed as the beneficiaries, Jerome."

"Well, then who is?" He was dumbfounded.

"That's the thing I don't know. Her name is Tamia Sheri Ellworth. And she is a minor, a seven-month-old baby as a matter of fact."

Jerome's face turned to stone. "Excuse me?"

"I am going to have to contact the company and her attorney to sort this out. Why would Momma leave all her money to a baby? Someone we never even heard of? It doesn't make any sense."

While Mitchell went on about the particulars of the estate, Jerome put the pieces together. *No way*. He shook his head. "How could she?"

"My point exactly."

"I think she left her money to her only grandchild."

Mitchell and his wife looked confused, and said simultaneously, "What grandchild?"

All Jerome could do was let out an ironic laugh. "I guess God is not the only one with a sense of humor."

Chapter 57

Roberta's financial advisor, Brandon Miller, had said to her, "Roberta, are you sure you want to put your granddaughter as the beneficiary of your policy? She stands to inherit around two million dollars, but not her directly . . . whoever her caregiver is. Do you understand that? It could end up in probate if your boys contest it."

Roberta shook her head. "I know what I am doing. They will do what's right. I know it."

"Okay, if you insist. Sign here please." Brandon gestured.

Roberta couldn't be happier, prancing around her house, thinking of all the wonderful things she was going to get to do with her granddaughter. They would go to the park. She would teach her how to garden. Teach her manners. Why she should read the Bible. Her first fall. Her first kiss. Her first heartbreak.

She couldn't be happier. She put a kettle of tea on and turned the TV to reruns of *Walker, Texas Ranger*. She picked up her cordless phone and dialed Jerome's cell phone number. It went to voice mail. She left him a message: "Hey, son. It's your mother speaking. When you get a chance, please call me. I have something very important to tell you, so please call, no matter the time. Love you, son, and I am so proud of you."

Roberta pressed the off button and pushed her recliner chair to relax and curl up with the Texas Ranger. Only, the television began watching her as she fell fast asleep from her exhausting day.

The kettle whistled at boiling point, but Roberta lay in a deep sleep and didn't hear it. The hot water spilled over onto the electric range and continued to spill until sparks of the electricity lit the cloths hanging from the stove, and the kitchen started going up in flames.

Roberta wiggled her nose at the smell of smoke. "Dear Lord!" She jumped out of her recliner, surrounded by fire and smoke. She coughed and coughed and tried to make it to the front door. She reached for the knob, but it was already too hot. "Lord Jesus, hear my prayer," she said, coughing. "Please look after my children and look after my granddaughter. Keep her

safe"—she coughed—"and away from harm—"
She coughed more and more

Her body began to lose oxygen, and as her lungs became clogged with poisonous gases, she slipped away, still praying to God her family would be spared.

Chapter 58

Jerome burst into Shana's salon, contempt in his eyes. "Where is she? How could you?"

Shana jumped, and her hand trembled. "Jerome, what the—"

"Ouch!" Dana, one of Shana's clients, was having a press and curl done.

"I am so sorry, Dana. Can you excuse me for a second."

"You got more drama than a soap opera, Shana," Dana told her. "I don't have time for this. I need to get to work."

"I'm sorry. This will only take a minute." Shana gestured for her to get up out of her chair.

"Where is she?" Jerome demanded.

"Who?"

"My daughter."

The salon grew very quiet, all customers with their eyes on Jerome and Shana. Their spectacle was like a VH1 reality show, HBO series and ABC drama all wrapped up in one.

So today is the day. Shana grabbed Jerome by his arm and ushered him into her office. "Let's talk in private."

He snatched his arm from her grip. "Let's not. You've had more than enough time, say seven months, to talk to me. As a matter a fact, you've had over a year to talk to me."

"Jerome, if you would just step into my office, we can talk about this like adults."

"Why? You don't want your clients to know what a lying, conniving bitch they got trying to make them feel pretty!"

Wham! Shana smacked the juice out of him. "Fuck you! Maybe if you weren't such a man whore I would have told you, trusted you to do the right thing, but let's face it, you are not father material. We are better off without you!" Tears began to roll down her face.

Gritting his teeth, Jerome balled his fist to slap the shit out of this lying heifer, but he managed to take a timeout and composed himself. "So it is true. Shana, I don't know what I would have done if you told me. I was a different person then. But, dammit, you should have given me a chance."

"Chance to do what? You and I both know you weren't anywhere near ready to have a child, or a family, for that matter, so get over yourself."

"Get over myself? Shana, you have fabricated a life worth of lies. Did you ever think about her? When she found out the truth? This is ridiculous. I am through arguing with you. I demand to see her."

Shana shook her head. "That's not going to happen."

"Shana, it is. My mother was a tremendous woman. And she chose you as a friend, so to me, that means you must have something good in you. Whatever happened between us doesn't matter. You know what's right, and I trust you will do what's right." Jerome walked off.

"I can't."

"Tomorrow, Shana. I want to see her tomorrow. I get off at five. Call me. If you don't, I will be up here every day until you do."

Distraught, trapped, stewing in the mess she created, Shana put her hands on her head.

The customers in the shop started stirring again, but none of them had the nerve to say anything to her.

"Come on, Dana," Shana said. "I will have you out of here in a minute."

"You sure, girl? You look like you could use a break."

"Let me finish up, and then I think I will."

***

Exhausted, Shana jumped in her Acura SUV and cried without reservation. "How could I have done this?" she said, crying. "Dear Lord, forgive me. Roberta, forgive me. Baby, forgive me. Honey, forgive me."

As Beyoncé's "Flaws and All" played through her cell phone speaker, Shana wiped her sorrows away and swallowed her anguish. "Hey, baby."

"Hey, yourself. How was your day?" Timothy asked.

"Not too bad. I've closed up shop and on my way to you and li'l mama," Shana said, trying to hold on as much as she could to the normalcy of their life together.

"She knows when you're gone too. She looks around, smiles at your picture, and says, 'Mama'."

Shana smiled. Her baby was the only thing that kept her going. She was too young now, but in time she hoped she would forgive her. "I'll be home soon. I have to talk you."

"You sound funny. What's wrong? Is everything okay?"

"Just have a lot on my mind. It's me. You've done everything right. It's me."

"Shana, I don't like how you sound. What's the matter, baby?"

She fought back her tears. "I will be home soon. Kiss Tamia for me. Bye."

How was she going to tell him the truth? It would crush him, and end their marriage. But how could she hide the truth? Not only did Jerome know, but he wanted to be a part of her life. She saw no alternative but to inflict pain on an innocent bystander. Her husband.

On her drive home, she sent Jerome a text message: YOU CAN SEE HER TOMORROW AT 6 P.M. MEET ME AT YOUR HOUSE.

Beeeeep!

From the corner of her eye, Shana saw bright flashes coming toward her, invading her space. She only saw darkness thereafter.

Chapter 59

Jerome was so nervous, yet in his heart he knew Shana would do the right thing. And even though he'd ripped her a new one for her deceit, he knew why she did it. Who knows how he would have reacted when she told him a year ago? Back then he was living the fast life, and women were a dime a dozen. It wasn't until he met Zahara that he realized he'd been making all the wrong choices.

Jerome cleaned up his two-bedroom apartment near the waterfront and ordered from Phillips Seafood. He bought a pink Jeep Baby Walker for Tamia, and some other toys that the Babies "R" Us clerk told him were age-appropriate. He plugged up the sockets in his entire apartment and got safety locks for his cabinets, to prove to Shana that he had changed and could make a good father, if given the chance.

Six o'clock rolled around. He said a prayer for his mother and for himself. "Please guide me and show me the way, dear Lord. I need You. I need Your blessing. In Jesus name we pray. Amen."

Seven o'clock rolled around, and the food was cold now.

Eight o'clock rolled around. Jerome dialed Shana's number. Straight to voice mail.

Nine o'clock rolled around. He threw his dinner in the trash.

Ten o'clock, he dialed Shana's number for the second time. Voice mail. He threw the phone across the room.

Hurt and disappointed, Jerome went to bed at eleven o'clock feeling like a chump.

Shana didn't make good on her promise, but he intended to.

Chapter 60

Jerome screamed on his cousin, "Keke, where are you? You said you would have my car to me first thing in the morning."

He'd owed her a favor from the time she'd bailed him out of jail last year, so she came to collect yesterday evening, asking to borrow his car.

"Hold your horses. I'm coming. It's seven o'clock in the morning on a Saturday. Really, what do you have to do this early?"

"Mind yours. Just bring me my car!" Jerome yelled. He had plans that morning and every morning thereafter, until Shana gave him what he wanted. To see his daughter.

Fifteen long minutes went by, and as promised, Keke showed up. Only, she'd neglected to tell him she was involved in a hit-and-run of some proportion.

"Do you mind giving me a ride to—"

Jerome was distracted by his haste to get to the salon. He knew women got up super-duper early to get in and get out on Saturdays. He almost missed the dent on the front fender. "Whoa! Whoa! Whoa! What the hell is this? You got into an accident?"

Keke couldn't deny this one. "Okay, don't trip. I hit somebody, but he's okay."

"You hit somebody!" Jerome was on ten.

"Don't trip, it's cool. He's fine. I made sure of it. Don't worry, it's cool."

"Keke, I swear it fucking better be. If the police come knocking on my door, I am going to point them in your direction. I don't have time for this shit. Not today!" Jerome hopped in his convertible.

"Hey, what about giving me a—"

Zoom! Exhaust from his Mustang's pipe blew in her face, pretty much answering her question about him giving her a ride.

Keke shook her head, pulled out her cell phone and checked on Lamant at the hospital.

Jerome made it to the salon in less than ten minutes. He wasn't taking no for an answer today or any other day. Ready for battle, he stormed toward the door and tried to push it open, but it was locked. In fact, the salon was closed.

***

He waited for three hours, and no one ever came to open it up. *She couldn't have run off that quick*, he thought to himself. He grabbed something to eat and made his way back down the street to Shana's shop. Still no one was there. Defeated, he left and decided to come back the next day.

Seven days later, Jerome waited around the shop for four hours. He was pretty convinced Shana had run off with his baby and he would never see her again. Just as he was about to pull off, a woman in a blue BMW 3 Series pulled up behind him. He watched her as she got out and walked toward the salon to unlock the door. He didn't recognize her, but he was pretty sure it wasn't Shana. She was tall with dark chocolate skin and a long, curly weave. Or what he thought was a weave.

He hopped out and caught her before she went in. "Excuse me. Is Shana coming in today?"

She turned and tried not to make eye contact with him. She pulled off her black shades. "No, she's not." Her body was present but her mind was some other place.

"When will she be in?"

The woman was on the brink of tears. "I am sorry to tell you this, but Shana was killed in a car accident last week."

"What?" Jerome's mind went blank. He was in shock. He muttered, "I don't believe this."

"The shop has been closed for a week now. I told the family I would look after it until they decided what to do. It's a mess. All I can think about is her baby. She's just a baby, and now her mother's gone." She burst out in tears.

Jerome consoled her. He felt so horrible. All this time he'd been stalking her, thinking she stood him up or ran away with his baby, she was gone. "Do you know what happened?"

"I'm not sure. The police said something about texting and driving. I dunno. She didn't see the trunk coming." She cried harder. "I just don't believe she's gone." She boo-hoo'd some more on his shoulder.

"Do you know where I can contact her family? I had no idea."

"Yeah, give me a second. I will get you her husband's address." She wiped away her tears and composed herself. "How did you know her?"

Jerome half-truthed, "We were old friends."

She sniffled and wrote down Shana's address. She looked up at Jerome and saw him a little clearer now that she stopped crying. "Hey, wait a minute. I remember you. You're that guy she was arguing with that day." She held the paper with the address close to her body, to conceal the information.

"Yes, that was me. And before you judge me, you know what you heard that day. I don't want any trouble. I just want to take care of my daughter."

"I don't know. Shana wouldn't want me—"

"Look, I don't know you, and you don't know me, but my daughter just lost her mother. She is a baby now, so she doesn't understand, but when she grows up, she will. Now, do you really think Shana would have wanted her to grow up without both her real parents? Without her father?"

The woman clinched the paper. She let that sink in her head. "I'm Ananda." She extended her hand.

"Jerome. Jerome Hart. Nice to meet you."

"For what it's worth, Tamia looks just like you."

Jerome smiled. "Thanks."

"Don't hate Shana for what she did. That day you left, she went right back to doing hair as if nothing happened. She wasn't the type to spill her personal business in the street. One thing about her, you never knew what really was going on inside her head. She was so guarded. I've known her for a long time, but I don't know her really. You get what I'm saying?"

Jerome nodded.

"I will give you her address, but please don't tell her family you got it from me. I can only imagine the shit that's about to go down when they find out about this. I don't want any part in it. Understand?"

Jerome nodded. "Thank you. I appreciate your help."

"What help? I didn't help you with a thing." Ananda winked.

Jerome appreciated her giving him a break. He sure did need one after the month he'd had, losing his mother, finding out he was a father, and losing his daughter's mother.

He decided not to wait until tomorrow to visit. He was sure of one thing—tomorrow may never come.

Chapter 61

Jerome drove into Shana's driveway nearly three blocks from her hair salon. Her and her husband had bought a brownstone near Georgetown in a neat, quiet neighborhood, perfect for raising a family. There were three other cars parked in her driveway and one in front of her house. Jerome swallowed. He didn't want to break the news to an audience, but under these circumstances, he didn't have a choice.

He climbed the steps and rehearsed inside his head what he was going to say. *Hi. I am Tamia's biological father. Sorry for your loss. Who's your daddy?* Nothing he said was going to numb their pain.

He pushed the doorbell, swallowed again, and put on his invisible armor, ready for battle.

A man resembling a pudgy Boris Kodjoe, about six foot two inches tall and 295 pounds, came to the door. "Can I help you?"

By the look in his eyes, Jerome could tell he was the grieving widow. "I am sorry to bother you, but I was a friend of Shana's. You must be her husband," he said, fishing for a name.

"Timothy." The bass in his voice matched his frame and masculine swagger.

"So sorry, Timothy, about Shana. Do you have a minute? I need to talk to you."

"What's this about?" Timothy was short with him.

"May I?" Jerome gestured for him to let him in.

Reluctantly, Timothy invited him in. "Go to your left. We can talk in the living room."

A woman's voice called from the kitchen, "Who is it?"

"I got it, Momma," Timothy shouted.

The house was full of people, most likely family members and close relatives. No sign of Tamia though. She must be napping.

Timothy thought he looked familiar, but let it go. Something about him, he instantly didn't like either. "Please sit down. What do you want to talk about?"

"Again, I am so sorry about your wife. Shana was a good person, and I know this must be devastating for you. I just lost my mother. She and Shana were close."

"I am sorry to hear that. So you knew Shana through your mother?" Timothy asked, sensing the answer was no.

"Kind of sort of. They actually met through me."

Timothy didn't like where this was going. "How did you say you knew my wife again?"

Jeanette, Timothy's mother, interrupted them. "Tamia's up from her nap. Do you want me to take her for a walk or something, baby? Get her away from all this?"

"Get her away from what?" Shana's mother, Lorraine asked. "She needs to be around her people."

Jeanette didn't want to offend Lorraine, even though she couldn't stand her. "I'm just trying to help, Lorraine."

"By taking my grandbaby away from her mother's family? We need to be together."

"Lorraine, please. My mother is just taking Tamia for a walk. She needs some air. Hell, we all could use some."

"Who's this?" Lorraine snorted.

Timothy answered his nagging mother-in-law, "This is Jamal, a friend of Shana's."

She raised her eyebrow. Something about him shook her core.

"It's actually Jerome. Jerome Hart."

Lorraine could sense there was something there. "And how did you know my daughter?"

"I don't know how to say this, but we met last year in May at club Love. And that night we—" He stopped himself, not wanting to be disrespectful. "There's no easy way to say this, but I am Tamia's biological father."

Lorraine sniped like a momma bird protecting her nest. "Excuse me?"

"You must be out your goddamn mind!" Timothy stood up, as if his height wasn't saying enough.

"I couldn't believe it either, but when my mother passed away, she made Tamia, her granddaughter, her beneficiary. After putting two and two together, I confronted Shana, and she all but confessed. I am sorry you had to hear it this way."

"How much did she leave her?" Lorraine asked, digging for gold.

"What does it matter?" Jerome shrugged.

Jeanette defended her son. "It doesn't, because you're a liar. Tamia is Timothy's daughter."

"I am sorry. But the night Shana died, she sent me a message, saying she was going to let me see her."

Timothy left the room and dashed to his bedroom.

"I asked you how much. I think you are after something. And you're not going to get it."

"Speak for yourself," Jerome responded, fully aware of her game plan.

Two minutes later, Timothy came back with a plastic bag with Shana's clothes and personal effects from the night she died.

He rummaged through the bag and pulled out her cell phone. He turned it on and pressed the mail button icon, to check her outgoing texts. He fell to the sofa slowly, as he read the truth. "I am sorry, man. I didn't know." Timothy placed his hand on his head in disbelief.

"What does it say, Timothy?" Lorraine demanded.

"Baby, what is it?"

"I would like to see Tamia."

Lorraine shouted, "Now wait just a minute. You can't come in here with some ass-backward story and think for one second you are taking my grandbaby out of here!"

"She's right." Jeanette agreed with Lorraine for the first time since she'd met the she-devil, as she'd nicknamed her.

"I know this is a bad time. I just want to see her. We can figure everything else out later."

Lorraine huffed. "Absolutely not!"

With Lorraine working his last ounce of patience, Jerome was about to be half past polite. "Now wait a minute."

"What's going on in here?" Sheri walked into the lion's den, carrying Tamia on her hip. "You need to keep your voices down. I can hear you from upstairs."

Jerome was in love the first time he saw her. So sweet, so innocent, with eyes like him and his father's side of the family. He knew she was his daughter.

Sheri took one look at Jerome and knew who he was. She was shocked to see him.

Lorraine told her daughter, "Sheri, take Tamia up to her room. She doesn't need to be around all this. It's a battlefield. Forget Iraq. You get what I am saying to you?"

Jasmine, the youngest of the three sisters, walked in. "Who are you?"

"I'm Tamia's father," Jerome said, proud as a lion looking over his den.

"Oh, shit!" Jasmine's comments were always unfiltered.

Timothy rose from his chair. "It's your fault! This is all your fault! She was texting you when she died instead of paying attention to the road. You killed her!" He charged Jerome, and they both capsized over the living room sofa. Timothy slammed him against the wall and punched him in the jaw.

"Marcus!" Sheri shouted, shielding Tamia from the brawl.

Jerome fell back in pain. He saw another fist coming for his eye, but was able to block it and uppercut Timothy on the chin, knocking him back over the same sofa and on to the hardwood floors, slightly dazed.

"I didn't come here to fight you. I just came to see Tamia." Jerome knew he could take him, if he wanted to. Timothy's size was like a useless machine he didn't have the instructions to.

"What is going on in here?" Marcus came to the rescue. "Jerome, what are you doing here?"

"I should have known he was a friend of yours," Lorraine said.

Marcus ignored her as usual and went to help Timothy up. "What's going on?"

"Jerome is Tamia's real father," Jasmine blurted out. "Shana and him were having an affair."

Timothy went wild with that one. "Is that true? You were sleeping with my wife the whole time?" He charged him again.

Marcus held him back. "Chill, Timothy. Chill out."

"That's not true. It was just the one time. We were together way before you and her even got married." Jerome massaged his jaw.

"Sure, sure." Jasmine teased.

Sheri had enough. "Shut up, Jasmine. How dare you tell lies about your sister? Have you any shame."

"It's not true," Lorraine said. "He's just after the money."

"Yeah," Jeanette chimed in, not ready to lose her grandchild.

Sheri shook her head. "It is true. Shana told me. She confided in me after your mother found out, Jerome. I am so sorry, Timothy. I am so sorry, everyone." She began to cry.

"Sheri, take Tamia upstairs." Marcus wanted to protect them both. "I will handle this."

"No," Timothy said.

"Excuse me?" Sheri was confused.

"Everybody get out! Get out of my house!"

"Son, it's going to be okay."

"It's not. It never will be. I've lost my wife and my daughter. I want everyone out. Out! Now, goddammit!"

Everyone started to clear the room.

Lorraine asked, "Timothy, what about Tamia?"

He didn't say a word.

"I'll take her," Jerome said.

Lorraine snapped her neck. "Over my dead body."

"Me and Sheri will take her with us," Marcus said, "until this mess is sorted out. That's what Shana would have wanted. Right, Sheri?"

She nodded.

Marcus shouted out to his son in the other room, "Marquise, go help your mother pack up some things for Tamia."

Jerome knew he wore out his welcome. At least everyone knew the truth. And, now, maybe he had a chance to be a father to Tamia.

Lorraine wagged her finger at Jerome. "This isn't over."

"I'm so sure." Marcus shook his head. "Jerome, I think it's best you go."

"I see what you are trying to pull, but if you think I'm going to let you drag my daughter's good name through some custody hearing, you really are as dumb as you look."

Marcus told her, "That's enough, Lorraine."

"Who are you? Timothy's name is on the birth certificate, not yours. You're just a ghost. A nobody. What can you offer Tamia? Absolutely nothing. You are after my grandbaby's money, and I'm not going to stand around and let you blow it on whatever big fat loser plans you can come up with. I'm filing for custody. You mark my words."

Jerome tried not to let Lorraine's words get to him. But what did he have to offer Tamia? He was self-employed, still in school, and had a criminal record. And his last stable relationship landed him in a hospital bed. He was a loser.

Marcus saw Jerome out. "Hey, thanks for everything. I'm sorry about your loss. I had no idea Sheri was Shana's sister."

"Hell, I had no idea Tamia was your daughter."

Jerome shook his head. "So what? You and Sheri are getting back together? What happened to Kendra?"

"Man, don't ask. And I'm just trying to be there for her and my son."

"Do you know if Shana told Sheri anything about me?"

"No idea. But what I do know is, you need to fight for your child."

Jerome stepped back. "I don't know. Maybe she is better off without me. I've been messed up for a while now. Maybe that crazy old bird in there is right."

"That crazy old bird will do anything and say anything, even sell her firstborn for money. You hear me? Trust me, I know. She's after the money. Shana left Tamia a good-sized life insurance policy too. Between her and your mother, that little seven-month-old is a millionaire. And, trust me, that's what Lorraine is thinking about, not Tamia's best interest."

"So you think I should file for custody?"

"I think you should do anything and everything to make sure she's not the one to raise your daughter. You saw how her little prodigy, Jasmine, acts, fast and willing to do just about anything for the right price. She's a mini-gold digger."

"Sheri seems like she has her head on her shoulders though. Maybe she could take custody of her and I could—"

"Jerome, if you really want to be a father to Tamia, you need to be a man first. She's your responsibility, not anyone else's. Fight for her before it's too late."

Jerome let Marcus's words sink in. He didn't know what to do. He just wanted to be a part of her life. He had no intentions of taking on being a single parent. He had a lot to think about. He hopped in his car with his thoughts heavy on his mind.

"Nice car," Jasmine said.

Jerome wasn't sure what to say to her. "Thanks."

"You want to get out of here?" she said, giving him the eye.

"What? Are you crazy? Didn't you bury your sister yesterday?"

"Fuck you! You probably a broke-ass nigga driving a car you can't afford anyway. I see why my sister dropped you." She switched her hips down the block.

At that moment, Jerome knew what he had to do.

Chapter 62

Zahara filled up her cup with green tea. Her plan for the evening was to watch *Kourtney and Khloé Take Miami*. She couldn't get enough of those Kardashians. She loved all the fashion and, of course, the drama. She slipped into a Snuggie and curled up with her remote inside her Laurel, Maryland townhouse. The minute she pressed the power button to her forty-two-inch LCD TV, the doorbell rang.

Who could this be? She wasn't expecting any company, and no one called her to say they were stopping by.

She reluctantly got up from her den and marched down the hall. She looked through the peephole and saw the last person she expected to see. Jerome stood outside her door, looking beaten.

Zahara planned to check in on him tomorrow to see how he was fairing after losing his mother. He hadn't returned her call in a week, so she

knew he might need a face-to-face, just so he
knew she was there for him. "Hey, you. Come on
in. How are you doing?"

Jerome shook his head. "I've had a very crazy
day. You won't even believe it."

"Try me. You seem to live in crazy, so I am
sure I won't be surprised." She joked. Something
about him drew him to her. She knew he was a
mess, but also knew he had something deeper
within.

Jerome made his way in and sat on her sofa.
"You look like you were in the middle of something. Did I interrupt you?"

"Yes, but it's cool. I'll catch up with the drama
some other time." She sat down next to him. "Besides, I bet what you have going on tops it."

Jerome grinned. He adored her sense of humor and how all his drama didn't scare her off.
Even though she claimed he was just a friend,
he wanted her to be more. His feelings for any
women hadn't been this strong in a very long
time. He never even slept with Zahara. Wanted
to, of course, but he wanted much more, a far cry
from his club- and bed-hopping days. It was different.

"I found out last week that I have a daughter. My mother knew about it, and left all her
money to her. When I confronted my daughter's

mother, Shana, she tried to deny it. When she finally agreed to let me see her, it was too late, she died." Tears began to surface.

"Go on."

"I went to her family to tell them the truth. Of course, they don't believe me. I got into a fight with Shana's husband. Shana's mother plans to sue for full custody, and I don't know if I would be doing the baby any good by fighting for her." Jerome shook his head. Tears began to roll down his face. "Look at me. What can I offer anyone?"

"You have plenty to offer, Jerome. You just have to see it. You have to believe it."

"I know you're right, and Marcus is right. And I know what I have to do. I just don't think I really can do it alone."

"What do you need me to do?" Zahara had developed feelings for him out of nowhere. She'd lied to herself that she didn't and wanted to be friends, but her heart knew the truth.

"I need your help. You are a family attorney, right? Well, maybe you could represent me or refer me to someone or—"

Zahara grabbed his hand. "It's done. I got you. Don't worry."

Jerome couldn't believe it was that easy. All this time he spent trying to fool women into doing what he wanted, he never had to do that with her. And he never wanted to.

Chapter 63

Timothy gave up his parental rights to Lorraine, still hurt by what Shana had done to him. But it took almost a year of Lorraine's courtroom shenanigans before Jerome could gain full custody of Tamia. During that time, he was granted supervised visits so they could get to know each other.

Jerome fought hard and jumped through every one of Lorraine's hurdles to prove he was a fit parent and could provide a stable home.

He left the driving range that morning feeling hopeful that today would be the day the judge would grant him full custody. Hell, Marcus and Sheri were getting remarried. Lamant was engaged to his crazy-ass cousin Keke, and finally published his first novel, *Love Like Julian*.

He too had a shot at redemption from his old ways. His lawyer and now girlfriend Zahara waited by his side as the judge emerged from his chambers to render his decision.

"All rise. The Honorable Judge Edwards now presides. Court is now in session."

"After reviewing this case thoroughly, I have come to a decision. And a hard decision it has been. Mr. Hart, your file is packed with evidence upon evidence why you shouldn't be granted custody."

Jerome swallowed the lump in his throat, while Lorraine stuck her chest out, feeling a cash windfall coming her way.

"Looking through your file, with your sordid history of personal affairs, your criminal record, your work ethic, a judge would be out of his mind to grant you full custody of a dog."

Lorraine smirked.

"If I didn't look at your file, I would see a man who loves his daughter and is willing to provide for her financially, emotionally, and physically. A man who up until over a year ago didn't know he had a daughter. A man who could have walked away from that. I see a changed man for the better, Mr. Hart."

Jerome's heart began to rejuvenate.

"Mrs. Dickerson, if I were to tell you I'm granting full custody of Tamia Sheri Ellworth to you, and that her money be placed in a trust fund for her to use at the age of twenty-three and not a penny until that day, would that be okay with you?"

Lorraine stuttered. "S-s-sure. Granted the cost of taking care of her is factored in, and I receive either a lump sum or monthly stipend to care for her in a way her mother would have. Of course."

"That's exactly what I thought you would say."

"I hereby award full custody of Tamia Sheri Ellworth to her father, Jerome Hart."

"What?" Lorraine burst out. "Are you kidding me?"

Jerome hugged Zahara. "Thank you. Thank you so much."

"That is my verdict, Mrs. Dickerson." The judge slammed his gavel on the sounding block. "And let me give you a piece of advice, Mrs. Dickerson. When a woman as seasoned as you still feels the need to steal candy from a baby, she should be asking herself, 'Are you kidding me?'" He gave her the toughest death look he could muster.

Lorraine stormed out of the courtroom without making arrangements to be in Tamia's life.

Jerome didn't gloat. He was just happy that he would be picking his daughter up from daycare for good after he left the courtroom,.

"You did it!" Zahara was so happy for him.

"We did it."

"Did you just *we* me?"

"Yes, I did." For the first time in his life, the idea of being in a committed relationship didn't scare Jerome. "I love you." He professed.

"My, my, Mr. Hart. If I didn't know any better, I would think you were trying to make an honest woman out of me," Zahara joked.

"I am." Jerome went down on bended knee. "Zahara Nicole Washington, will you marry me?"

Completely sideswiped, Zahara responded, "I don't know what to say."

"Say yes."

"Yes!"

As the judge walked out, he did a double take and watched from afar as Zahara accepted Jerome's hand in marriage. He approached them and said, "I can marry you today if you'd like."

Jerome answered, "I'm ready."

"So am I."

"Wait. I want Tamia to be here. Can we come back later today?"

Judge Edwards put up his hand. "I understand. Whenever you're ready."

"Thank you again, Judge Edwards."

He nodded and left.

"Jerome Hart, I never thought I would see the day when a girl changed you."

Jerome shrugged his shoulders. "I guess the right girl came along."

"Yes, she did. And her name is Tamia."

Jerome smiled. Zahara was right. Tamia made him want to be a better man. If loving him was costly, he planned to make sure he was well worth it.

Notes

Notes

Notes

ORDER FORM
URBAN BOOKS, LLC
78 E. Industry Ct
Deer Park, NY 11729

Name: (please print):_____

Address:_____

City/State:_____

Zip:_____

QTY	TITLES	PRICE
	16 On The Block	$14.95
	A Girl From Flint	$14.95
	A Pimp's Life	$14.95
	Baltimore Chronicles	$14.95
	Baltimore Chronicles 2	$14.95
	Betrayal	$14.95
	Black Diamond	$14.95

Shipping and handling-add $3.50 for 1st book, then $1.75 for each additional book.
Please send a check payable to:
Urban Books, LLC
Please allow 4-6 weeks for delivery